*Owain*

*An imprint of Milo Press*

Owain and the Milo Press colophon are trademarks of Milo Press.

*Bruno Cassini: A Florentine Tale*

*Copyright © 2014 by Rosalind Trotter*

**ALL RIGHTS RESERVED**

1820 Milo Way, Eugene, OR 97404

First Milo Press Edition published October, 2014

**ISBN13 978-1-630-75001-5**

**ISBN10 1-630-75001-8**

Library of Congress Control Number: 2014935123

*Author photograph: Katie Duong*

www.owainbooks.com

www.milopress.com

Printed in the United States of America

*For Alex, Andrea, Sophia, Cameron, Rosalind, Jessica, Khai, Katie, James, Jenny, and Maddy*

# Bruno Cassini

*A Florentine Tale*

*Rold Titt*

## Rosalind Trotter

For Martin

Best Wishes

November 24, 2014

# Prologue

*Florence, Italy*
*May 1941*

The boy sat in the kitchen doing his homework. Outside, *Il Duce*'s voice blared from loudspeakers mounted on a car roof. *Credere, obbedire, combattere.* Believe, obey, fight. In the bathroom, his Papa hummed *Un Bel Di*.

As a child, when his father had been away fighting in Africa, *Il Duce*'s voice had made the boy feel a part of something proud and strong, but the boy was eleven now and those feelings were gone. How could he grow up to be a soldier or a fighter pilot? How could he be anything if he couldn't even stop his father from preparing for a night on the town? His weakness shamed him and he saw himself as something ugly, a colorless maggot that belonged underground, hidden from sight.

The car moved down the street. As the loudspeaker sound faded his father's voice grew louder. The boy could almost smell the pomade and cologne from the days before the wars. These days Papa only sleeked his hair back with water and shaved a second time, using the family's carefully hoarded soap, but the result was the same. Soon he would leave to be with one of his women and the apartment would grow heavy with *Mamma*'s sadness.

The boy often clowned around then, getting his mother to smile, though her eyes remained troubled. Sometimes he would see tears roll down her face and then he would freeze, both in his mind and in his body, not knowing what to say or do, with no way to escape the terror he felt.

He finished his history assignment and started to reach for his math book. Next to him his little sister was bent over the page she was working on. His mother stood at the stove, her back to him. He wiggled his chair away from the table, stood up, and slipped through the door of the kitchen. He crept down the darkness of the front hall to where his father's jacket hung on the coat rack. Just as he reached in the pocket to pull out a cigarette, he heard the click of a key in the apartment door. He turned around, expecting his grandfather. His heart raced as he tried to look innocent. But it was only *zio* Michele, his uncle, who was leaving tomorrow with his regiment and was coming to say good-by. *Zio* winked at him and tousled his hair as he passed down the hall to talk to the boy's father. The boy slid the cigarette into his pocket and went back to the kitchen. Later, after his father left, he would go out on the terrace and smoke.

He sat back down at the kitchen table and started his math assignment, reducing fractions. The exercises were too easy to fully engage his mind, but watching the answers emerge soothed him.

His sister, Annamaria, looked up from where she was carefully writing out her letters. "I know what you did," she said. "I want a puff."

"You're too young."

"I'll tell."

But he knew she wouldn't, just as he knew he would let her have a puff.

"*Perbacco*," Papa bellowed now from the bathroom. "Men have needs."

The boy cringed. He knew this was true. He had heard it all his life. He was even beginning to feel stirrings himself, stirrings tangled up with his mother's sadness.

His sister bent further over her work, but her pencil was still.

"Of course they do," his uncle shouted now. "But you don't have to parade it. She doesn't have to know."

*She doesn't have to know.* As clear as a fraction reduced to its simplest terms, the boy understood that this was the key, the solution. If his mother didn't know where his father was going, it wouldn't hurt her. Why didn't Papa understand this?

"I'm never going to be like him," he whispered.

"You better not be," his sister said, copying her letters, pushing so hard that her pencil tore the paper.

# 1

*Summer, 1967*

*"Way up there,"* Bruno said to Graziella, *as he pointed to the sky.*

It was the early evening of June 24, the feast of John the Baptist, patron saint of Florence. Bruno Cassini, his wife, Ivana, and their five-year-old daughter, Graziella, were walking along the riverside on their way to see the fireworks. The city was out tonight, and Bruno and Ivana walked slowly, moving with the crowd. Graziella, her warm hand tucked confidently in Bruno's, looked up at him expectantly and he was filled with tenderness.

"Way, way up there, much too far to see, there are two..." Bruno said. He turned to Ivana. "How can I explain space probes to her?"

"Like little airplanes with no people in them, but they can take pictures," Ivana said.

Bruno smiled. He could always count on Ivana to get to the heart of things. He turned back to Graziella. "Soon they will get to another whole world called Venus and send us pictures, so we'll know what it looks like."

"Why?" Graziella asked.

"Why what?" Bruno asked.

"Why is there another world?"

"That's just the way it is, *amor mio,*" he said, but he was unhappy with his answer. He searched his mind for a way to share with Graziella the wonder he felt at the unimaginable distances through the dark, cold of space that these manmade objects would travel, at the ability of science to calculate the precise trajectory to take them to such a distant target.

"*Professor* Cassini."

The accented voice tugged at the edge of his memory, but he wasn't able to place it until he turned and saw her. There she stood, smiling at him—the American girl from so long ago. Only she was no longer a girl. Shifts in her shape and features had produced a subtle beauty that reminded him of something he couldn't quite place, like an elusive melody. And those startling blue eyes, still the same, but now set off by mascara. He wanted to keep looking, but he couldn't show this to Ivana, and he would not have been comfortable showing it to the girl. He closed his face.

He shook hands with the girl and then turned to Ivana. "This is Signorina Jensen. She was a student of mine many years ago."

Two other young women stood next to Signorina Jensen, both blonde with red lipstick and little eye makeup, a combination that immediately identified them as American. While Signorina Jensen introduced them, Bruno stole glances at her, slowly reconciling his memory of the awkward fourteen-year-old he once knew with this elegant young women.

She finished her introductions, and he turned towards Ivana. He had always considered her an attractive woman and was surprised at how dull her skin and heavy her features looked next to the porcelain-doll looks of the American girls. He put his arm around her. "This is Signora Cassini," he said.

Graziella, impatient with the grownups standing around, pulled at his trouser leg. He lifted the child up into his arms. "And this is my daughter."

"She's so beautiful," Signorina Jensen said.

Bruno smiled. He never tired of watching Graziella, her small body, the soft waves of her unruly brown hair, her rosy cheeks against the darker tones of her skin. When she smiled—a smile that was friendly but also private and self-sufficient, as though the small corner of the world she inhabited totally met her needs—she seemed to him the most beautiful child he had ever seen.

But he was aware that most parents thought their children were beautiful, even the ones who were quite plain, and it bothered him that he couldn't get an objective fix on the matter. So he was pleased because he didn't think that Signorina Jensen would say Graziella was beautiful just to be polite.

"Are you going to take pictures of the fireworks?" Ivana asked, pointing to the camera hanging from Signorina Jensen's neck.

"Actually, I was thinking about taking pictures of the people watching the fireworks."

"What a great idea," Ivana said. Ivana loved photography. The two women talked about exposures and apertures for a few minutes while Bruno took advantage of the opportunity to look more closely at Signorina Jensen. She had her dark hair up like an Italian, but it had red highlights around her face, like she had been in the sun. He had forgotten how creamy white her skin was, even with the warm touch of summer across her nose and cheeks.

"Are you going to be in Florence for long?" Ivana asked.

"I don't know. I came with a group to help after the flood, and now I've found a job."

"How soon after did you come?" Bruno asked.

"About a week. The water had mostly receded, but there was mud everywhere." She spread her arms in a sweeping gesture. "I've heard the first days were terrible."

They had poured into the city in droves, students and teachers and art lovers from around the world. Even the *capelloni*, the long-haired hippies with the enthusiastic energy of street urchins. Signorina Jensen, Bruno was sure, would have been one of the more proper ones.

The blondes said a few words in English to Signorina Jensen and left. "They're going ahead to save a place," she explained.

Bruno was glad to see them go. The conversation had been awkward as they spoke no Italian, and Bruno and Ivana spoke little English.

"I am so happy I ran into you," Signorina Jensen said. "I thought about you when I found out I was coming to Florence."

Bruno wasn't sure how to respond to this. He glanced at Ivana. "We are all grateful that you and so many others came," he said.

"I've heard people say it was worse than the war."

"That's ridiculous."

A flush colored Signorina Jensen's face.

"I think what they meant," Bruno said, softening his tone, "was that the war came to Florence slowly. We had time to get used to it, to find ways to protect much of our art. We were always able to look forward to its end." He searched for a way to help her understand the difference between an ongoing ordeal that might eventually end and a disaster realized. "There was nothing to hope for during the flood," he said, finally, smiling at her. "It just happened."

Although the Arno was swollen almost to the riverside walls the night before, its brown water swirling in creamy crests like a dessert to be spooned up, it was not unusual for it to be so full in November, and Bruno had been no more worried than anyone else. He didn't suspect anything until the next morning.

"When I opened the door to go out to get bread for breakfast," he said, "the river was inside the building, covering the ground floor and still rising. It was gray from the naphtha of leaking furnaces."

"I worked with the books in the Biblioteca Nazionale," Signorina Jensen said, referring to the largest library in Italy, which had been badly flooded. "The naphtha was all over them." She wrinkled her nose. "The smell was awful." Her Italian was better than he remembered, although she still struggled with her R's.

"What was your job with the books?" Ivana asked.

"Mostly I just carried them from one place to another."

Bruno imagined her slim body struggling with tall stacks of books.

"It was wonderful that so many people came to help." Ivana said. "Things are improving so much faster than after the war."

Bruno nodded. Ivana was right that the help that arrived was invaluable. At first, when the central government in Rome minimized the situation, the local leaders of the communist party, the parish priests and the *carabinieri* came together again as they had during the Resistance, to provide food and assistance. Eventually the rest of Italy mobilized, while money, expertise, and labor arrived from other countries to help save countless art treasures. The citizens of Florence pushed up their sleeves, set themselves to work and soon had most of the shops in the tourist area open. Digging into their long history of merchant ingenuity, the owners marked down the ruined goods and sold them as flood souvenirs. In fact, the leather of the purse Signorina Jensen carried over her shoulder had the telltale signs of water stains and stiff, curling edges.

"*Babbo,*" Graziella said, touching Bruno's cheek. "I want to see the fireworks."

"Be patient, *piccola,*" Bruno said. "We have to wait till dark." Graziella squirmed in his arm. He let her down.

Ivana took her hand. "It's hard for her to stand here with nothing to do."

"Soon, *tesoro,*" Bruno said to the child and turned back to Signorina Jensen. "Are you still working at the *Biblioteca*?"

"No. I'm teaching at the American school. Are you still at Signorina Cohen's school?"

"No. Starting this year I have a position at a state school, at the Galileo."

"State jobs are pretty hard to get, aren't they?"

"Yes," Ivana said. She put her arm through Bruno's. "I'm so proud of him. It will be better pay, and there'll be a pension."

"That's good," Signorina Jensen said. She turned to Bruno. "But the state schools are supposed to be a mess right now with over-crowding and crazy bureaucracy." She looked at him, her eyes direct and searching. "How is that going to be?"

Although Bruno had asked himself the same question, he was taken aback by her question, and by her look which suggested that she was speaking to some deeper self than his public persona. He shrugged. "You do what you have to do. Bureaucracy is always an issue in Italy."

"Let's just hope the administration doesn't decide to transfer him somewhere else," Ivana said. "They do that sometimes for reasons known only to themselves."

"Well, we'll deal with that when and if it happens," Bruno said. "No point in ruining today worrying about tomorrow. But we should move on, or we won't be able to find a place." He touched Graziella's head. "This little one's patience is running out."

It was impossible to walk four abreast on the narrow sidewalk. Bruno, on the outside, frequently ended up in the street or behind the others. Conversation stopped.

When they arrived at the spot on the riverside that Bruno thought gave a better view than the bridge, Signorina Jensen said good-by and went on ahead. Bruno watched as she walked off in her short skirt and clean shaven legs. Americans shaved under their arms as well, he knew. Italian women were beginning to shave, too. He wondered if Ivana would ever decide she wanted to. He wasn't sure how he felt about it, but he wouldn't complain if that's what she wanted. He used to wonder if American women shaved their pubic hair until he had seen an American woman lying on her back as she sunned on the beach. Her bathing suit revealed enough to show him that she shaved to her bikini line, but that was as all. Now, as Signorina Jensen merged into the crowd ahead, he was pleased that, shaven legs or not, she was dressed in the well-fitting clothes of a young lady and had not adopted the tattered, utilitarian clothes of the *Angeli del Fango* or the Doris Day, perky, terminally adolescent look of her friends.

While they waited for dark, Bruno leaned on the ledge of the riverside drive, Graziella safely enfolded in his right arm as she sat on the wall beside him. The organic smell of river wafted up, and the brilliant colors of the sunset reflected off the lazy water. Bruno entertained Graziella by pointing out the sights—a canoe gliding by, the swallows flitting under the arches of the bridge and enormous river rats scuttling around on the banks below. But his glance returned continually to the bridge, where the two tall blondes made it easy to keep sight of this new young woman the Jensen girl had become.

"Was that the American student you told me about years ago?"

The fireworks were over and they were walking back home, Graziella slumped over Bruno's shoulder, asleep. She made a little noise as she breathed.

"Shh," Bruno said. "Listen. She's snoring,"

Ivana laughed. "That's not a snore."

"It's a baby snore." Bruno grinned.

Ivana moved closer and hooked her arm into his.

"The girl," she said. "The American. I remember you talking about her. She was smart."

"Yes, in a class of dullards."

"We were all dullards in those days. You know how it was. We were still in shock from the war."

He nodded. "What I remember most is how cold I was all the time."

She pinched his arm gently. "You've put on a little weight. You were skin and bones those days. That made it even worse."

As they passed through the portico under the Vasari Corridor, Bruno shifted Graziella's weight so that he bore it on a different set of muscles. She was getting bigger, and it saddened him to know that the time would soon come when he wouldn't be able to carry her.

Ivana laughed.

"What's so funny?"

"Remember when you first got the Vespa and we went up to Fiesole?"

Bruno had found his first job in the fall of 1952. By February he had saved enough to buy a scooter, and he invited Ivana on an outing. She made a picnic lunch and they set out. Bruno chose the main *Viale* for its open views of the city, but he didn't anticipate how open that route would be to the winter wind.

"You were so frozen when we got there, I was afraid you weren't going to be able to get off the Vespa."

He managed to park the scooter and make it to a nearby café. After a glass of cognac he could move enough to ride down the narrow, walled Vecchia Fiesolana to his cousin's home in San Domenico. He and Ivana sat by the stove, warming themselves, eating salami sandwiches Ivana had fixed.

Bruno laughed. "I felt bad because you had gone to such trouble to find meat for our picnic, and I ruined it."

"And I felt bad because I wasn't as cold as you. I had the warmth of your back instead of the wind."

"I was embarrassed. We were barely engaged, and I was still trying to make you think I was perfect."

"I never thought you were perfect, but I loved you."

"Loved?" He raised an eyebrow.

She smiled and drew closer. "Still do."

They walked in silence for a while and then he said, "I hate the thought that Graziella would ever have to live through something like that."

"We did, and we got through it. Anyway, it's over now."

"For how long? If the Russians and Americans decide to go after each other, we'll all be in the middle, and it will be even worse this time."

"We made it through the war and the years afterwards and the flood. We'll make it through whatever comes."

As they came up on the Ponte Santa Trinita, she pointed to the Primavera statue. "Even the Primavera has her head now. It's over."

Four statues, representing the four seasons, had originally stood at the corners of the bridge, which had been destroyed during the war. After the war the statues had been rescued from the bed of the Arno, but the head of the Primavera had not been found until after the bridge had been rebuilt, and the statue had remained headless for three years.

"I liked it without the head," he said. "It was a reminder of the war."

"We don't need reminders."

"We don't, but what about the next generation? If it's all rebuilt like nothing ever happened, how will they ever understand? Graziella doesn't know how it was. For her, when you turn the tap on, water comes out. You don't even ask if it's safe to drink. When you flip the switch you have light. There is food in the markets, roofs and walls on the buildings, no uncollected garbage stinking in the streets. Her family is all nearby, nobody missing. She doesn't know what it's like to freeze every time an airplane goes overhead, to feel fear everywhere, all the time. And it's the same for all her generation. And if they don't understand, they will let it happen again."

"She'll know. I'll tell her and you'll tell her. Just like everybody else's parents will."

But he knew it wouldn't be enough. The truth was that there had been wars since the beginning of mankind, wars that had grown with man's ability to destroy. There was no reason to think they would ever stop. The best he could hope for was that the next one would not be in his lifetime. Or in Graziella's.

"You worry too much," Ivana said.

She was right. He squeezed her arm. There was no point in wasting the good days. Tomorrow could bring anything, or just as likely take away everything. For now the war was over, the years of poverty were ending and the recovery from the flood was well underway. Even the grief over his other daughter, the secret one, once a constant, encompassing pain, now came only in waves, washing over him at unexpected moments and then receding for a while.

He was especially pleased with his new job. Signorina Cohen, the director of the school where had been teaching, was a war refugee from Austria. He had always assumed she had a coterie of private demons, but in recent months her eyes had taken on an empty look and she had begun talking to herself. A few weeks ago the neighbors found her walking around the neighborhood, staring ahead, not returning their greetings. Bruno worried about her, but was glad he no longer depended on her for work. His life was as good as he could hope for.

They walked on, arm in arm, the child on Bruno's shoulder, the touch of the evening breezes gentle on his skin. Yes, he said to himself, for now, at least, it is good. He would not listen to that little voice that asked, *but for how long?*

When they arrived at their building. Bruno unlocked the great *portone* downstairs, they climbed up and he let them into their apartment where they were greeted by the familiar sound of his mother snoring. Maybe *Nonna* would be asleep, too. But there was a light in the living room, and when they entered he saw his grandmother sitting on the sofa. Bruno could tell by the set of her mouth that she was not pleased. "She wanted me to come stay with her because she was afraid of the fireworks," *Nonna* complained, pointing to the snoring coming from her daughter's room. "And there she is sleeping like a baby, while I'm wide awake."

"Did the fireworks keep you awake?" Ivana asked.

"I've lived through two world wars. Fireworks don't bother me. But how can anybody sleep with that thunder?"

Bruno went over and sat beside her. "Poor *Nonna*. I'm sorry. Do you want me to take you home?"

Her face softened a little. "No, I'll stay. I'm sure I won't sleep at all, but I don't want to miss seeing that precious child tomorrow."

"Would you like Ivana to make you a cup of chamomile tea?"

"That would be nice. You wouldn't mind, would you, *cara*?"

"Of course not," Ivana said, "but let me put Graziella to bed first."

Bruno carried Graziella to her room and laid her on the bed. He and Ivana each took off one of her shoes and socks, and Bruno lifted her to a sitting position while Ivana undressed her, put her nightie on, and tucked her in. She was about to turn the light off when *Nonna* announced that she had to kiss her. Bruno watched *Nonna*'s body bent over the child and felt a rush of gratitude for the family that surrounded his daughter.

Later, after Ivana and Bruno had settled the old woman and were alone in their room, he sat on the bed and took his shoes off while Ivana brushed her hair. "She is pretty, the American girl, isn't she," Ivana asked.

"She wasn't then," Bruno peeled his socks off and tossed them in the corner of the room.

Ivana climbed into bed. "How long ago was it?"

He carefully hung his shirt on the back of a chair, removed his trousers and hung them on a hanger. "About ten years. It was the year I got the first car."

"You remember her well."

"There was a problem with Signorina Cohen."

"How is Signorina Cohen? Have you heard any more?"

"No, just what I told you already. She is getting worse."

"*Poverina*. I'm worried about her."

Bruno nodded and climbed into bed. "I'll try to check in on her this summer."

Ivana turned off the bedside lamp, reached for him and he turned over to meet her. But later, as he lay relaxed on the edge of sleep, memories of the girl wandered through his thoughts and of the year he first knew her. It had been a darker time then and he had not wanted to like her. Foreign, imagined to be as rich as he believed all Americans to be, undamaged by the war, she represented everything he was angry about.

# 2

*Winter, 1957*

A Tramontano, the wind that brings storms from the north, blew
hard that morning, carrying great droplets of rain that puddled deep
on the paving stones of the street. Bruno, riding his Vespa to Scuola
Cohen where he taught, struggled to keep the scooter upright as the
wind pelted him with rain. Its chilly touch crept down his neck, up
his sleeves. He hated being cold, hated the way the cold occupied his
body like an invading army, pushing all other concerns aside, leaving
no option but to endure. He was worried, too, about what this chill
would bring. He knew he would catch a cold before the winter was
out. The cold would be followed by a cough, and the cough would
cling until spring. He was twenty-six years old, and there had been
no winter he could remember that this had not happened. But he
hoped it would not happen so early in the season. Not the first day
of school.

He arrived half an hour before the bell. The small private *liceo*
occupied a flat on the top floor of a three-story, stone building. With
its high ceilings and large windows, it was expensive to heat, especially here in Italy where most power was imported. But Signorina
Cohen always kept the rooms comfortably warm. A fierce Jewish
woman who had come to Florence by way of the war, she was fist
tight about most things. Bruno could only guess what memories she
held at bay with this particular extravagance.

Now, in the small room that served as her office and faculty meeting space, a pot of water simmered on a hot plate. Bruno made himself a cup of chamomile. The first swallow left a trail of welcome heat, and soon his whole body felt warm. He felt relieved to have avoided the bone-grasping chill he feared. Maybe it would not be such a bad year.

He looked over his class lists as he finished his tea. The second classical lyceum and first scientific lyceum had been combined for mathematics and physics, the two classes he taught. Bruno was not surprised at this arrangement. The school was small, about thirty students in all, and there were only four classrooms for five grades. But he was concerned about the lone girl in first classical, who had also been scheduled with that group.

If she was in this school for students with problems because she couldn't do math, it was going to be difficult to juggle such a group. The name, too, Nadia Jensen, didn't bode well. It looked foreign, maybe American. She might even be here because she didn't speak Italian, although most Americans went to the English speaking school in Florence.

Signorina Cohen came in. Her squat body barely came chest level to the giant of a man who accompanied her. He was an American, dressed in khaki pants and brown loafers. His blond, close-cropped hair was nearly white, and, under equally light eyebrows, his eyes were electric blue. After Signorina Cohen introduced him as Signor Jensen, he explained to Bruno in heavily accented Italian that he and his daughter had lived in Rome for several years and he wanted her in an Italian school to improve her Italian.

Bruno nodded but was silent. A childhood spent under fascism had done nothing to change his natural inclination to keep his words close. Nor did he trust, after Signor Jensen left, when Signorina Cohen told him that the girl was very good in math. Signorina Cohen was always impressed by mathematical ability as she herself was mystified by even the simplest calculations.

One day, in the first months Bruno had been teaching here, she took him aside and asked him in a lowered voice to stay after school. She needed "a little help" with her books. Bruno agreed, and that afternoon he spent hours untangling her accounts. Then, because he preferred to do them himself rather than struggle with the broken connections of her arithmetical logic, he offered to take them over. She scowled and told him that she couldn't pay extra.

Bruno shrugged and said that he hadn't intended for her to pay. She smiled like a child and produced a tin of cookies and a bottle of cognac from her desk. From then on he stayed after school once a month, and he was always offered a cookie, as often as not stale, and a small glass of cognac. After the books were balanced, he had to explain them to her. He didn't look forward to these afternoons, but he accepted them. What else could he do? Signorina Cohen had no family to count on. Somebody had to help. Besides, her bookkeeping was a peril to the school, and his job.

Sometimes, while he worked through the short winter afternoons in her office, he wondered how this ugly, ill-tempered woman had come through the wreck of Europe to start a school here in Florence. But she never talked about the past. She talked about the school—a lifelong dream, she told him, because a teacher can make a difference, and if she could make a difference in only one student's life then her own life would have meaning.

Bruno was of the opinion that too many people already made too much of a difference in other people's lives, but he said nothing. And he said nothing now about the American, preferring to wait until he knew what he was dealing with. But he did not set great store by Signorina Cohen's ability to assess anyone's mathematical talents.

Although he was intrigued by Americans, he didn't especially like them. Their smiles were too unselfconscious, too trusting, big mouth-hanging-open smiles that didn't care what they revealed.

During the war, when he was still a boy, the Americans were his heroes. Florence had been occupied first by the Germans, then the English and finally the Americans. The Germans, from the start, even when they were officially allies of the Italians, had been coarse and domineering, strutting through the streets as they spoke their guttural gibberish and taking what they wanted as their right. The British arrived as liberators, but they were standoffish and fussy. It was difficult to warm up to them. The Americans were friendly, well-supplied and generous. Bruno was also impressed with the confidence of the American soldiers. They seemed to fear nothing.

Now that the war was over, however, his feelings had softened for the Germans, whose cities had been razed. They vacationed in Italy now, middle-aged men with ruined pink skin, paunchy figures and dumpy, frizzy-haired wives. Fellow Europeans, they too had been marked by the war and its aftermath. At the same time, he became impatient with the Americans, unscathed and innocent, like well-fed farm animals who know nothing of their own vulnerability. They came as tourists, in droves, more every year, and most of the time he didn't allow himself to give them any more attention than he might give the flies in the fruit market. There were other Americans, too, not tourists. Some lived permanently in Florence, blending in quietly, but Bruno had never known one of these personally.

Now he had an American girl as a student. He saw her immediately when he entered the classroom. She was thirteen or fourteen years old, physically remarkable only for her coloring. She had the same blue eyes and pale skin as her father, but her hair was thick and almost black. She seemed young for her age. The other girls in the class wore stockings and flats, while she still wore white socks and sturdy shoes.

He wished that she, and all the other foreigners, would go home, take their strange languages and fat purses and leave the city to the Florentines. Let them try to put their lives back together in peace.

But she was here and it was his job to teach her. He gave her a unit from the text to read and told her to do as many of the exercises as she could. When he was finished with the main group, he would explain anything she had trouble with.

In about twenty-five minutes she looked up from her work. Thinking that she was stuck, he told her he would get to her in a moment, but she said that it was all right, she was finished. He doubted that she had actually finished the sizeable amount of work he had given her and assumed that he was going to have to deal with inability to understand directions, dishonesty, or some more esoteric American tendency. In the meantime, if she said she didn't need him that was fine, because the main group certainly did. She listened as he explained their unit, her expression indicating both interest and understanding. He considered calling on her, putting her on the spot. But he felt her watching, as though aware of his curiosity, almost amused, and so he waited. He would know what he would know when he looked at her work.

When he finished explaining to the others, he assigned problems for them and turned his attention to her. She didn't have a desk mate, and he sat down in the double desk beside her, noting the nicotine stains on her fingers. American cigarettes, undoubtedly. Her family was probably so rich they bought them by the carton.

As he checked her work, it became clear that she was very good at math. She looked at him expectantly, but since she clearly knew how good she was, he saw no reason to tell her.

"Signorina Jensen," he said. "You have two choices. You can continue to do your unit in the first half hour of class and amuse yourself as well as you can when you are finished. I don't care what you do as long as it doesn't disturb the rest of the class." He looked at her coldly to make sure she understood. "Or, if you want," he continued, "you can go through the book on your own time—I will help you if you need me—and try to keep up with the group during this hour."

She nodded at the second suggestion, seeming pleased, even grateful. Well, maybe she could work on her own. Certainly it would be easier for him that way.

It rained all that day and the next, but on the third day the sun rose strong and unclouded. By the time school let out at one-thirty, the day was so pleasant that Bruno took his Vespa out into the open square of Piazza del Duomo, circling the massive cathedral and then veering off towards the riverside by Piazza Santa Trinita. A temporary bridge had been erected after Ponte Santa Trinita was destroyed during the war, but now they were rebuilding the old bridge. Bruno turned right at the riverfront. A construction barricade blocked his way, and he drove along the river to the next bridge, the Ponte alla Carraia. He crossed the river, doubled back to the other side of Ponte Santa Trinita, and parked his Vespa between the newsstand and a rotisserie cart that had appeared when construction began. The smell of apple fritters drew him to the stand. He didn't want to eat fruit before his lunch so he bought two pieces of fried polenta instead. When he got home he would ask his wife, Ivana, to make apple fritters. The apples would be good this time of year and Ivana made wonderful fritters—almost as good as his mother.

He walked over to the river to eat the polenta. A piece of canvas hid the top part of the bridge, but the three spans below were visible, rebuilt now, and their familiarity reached places deep inside him. He found them strangely fresh and clean and newly made, like a child's skin. He finished the polenta, wiped his face and hands on his handkerchief, and looked out across the river. It was good to stand here by the bridge, feel the sun on his back, and know that his city was coming back. Other things were also better. There was more money. Soon, perhaps this spring, he might even be able to afford a car. Bruno didn't often smile, but now, thinking about himself at the wheel of a Fiat 600, he felt a tugging at the corners of his mouth.

With these thoughts, he mounted the Vespa and headed for home.

The sun held all that week and the first half of the next week. Then the rain set in again, and fall began in earnest. The wind pushed down from the hills, buffeting its way along the river fronts, soon commanding all the open spaces of the city. To avoid the wind, Bruno chose a route to school that dog-legged through the narrow back streets where the wet stone of pavement and palace seemed to swallow all color. He had a windshield on his Vespa and no longer had to put newspapers under the front of his overcoat, but the scooter was still open to the cold. If all went well, though, and he was able to afford a car, this would be the last winter he would have to endure these chilly rides. In the meantime, the warmth of the school was always welcome, as was the yellow light of the classroom, weak though it was. And in last class before morning break, a class that seemed less interested and more uncomprehending than any he could remember, the intelligence of the American girl began, also, to be a welcome presence.

He was reserved with his students, especially the girls, but she was the best student he had ever taught, and if she had been Italian he might have shown more friendliness toward her. At that time in Florence, American cigarettes, blue jeans, and Zippo lighters were highly prized, and most of Bruno's friends collected American slang, loved American movies, and dreamed of going to America someday. In America they would become rich and live the kind of life they saw in the Hollywood movies. Bruno had shared these visions, when he was younger, and a part of him still did. He never missed an American movie. Humphrey Bogart was his favorite actor. Sometimes he even fantasized himself delivering Bogart lines, although Bogart's style, he insisted to his friends, was more genius than American. But mostly Bruno resisted the current Americanization. He smoked Nazionale cigarettes, lit them with wax *cerini*, wore "civilized trousers," and, in the drawl of his best street Florentine, the c's heavily aspirated, expressed his contempt for these trends. He was of the people, he said, and proud of it.

And so he was especially distant with the American girl, carefully avoiding eye contact in those moments when he felt her excitement at some grasp of the material, understanding that often leaped ahead of his explanation. He admired that she didn't seem intimidated by his aloofness, but it bothered him, too, as though she saw some part of him that he considered private.

One day in late November, when he was monitoring the mid-morning break, he looked up from his book to see that she was positioning herself to arm wrestle with one of her classmates, a boy named Rosselli. Girls arm wrestling with boys, with anyone for that matter, was clearly improper, and Bruno started to intervene. But Rosselli was an arrogant boy without a remnant of kindness that Bruno had ever witnessed. The off-chance that Rosselli might have to endure the humiliation of being bested by a girl had a certain appeal. Bruno lowered his head to his book, keeping the scene in view. Several of the boys standing around glanced at Bruno, but he kept his head down. The bodies of the other boys blocked most of what was going on, but Bruno had a clear view of Rosselli's face. He watched uncertainty cross it, then a stunned, furious awareness, and then he heard the cheering of the other boys. Bruno rose and went to the desk they clustered around. The girl was the only one who didn't look uncomfortable. She smiled at him, inviting him to share the pleasure of her victory.

"Arm wrestling does not become a lady, Signorina," he said.

"Yes, *professore*, "she answered, although she continued to smile.

Later that day Signorina Cohen asked him how the Jensen girl was doing. She had heard rumors of unladylike behavior. Bruno said that he hadn't had any problems with her, and Signorina Cohen seemed mollified. About a week before Christmas break, however, the girl came to school with a bad cold. Bruno, who by now was allowing himself to hope he might make it to Christmas without a cold and had no intention of exposing himself to hers, sent her out of his class to work in the hall. Signorina Cohen pulled him aside at the end of the morning and asked him what Signorina Jensen had done to be sent out. Bruno explained that he had sent her to the hall because he didn't want to catch her cold.

"I don't know," Signorina Cohen said. "She fell asleep in Professor Berlazzi's class today." Professor Berlazzi was the history teacher and talked in a flat monotone that made Bruno want to fall asleep every time he had a conversation with him.

"I think she's up to something," Signorina Cohen went on.

"She has a cold," Bruno said, reasonably. "She's sick."

"I don't know," Signorina Cohen repeated, with the inward look of a brooding hen. Her expression bothered Bruno, who had seen her make people's lives miserable because of her skewed and troubled interpretations of chance words or actions. He was glad when the girl missed school all the last week before Christmas vacation, hoping that lack of contact would distract Signorina Cohen. And in the meantime, he still had not caught a cold.

Although it didn't rain the first day after vacation and the morning was not so dark as some, the wind whipped at Bruno's trousers and coat as he drove his Vespa to school. But, wearing the wool scarf his mother had knitted for him and, under his flapping trousers, the long underwear his wife had bought him, he felt prepared for anything the weather might bring and charged with energy, ready to return to work.

The students, however, were restless, slow to settle down, and seemed to have forgotten more over vacation than they had learned all fall. The Jensen girl, who could usually be relied on to help carry an inattentive class, was pale and struggled with a cough. Bruno didn't call on her even in the brief interludes when she wasn't coughing, knowing from his own experience that such interludes were often only fragile truces that the speaking of a single work could break. It was the damp cold here in the valley that produced those coughs, and it didn't help, of course, that she smoked. That was hardly likely to stop her, however. It certainly had never stopped him. Although he had had a winter cough since before he could remember, he had tried his first cigarette when he was ten years old and had smoked ever since.

That cough had served him well years before. He was fourteen years-old, and had set off about an hour before dusk, carrying a message across town from his father. He knew without being told that the message he carried was dangerous. "Go straight to Mario," his father said. "Don't give this to anyone else."

Fear mingled with excitement, heightening his perceptions at the time and etching hard edges on the memories he carried now—the sudden light as he came out from the narrow Borgo San Frediano into the open square of Piazza Nazario Sauro, lost again as soon as he entered Via Santo Spirito; the enormous white cat sitting inside the barred window of a ground floor apartment, its haughty air tempting him to stop and tease it (at any other time he would have); the acrid smell of the public urinals as he turned towards Piazza Santo Spirito; the cold that stiffened his face and hands and reddened blotchy patterns on his legs, still in short pants; and, as always during those years when there was never quite enough to eat, the dull, empty presence that worried at his stomach.

As he entered the square, he found himself in front of two German officers. Looking as unconcerned as he could, he attempted to walk by them. The younger one blond, his skin pink, eyes icy blue, took hold of Bruno's shoulder and stopped him. The other officer laughed as the young one smiled and offered Bruno a cigarette, saying something in German that Bruno didn't understand. The accompanying gesture, however, made it clear what he wanted.

Bruno's heart was pounding. He had never been propositioned before. The officer stroked Bruno's hair and said, in his broken Italian, "*No paura*." Normally Bruno would have tried to run away, to depend on his youthful speed and knowledge of the city to aid his escape, but the message he carried made him fearful. He accepted the cigarette and, with a spark of what, even now, he judged to be genius—or at least close to genius—he pretended he had never smoked before. A few fake coughs were enough to fuse the spasms of the real cough that never left him for long. Soon he was able to retch, managing a thin string of phlegm and saliva which fell across the toe of the officer's boot. He was ashamed at the insignificance of this pale, sour product against the powerful boot, its heavy, polished leather creased and scarred with use. But, small or not, this blob was enough to do the trick. The two officers laughed, but they turned and left.

Now, in his classroom, watching a student struggle at the blackboard, it intrigued Bruno that he remembered the incident with such clarity. He doubted that either of the officers had any memory of it. He wondered if any careless action of his had ever become part of the mythology of one of his students. Certainly not today—their attention seemed to be on everything but him.

After class, during morning break, Signorina Cohen passed him in the hall. "Did you see Signorina Jensen today?" He didn't answer her, but her conspiring tone made it clear that she had not put aside her doubts about the girl. All in all, it was not a good first day. Though on his way home he noted a slight but discernible increase in the strength of the sun.

February came in colder than January and rainier, but the wind slackened its attack, and the days were longer now. At school, Signorina Cohen continued to hint at some suspected problem with Signorina Jensen, while the girl continued to be besieged by her cough. Bruno was sympathetic and even reconciled by now to his inevitable exposure to her germs, but there was little he could do for her. In the meantime, he spent his afternoons pricing cars and revising budgets.

By the end of February, the rain had thinned, and the light that penetrated the clouds slanted increasingly true. Bruno remained well. He considered that not only was a car a possibility, but that perhaps he would make it through the winter in good health.

One afternoon, in March, a friend who sold cars called him and told him he had a situation with a car and could give Bruno the "deal of a lifetime" on it. That afternoon, after studying all the details, Bruno signed the papers for a little Fiat 600, shiny, new-smelling and totally beautiful.

He arranged to pick the car up after his sister, Annamaria, returned from work so she could drive the Vespa home. On the way back, he stopped at the newsstand under the loggia in Piazza Repubblica. He bought a newspaper and exchanged a few pleasantries with the vendor. He wanted to say something casual about his car, but all he could think of was, "I have to leave now. I have to pick up my car." As he turned to go, he almost walked into the Jensen girl who stood behind him waiting to pay. She had been there when he first came up, he now realized, looking at the comics at the other side of the newsstand. He hadn't recognized her. She seemed younger and shorter, bundled in her winter coat.

Not wanting her to think that he had deliberately ignored her, Bruno made an effort to say something. Although the writing on the front of the science fiction magazine she bought was in English and he couldn't read it, he was familiar with the magazine in Italian and remarked that it was one of his favorites.

"I like it, too," she said, and he was surprised at an awkwardness or shyness in her voice that was unlike her usual stance in class.

He couldn't think of anything else to say. She would not be

impressed by his car—all Americans had cars, cars with big engines and lots of chrome. He wondered what it would be like to sit in a big American car, a Cadillac, maybe, with leather seats. She had probably ridden in lots of Cadillacs. "Smell the air," he said. "Soon it will be spring."

"I won't be here then."

"Why not?" he asked, surprised.

"We're going back to America in two weeks."

He tried to imagine her in America, but all he could conjure up was a ship with her on it getting smaller and smaller until it disappeared and she disappeared, too.

"How long have you been here?"

"Two years now."

"That's a long time. Your relatives and friends will be excited to see you." He thought of his grandmother that he visited in the country, but not as often as he should. She was always so happy to see him. He would visit her more often now that he had a car. He liked the image of driving out to see her.

"I have a horse in America," the girl said. "I hope he hasn't forgotten me." Now he imagined her bareback on a spotted horse, her hair loose behind her, galloping across a vast plain like the ones he had seen in the movies.

"You'll be glad to get back to him."

She nodded. "Yes, but I'm also sad that we're leaving."

"Why?"

"I like it here. The buildings and the streets, the colors. They're so rich and soft at the same time. I don't know . . ."

Again he was surprised by a hesitancy in her manner that he was not used to and a little touched, too, by her affection for the city. He wanted to smile at her and tell her not to forget Florence and to have a good life with her horse. "Well," he said instead. "Life goes on. And don't forget to study for the test tomorrow."

Annamaria was furious when she got home from work and heard about the car. "We'll never get a bigger apartment," she said, in tears. He tried to calm her because he needed her to help bring the car home. Ivana didn't drive the Vespa. Finally he was able to persuade Annamaria to come by promising to teach her to drive the car. Her mood softened, though, when she actually saw the car. Together they circled it as he pointed out all its features.

Then he handed her the key to the Vespa and got in the driver's seat. He turned on the ignition and ran through the gears. He had only driven once before and getting home was a little more difficult than he had anticipated, but by the time he got to their house he had located the lights and was able to stop without stalling and to shift without lurching. Annamaria ran upstairs to get his wife and mother, while he waited in the car, his hands relishing the feel of the wheel and of the knob of the stick. Tomorrow he would call his cousin, Renato, and they would go outside the city and test his skills on the curves of the hills. And he would take *zio* Michele for a ride. His uncle had made his way back from the Russian front a few years ago, hobbling on crutches. Both feet had lost toes to frostbite and he didn't get around much. It would be fun to take him out.

Now his family came out the main door, excited, all talking at once. They loaded in and he took them out for a drive through downtown and out onto the *viale*'s that circled the town. When he brought them back, it was not easy for him to lock the car and leave it outside.

He was up early the next morning, and, although it was not yet April, when he opened the door to go out, he thought that he caught a whiff of spring freshness in the air. Certainly he felt a renewal of energy as he saw his little blue car waiting by the curb. He had left his long underwear off, thinking he could use the car's heater, but once he was in the car he found he didn't need the heater. He arrived at school early and, as soon as his first colleague arrived, he brought him down to see the car. Soon, a crowd of students and teachers stood around admiring the car, inspecting every detail. Even Signorina Cohen looked impressed and made him promise to take her for a ride.

"I need to talk to you," she said, as they walked upstairs together. "I've been watching Signorina Jensen. She comes to school tired every day and her eyes are red, like she hasn't gotten enough sleep." Signora Cohen spoke in a hoarse whisper. "She's that age, you know . . . And they say Americans don't have any morals. I think she's . . . you know . . . at night . . . pleasuring herself."

Bruno, who had been struggling to grasp what she was trying to say, stopped walking and stared at her.

"Boys aren't the only ones. " He heard an edge of defensiveness in her voice now. "Of course, nice girls don't . . ."

"She looks tired because she's been sick and she's worn out with a cough." Bruno kept his voice quiet and reasonable, knowing that frontal engagement was counterproductive with Signorina Cohen.

"I have a responsibility to my other students, nice girls. I can't let their innocence be soiled by the things she knows."

Bruno didn't answer.

"I've been watching her. I know girls."

"I think it's just her cough," Bruno said, filtering all feeling from his face and his voice, but, as he went into his first class, he felt stunned and sick. The girl is only here for two more weeks, he tried to reason with himself. As long as Signorina Cohen doesn't tell her what she's thinking, it won't be so bad. But the feeling of the morning was shattered.

It was test day for all of his classes. He had a collection of text books at home, and it was his habit to take problems from these texts for his tests. Usually he solved the problems himself the night before to make sure they were suitable. Last night he had been busy with the car and had simply pulled a certain number of problems from the appropriate chapters. He began working the problems out now, while the students were taking the tests, to make sure they didn't contain the need for material he hadn't covered yet.

As he worked, he thought about what Signorina Cohen had said. He told himself that her ideas about the girl weren't really his business, and, besides, he didn't think there was anything he could say that would change her mind. Still, he tried to remember times in which he had had some influence on her, hoping to reconstruct what might have been the word or tone or stance that had caused her to listen to him. While he was considering these things, he found himself struggling with the last problem on the test.

The problem was not conceptually beyond what had been done, but it was complex and demanded a thorough understanding of the material. It was also a little tricky. The wording indicated an approach in setting it up that didn't work. He had fallen into the trap himself at first. He wouldn't have selected this problem for this class if he has gone through it beforehand, but he would take the difficulty into account when he graded. He wondered now if the Jensen girl would figure it out. He got up and stood behind her. She moved so that he could see and pointed—yes, she had figured out how to set it up and had started the lengthy calculations that would be needed to finish it.

He remembered how impressed Signorina Cohen had been with her at the beginning of the year. And now an idea came to him. If he could get Signorina Cohen to focus on the girl's talents in math, maybe she would forget this other rubbish she had come up with.

"Take your work and come with me, Signorina," he said and led her out of the class. He knocked on Signorina Cohen's door and entered. "Signorina Jensen has solved the most difficult problem on my test," he said. "The other students are all craning their necks to see how she did it. I thought it would be better for her to be out of the room. Could she finish the test in here?"

He returned to the classroom uncertain if he had done the right thing, hoping Signorina Cohen would be impressed and not seize the opportunity to question the girl about her supposed nocturnal activities. Then, as he realized the girl would know he was lying, he felt embarrassed at his ploy. No one had been looking at her test. They hadn't even started that problem. He had no idea what she would think about this.

When the hour was over, he went back to Signorina Cohen's office to get the girl's test. She sat talking to Signorina Cohen. The tin of cookies was open, and a slightly nibbled cookie lay on the desk in front of her. Signorina Cohen was smiling. The girl looked at Bruno, making no attempt to hide either understanding or gratitude.

Oh well, Bruno thought, the owner of a new car could afford to be generous. He leaned against the side of the door and let the corners of his mouth rise slightly, his eyes half closed, in what he imagined was a Bogart expression of cynical friendliness. But, as he met the girl's eyes, the sun pouring through the window, dust motes dancing in the light, his car waiting downstairs, he was unable to suppress a full, unrestrained smile.

# 3

It usually rained the day after the fireworks. "To wash the sky clean of all that nonsense," *Nonna* said. But this year the pleasant weather held through June. July, however, brought a fierce heatwave that gripped all of Europe. Florence, trapped in the valley, registered some of the hottest temperatures while the exhaust from the ever growing number of cars left everyone with raw throats, red eyes, and burning noses. Anyone, who could, stayed home. Bruno went to the movies.

Second-run movies were cheaper, but on the fifth afternoon of the heat wave Bruno indulged in the comfort of the first-run, air-conditioned *Gambrinus. Who's Afraid of Virginia Woolf?* was playing. When the film was over, the audience shuffled out. As they flowed into the lobby and began to disperse, he bumped into Signorina Jensen.

He braced himself for an encounter with her two friends, but they were nowhere in sight. The stream of people pulled them along so that it was difficult to talk, but there was an area to the side of the lobby, out of the flow of traffic, and he pointed to it. She slid through the crowd easily. He followed.

"Do you usually go to the movies alone?" he asked, as they moved away from the larger crowd.

"Yes." She replied, with a hint of challenge in her eyes. "Do you?"

"Yes," Bruno smiled. "But I'm a man."

"And?" Signorina Jensen paused for a moment, before adding. "It's a different experience seeing a movie alone. I like it."

Most Italian women didn't go to movies alone, but Bruno was aware that Americans did things differently, and her answer made sense to him. He couldn't think of anything really wrong with a woman being alone in the theater, especially in the afternoon. It was the kind of thing his sister might do. He could almost hear her. *It's 1967, after all. I'm a modern woman. If I want to go to the movie why should I wait until someone else wants to?*

"Did you like the film?" Bruno asked.

"Well . . ."

"You didn't like it?"

"I thought Sandy Dennis was good. And I always enjoy Richard Burton."

Bruno shrugged. In his opinion, Richard Burton had a fat baby face unsuited to the dramatic roles he liked to play, but Ivana and Annamaria both liked him so it must be one of those things that the opposite sex didn't understand. "I like Elizabeth Taylor," he said.

Nadia met his eyes and smiled. She was wearing her long hair loose and she tucked it behind her ears. "I liked the ending," she said. "That shot by the window. That was great." She paused. "What did you think?"

The crowd had dispersed, and Nadia and Bruno started toward the door.

"Why did he behave that way?" Bruno asked.

"They were drunk."

Bruno was surprised at the way she said this, as though drunkenness was completely normal. "Why would he get drunk in front of his guests?"

"Americans are less inhibited than Italians, in some ways."

"I don't understand Americans." Bruno sighed loudly, knowing he was being rude, but feeling suddenly irritated at Richard Burton, at the man he played, at all Americans. "He was a professor. He should be ashamed."

They reached the front of the lobby and stepped through the tall glass doors of the cinema. The heat was like a wall. "Oof," Signorina Jensen said.

"*Un caldo cane*," Bruno agreed. "It's the valley that holds the heat in." But he didn't want to talk about the weather. "Wouldn't he have gotten in trouble with the university? What about his students? Would they have any respect for him after that?"

"People would probably let it go, for a while," Nadia said. "They'd figure he was going through a hard time, having an identity crisis or something."

Her hair had fallen into her face, and Nadia lifted and twisted it somehow so that it stayed up briefly before falling again. "I don't like it when movies are like plays, mostly dialogue. I'd rather see that kind of thing in the theater."

The same thought had occurred to Bruno during the film. He loved the visual possibilities unique to the cinema. "But there were some nice shots."

"Yes, but I like European films: Bergman, Fellini, Rossellini, and Antonioni, too."

"How do you understand Antonioni and Rossellini?" Bruno asked. "You're an American." *A beautiful, privileged American.*

"You learn by watching, like reading or traveling—you see what life is like for other people. People are the same everywhere, just their circumstances are different."

"How can you say that? You live in a country where everybody has everything they want." He didn't control the edge in his voice. "I don't see how we Italians are anything like Americans."

"I'm not like people in those movies either." She didn't seem to be put off at all by his tone. "Most people aren't. Hollywood makes everything slick and perfect. It's all escapism."

He stared at her. Hollywood had certainly provided a major escape for him but that was different. Coming of age in the poverty of postwar Italy, he and his peers had devoured American films with the hunger of teenagers struggling to find their way in a broken society. They were fascinated by this distant world where everyone had large houses, new cars, and perfect bodies. They fantasized about women whose voluptuous endowments were half visible in the scanty American clothing not permitted in Italy at that time. "Americans have everything they need," he said finally. "What are they escaping from?"

"They don't all have everything they need. There's a lot of poverty, especially in the inner cities."

"But most Americans are rich." Although they were in the shade, under the stone loggia outside the theater, Bruno could feel the sweat beginning to trickle down his back.

"You've seen too many American movies," Nadia said, her face glowing with a light film of perspiration. "American movies don't reflect reality. They're a diversion for middle-class Americans, a way to pretend there's nothing wrong with their world."

Her voice had risen and there was a little furrow between her brows. Now suddenly Bruno could see the girl he had known years ago.

The front of the theater was filling for the next show and Bruno and Signorina Jensen were blocking the entrance. But Nadia, her eyes intense, her face lit up with enthusiasm, seemed unaware.

"Well, we're certainly not rich here," Bruno said. He placed his hands on her shoulders and gently moved her aside. "Except for the industrialists in Milan. We have cars, now," he added. "Meat on the table, a little extra money. But we're not wealthy like Americans. Our schools are overcrowded. There's serious poverty in the South."

"Things need to change. We need to break away from materialistic values. We need to elect leaders who will focus on eliminating poverty."

Bruno thought of how as a boy everyone he knew had been excited that Mussolini was leading Italy to its former greatness. What a terrible joke that had been. Then, after the war, the focus had been on freedom and democracy, a fresh start. But what had come of it? Corruption. Bureaucratic inefficiency. Ceaseless bickering among the different parties. And there was the rest of the world—the purges under Stalin, the increasing aggressiveness of the Americans in Viet Nam, the constant fear that the cold war would spiral out of control.

"I'm not sitting around waiting for things to change," he said. Then, returning to the subject that interested him, asked, "If the people in the movies aren't what Americans are really like, what are they like?"

"Unfortunately the people in *this* movie were pretty real," she answered.

"Really? You know people like that in America?"

"A few." And then, her eyes amused, she asked, "Are there really people like Monica Vitti in *L'Avventura*?"

Bruno laughed, his irritation slipping away. "We have a few degenerates, but most people are just trying to get by. Like the young men in the *Vitelloni*. Did you see the *Vitelloni*?"

"Years ago."

"It's playing this Sunday, if you want to see it again. It's at the movie club on via Cavour."

"I'll be there."

Looking back, it seemed to Bruno that this was the pivotal moment, the moment when everything changed. Up until then he could have walked away without ever seeing Nadia again, without regret. But the ability to see clearly is the first casualty in these matters, and, having delivered his invitation as easily and unpremeditatedly as he might have held the door for her, he walked home with a light heart.

# 4

Four days later, at nine-thirty in the morning, Bruno rose from the breakfast table, kissed Ivana, Graziella, and his mother, and set out for his movie club.

The cool of the night still lingered in the air, and he felt energized as he walked towards the theater that his club rented on Sundays. He told himself that he didn't really expect Signorina Jensen show up, that he didn't really care if she did or not. But as he neared the theater, he could not deny the sense of expectation in the pit of his stomach and a tightening in his chest. He spotted Signorina Jensen immediately, paying the membership necessary to get in. He made his way towards her, trying to look casual as he greeted friends gathered at the entrance.

"You came," he said.

She smiled.

Two of his friends joined them as they went into the theater, their demeanor leaving no doubt as to their interest in Nadia. Bruno managed to sit next to her, though he tried to make it seem like he was merely taking the closest available seat. It would not do, he told himself, to leave her to the mercy of his friends.

He had seen the *Vitelloni* several times, and he admired the way the film captured the experience of these young men with too few possibilities and too many hormones. But now, sitting next to Signorina Jensen, as the young men prowled the streets exuding the longing of such men, it was as though Bruno had returned to the long summer nights of his own youth. His body was as aware of Nadia's as if they were physically touching.

When the movie was over and they stood up to come out of the theater, Bruno invited her to have an ice cream. There was a nearby café that sold cold drinks and ice cream, but it was overpriced and they only carried Motta ice cream, packaged, not freshly made. It was also where his friends would be hanging out. "If you don't mind walking a few blocks," he said, "there's a place behind the Duomo that sells wonderful ice cream."

"That sounds good." She smiled.

They came out onto the sidewalk, and, taking her arm, he quickly steered her in the opposite direction from the one his friends would be going in with an air of purpose that made it difficult for them to follow. He was pleased with how effectively he had cut them off.

"Tell me about your new job," she said, as they walked towards the cathedral. "How did you get it?"

"It was a stroke of luck. There's an old colonel who lives near me who has pull, and, since he owed me a favor, he recommended me. I'd probably be teaching at the Cohen school until the day I died otherwise."

"Couldn't Signorina Cohen give you a recommendation?" She turned to look at him. Her eyes, reflecting the blue blouse she wore, seemed even bluer than usual.

"Signorina Cohen has no influence."

"What does that matter?"

"It's everything, unless you have the money for a big bribe," he answered. "And I don't," he added shrugging.

"But the jobs should go to the best people."

"It doesn't work that way. Italy is a corrupt country. But the important thing is I got lucky and I have the job."

"Why did the Colonel owe you?"

"Right after the flood it was hard to find food. All we had in the house were a few packages of apricot tarts and a little bit of fruit. We had pasta but couldn't cook it because there was no power to heat the water."

"You had water?"

"The water trucks arrived the first day. But my daughter was only four and she needed protein. I decided to go to my grandmother's house in San Domenico, up in the hills, out of the flood area. There would be plenty of protein there." They entered Piazza del Duomo. Its crowds of tourists forced them to walk closer and his sleeve brushed her arm. "The busses were out, and so I walked."

"That's a long way."

He nodded. "The mud downtown was deep, hard to walk through. And it stank. The naphtha was everywhere, all sorts of food carried away by the water was beginning to rot and dead animals were decomposing. After I made it through the flood area I still had a long climb. By the time I got there, several hours later, I was filthy and had blisters on my feet. My grandmother fed me, helped me clean up and sent me back with two roast chickens, three apples, a large slab of cheese and a dozen eggs. My cousin gave me a lift on his Lambretta as far as the edge of the flood zone. After that I was on my own in the mud again. It didn't take long for the chickens to begin leaking though the brown paper they were wrapped in."

He didn't want to sound like he was feeling sorry for himself, so he smiled and shrugged. "That's the way it was."

"It sounds pretty bad."

"Mainly I was worried about infection since we didn't have any way to heat water to wash the open blisters on my feet."

"I remember how cold it was. And it was still raining when I got here."

"Yes, the weather didn't help. It was dark by the time I reached the river, and when I crossed the bridge the wind cut like knives of ice."

"You were going to tell me about the Colonel."

"I was almost home when I passed his building. I didn't know him well, but I saw him sometimes in the square when I would take my daughter to play. He had a granddaughter, a little older. She was always friendly. Anyway, they had the front door open, and the maid was scrubbing oil from the walls in the entryway while the son-in-law was sweeping the floor with a big push broom. The Colonel was directing the operation, mainly by leading them in old military songs, from the First World War, I think, or even from campaigns before that." He laughed. "It was quite a scene. This old man with his pot belly and white hair, but his features still strong and his military posture as straight as ever, reliving his youth in another great adventure."

Signorina Jenson laughed, too. "I can see him," she said. "A sort of chubby Vittorio de Sica."

"Something like that. They were in the same situation as everyone else, and it would still be several days before they could get the child out of the city, so I gave them one of the chickens, one of the apples and four of the eggs,"

"Why did you do that?"

"The child needed protein. What could I do? You have to pull together when things are bad, and besides it never hurts to have a few favors to call in."

"A lot of people wouldn't have done it."

Bruno thought that most of the people he knew would have done it. He didn't know how to answer her.

"What happened next?" Signorina Jenson asked.

Feeling somewhat lightened of his load and anxious to be home, he had walked faster and with less care. At the end of the last block, just yards from his front door, he slipped in the mud, slamming into the wall of the *palazzo*. He heard the crack as one of the eggs broke.

He entered the apartment, his clothes covered with putrid mud, chicken juice and egg slime, set his loot on the kitchen table, put a towel on the seat of his favorite chair and collapsed in it. Ivana took his shoes off and washed his feet as well as she could with the little cold water available. Then he climbed into bed where the whole family was huddled together under layers of blankets and coats. Eventually he warmed up, and the blisters, miraculously, didn't get infected. But it was weeks before he felt free of the smell of chicken mixed with naphtha.

"What happened next, " he said to Signorina Jensen, "was that the Colonel always spoke to me when he saw me, and, when he found out that I was a math and physics teacher, he told me that there was going to be a job opening at the Galileo the next year, and I should apply for it." He had not thought he had a chance, but Ivana urged him to try, pointing out that the Colonel owed him something and might well have some influence. "I submitted my application and got the job."

"Wow," she said. Bruno was familiar with this sound Americans made, but this was the first time anyone had actually said it to his face. Although the Italian language, and certainly its many dialects, has its share of interjections, inserting this primal sound in the middle of a conversation seemed very strange to Bruno, and he wondered where it came from, whether it was an imitation of an animal or of an American Indian.

In the meantime they had arrived at the ice cream shop. The humid midday heat had set in, and Bruno's shirt clung to his back. He bought their ice creams in the front part of the café, raspberry for her and hazelnut for him, and then led her to the back area where a few tables were crowded together under an ancient overhead fan. The fan slowly moved the stale, smoke filled air around, its rhythmic squeak high-pitched like the call of a cricket hidden somewhere in the house.

They sat down at the last empty table, and now that they were face to face a wave of panic tightened Bruno's throat. What would he say to her? He ate a spoonful of his ice cream, not really tasting it, and then looked around the room in an effort to mask his discomfort. The blades of the fan threw a slow series of shadows on the walls of the room. "Look Signorina Jensen," he said, with a kind of desperate inspiration as he pointed to the fan. "*Casablanca.*"

She smiled. "But please don't call me Signorina Jensen. I'm Nadia."

"And I'm Bruno." Then he had no choice but to suggest that they use the familiar form. He had never used the familiar form with one of his students, never asked one of them to use it with him, but, of course, he told himself, she was no longer a student.

"How long will you be staying here?" he asked. The daring of the *tu* on his tongue was exciting, its intimacy intoxicating. He followed this question with as many others as he could think of in order to repeat the experience. Except for the fact that she had no immediate plans for returning to America, he didn't remember her answers. What stayed with him was the way she moved her wrists as she ate, gesturing with the spoon while she talked to him, the touch of her hand on his when he lit her cigarette, after she finished her ice cream, the curves of her body beneath her blouse when she leaned back to smoke, the fresh, slightly floral scent of her hair as they walked together.

That night he made love to Ivana with both the passion and the tenderness of their early days together.

# 5

Nadia was out of town the next Sunday, so Bruno didn't see her for two weeks. The weather, though still hot, was decidedly less humid than it had been, and during this time he was able to catch up on projects he had put off during the heat wave. He also had several students he was tutoring during the summer.

Nadia remained in his awareness—the graceful movements of her long arms and legs, the freshness of her cream-colored skin and especially the direct, almost challenging way she looked at him with her blue eyes. As he wandered through these days he found himself often smiling for no reason.

On Tuesday of the second week, the mother of one of his students asked him how her daughter was doing and if he thought she would pass the make-up exams in the fall. The daughter in question was a distracted adolescent girl who had as little interest in mathematics as she had talent for it. Bruno told her mother that he would be very surprised if she passed and the mother asked him if he would be willing to stay in town over the August holidays and tutor her daughter every day, instead of every other day. She offered to pay extra.

Bruno hesitated and then told her he would get back to her. Walking home he thought about it. He seriously doubted that any amount of tutoring would do any good and didn't generally like to get into impossible situations, but the extra money would be useful.

He and Ivana wanted to give Graziella a bicycle for her birthday in November and he was saving for this.

And there was something else. His family would be going to the sea for two weeks, and he had planned on going with them, but he knew Nadia would be staying in town. If he stayed, too, without his family, who knew what might ensue?

He had never had an affair. He had not been tempted and he did not want to risk hurting Ivana. But Ivana would be out of town. She would never know. He felt something stirring in him that had been dormant a long time, a willingness to reach for something more than safety. He decided to accept the job and send his family off to the sea without him and see what happened. When he told Ivana, she suggested that since they had already reserved rooms at the pensione, she should take *Nonna* instead.

Four years earlier, Bruno's cousin and his aunt and uncle had moved into town. Bruno's grandmother refused to leave the old house in the country and now lived alone with her chickens and a small kitchen garden. Her relatives checked in on her regularly and she seemed happy, but she had not been willing to go on vacation with them, saying she didn't want to leave her home unoccupied. "Those long-haired, foreign kids are everywhere. Some of them camping in the fields next to my home."

"You could keep an eye on her place," Ivana said now, "and take care of things." When they proposed this arrangement to his grandmother, she agreed, and so it was decided. Bruno would stay in town when the family left for vacation. The situation had an added bonus. His grandmother's house would be available, and, should the occasion arise, he wouldn't have to bring Nadia to his home.

Sunday finally dragged around. Bruno sat at the kitchen table, while his mother and Ivana busied themselves making breakfast. The room was cool and smelled of fresh bread, coffee and a hint of lemony soap where Ivana had scrubbed the Formica surface of the new table. Ivana loved the new table, but it made Bruno feel unreal, as if he were in one of those magazines with pictures of modern kitchens. He missed the oak table they had before, centuries old, dented and dinged by generations of children, including himself. But Ivana was pleased, and it was her kitchen after all.

Now in the distance Bruno heard the first bells of Santo Spirito as they announced the nine o'clock Mass. He was restless to be off but resolved not to look at his watch until he heard the second bells. Unless the sermon was unusually long, they would ring about ten minutes before he needed to leave. Graziella sat next to him, her head bent over a drawing, her colored pencils spread out around her, while Ivana busied herself at the stove. The blinds in the rest of the house were still shut so as to preserve the cool of the night, but Ivana had opened the small casement window in the kitchen, and a shaft of light backlit Graziella's head, picking out each wave of her dark hair and painting it with red highlights.

"Come on, put your things up," Ivana said to her now, as she brought hot milk and coffee to the table. "It's time to eat."

"Wait," Graziella said, bending her head closer over her drawing. "I need to finish."

Graziella was a cooperative child most of the time, but she approached her art with intensity and was often stubborn about leaving it. Ivana had little tolerance for dawdling at mealtimes, having like most Italian mothers an almost religious belief in children's need for structure, but Bruno sensed in Graziella's attitude a need beyond childish willfulness and often interfered in her behalf. He said nothing now, not wanting to fight with Ivana. He turned towards Graziella, intending to cajole her into obeying her mother, but the child leaned back to show him what she had drawn, a picture of the family taking a drive in the car.

"Look." He held the drawing up for Ivana to see. "She has drawn us in profile. And see how she has caught everybody." She had drawn him with his hands on the wheel of the car, taller than the rest, thin, his hair thick and dark. Ivana sat in the front seat next to him, leaning a little further back, so that both profiles were visible. She was smiling, with crinkled smile lines at the back of the one large eye that was visible, and her black hair was up in a French twist on the back of her head. Graziella herself had thick brown curls and sat in the back seat on the lap of her grandmother, Bruno's mother, whom at the age of two Graziella, for unknown reasons, had christened *Mamma Do'*. *Mamma Do'* was, in the picture as in real life, short and round with wispy, grey curls.

"I know she draws well," Ivana said, removing the pencils, "but it's time for her breakfast."

Graziella took the picture back from her father and clutched it to her chest, her lower lip out and beginning to quiver. "*Mamma Do'* doesn't have her glasses," she said. "I need to put her glasses on."

"She's almost done," Bruno said to Ivana. "Let her finish."

Ivana glared at him. "You make it harder for her when you encourage her."

Graziella began to whimper.

"Come on," Bruno said, leaning down and kissing the child on the head. "You need to eat to grow big." Graziella relinquished the drawing, but her lower lip still protruded.

"Look, we have raspberry jam, your favorite." Ivana put a plate with a roll on it in front of the child. "And you can finish your drawing right after breakfast." Graziella smiled now, and just at that moment the bells began ringing.

Now that the time had come, Bruno no longer felt restless. He slowly finished his coffee, enjoying the sense of anticipation at least as much as the hot drink. "I guess I'll leave for the theater," he said, prepared to explain why he was leaving early, but Ivana didn't seem to notice.

The morning light was bright as he stepped out of the dark of his building and began walking toward the Ponte alla Carraia. The sidewalks here on the far side of the Arno were quiet—the shops were shuttered for Sunday, the neighborhood people home or in church, and the tourists mostly on the other side of the river. The day felt new and fresh and full of promise.

Bruno arrived at the theater a little early, but Nadia was already there. She was wearing her hair down again, and several long strands blew across her face as she turned and smiled at him. She pulled it behind her ear, in a gesture that by now was familiar to him, and waved.

They entered the theater and found aisle seats halfway down. Bruno took the inside seat, and Nadia slid in beside him. In his younger days, if Bruno had been at the movie with an attractive woman he would have reached his arm around her, but he was older now, more able to appreciate the nuances of a slower pace, and, even more, he felt unsure with Nadia. As a man, he expected to make advances and be rejected, but he was uncomfortable with the idea of being rejected by an American woman, especially after all he had heard about how easy they were. And he couldn't tell if Nadia saw him as a possible suitor or just an old teacher of hers. The film was *War of the Worlds*, and he knew it was full of suspense. He decided that if Nadia jumped or cringed, he would risk comforting her. But she sat impassive, and he contented himself with letting his sleeve brush against her as they sat side by side.

When the film ended, he took her elbow to steer her through the crowd exiting. "Shall we have an ice cream?" he asked.

"Why don't you come to my place instead? I bought a new book about Italian film that I wanted to show you, and I made some lemonade this morning."

"That sounds nice." His pulse quickened. "Where do you live?"

"I have an apartment in via San Niccolo."

He wished now that he had taken his car instead of walking. Via

San Niccolo' was in the opposite direction from his home, and, by the time he walked there and back with even a short visit at Nadia's, he would probably be late for the midday meal, the big one of the day. But much as he regretted the discourtesy of being late, especially on Sunday when Ivana would have fixed something special, he had no intention of refusing Nadia's invitation. He would just have to make the visit short and walk home as fast as he could.

"Did you enjoy the film?" he asked as they passed through Piazza San Marco.

"Sort of."

"You don't like science fiction?"

"Oh, yes, I do. But not the kind where monsters from outer space invade the earth and then there's a big war."

They were walking down via Cavour, heading towards the Duomo. Bruno was about to suggest that they turn through the university area so they would miss the throngs of tourists, when, as though reading his mind, Nadia pointed towards via Pucci. "I always go that way," she said. "It's less crowded."

"What science fiction do you like?" he asked, as they made their way through the back streets.

"I like the ones that make you think about what different worlds would be like. There's a new writer in America. Ursula Le Guin. She wrote a novel about a planet where each season lasts five thousand days. She works out all the ways their culture is affected by that."

"Like *Notturno*."

She looked puzzled.

"By Isaac Asimov."

She was silent a moment and then her face lit up. "*Nightfall*," she said in English. "That's my favorite short story."

"Mine, too. A world with six suns. They never experience darkness and they never see the stars except for every couple of centuries when all the suns have set at once."

"And the few people who believe they're really going to see the stars think the predictions have been exaggerated and they will see four or five, at most." She chuckled.

Bruno looked over at her and felt a great sense of contentment. He had always thought that only men and boys liked science fiction, but she not only liked it, she had the same taste that he did.

They passed through the small piazza snuggled against the porticos of the Santa Maria Nuova hospital and turned right. Bruno pointed to the street sign that said via Portinari. "That was the family who built the hospital in the thirteenth century. It was quite a new thing in Europe. Florence was a leader in those days."

"But Florence is still an important city, isn't it?"

"Not like it used to be."

"But you have the greatest art in the world. It must feel amazing to be a Florentine. To be part of something so big."

He didn't know how to answer her. "I've never been anything else," he said finally.

"Well, I think Florence is wonderful and Italians are special."

He looked over at her and grinned. "At least we're still the best lovers."

She was silent and moment and then said, "So I've heard."

Her casual tone had a studied feel that made his heart thump. She felt it, then. That he was a man and she was a woman and all that went with it.

Once they arrived at via San Niccolo', they turned left and she pointed out her building, one of the old family *palazzi* on the south side of the street. A *portiere* sat in his little cubby at the entrance. He was ancient and greeted them with the kind of smiling courtesy that made it clear he would consider it his duty to be helpful to Nadia. Bruno was pleased.

"I'm on the third floor," Nadia said. "There's an elevator, if you want, but I like to walk. The elevator moans and groans and stops and starts. Even if I trusted it I would feel guilty about making it move its old bones."

"I don't mind walking." He was, in fact, used to it as there was no elevator in his building. They walked up side by side for the first two flights. The sound of their feet on the marble steps filled the space of the large open stairway. After they passed the second floor the steps became narrow and they went single file, Nadia in front. Bruno followed behind, the sway of her hips in his line of sight.

"So you think the elevator has feelings?" he asked. "And you, a woman who teaches math, who should know how to be logical?"

"I'm the one who has feelings. Not the elevator."

"Feelings of fear or feelings of guilt?"

"Both."

"Only about the elevator?"

She turned back to look at him, her blue eyes sparkling through a strand of her hair, and then laughed softly.

They were at the door of her apartment now, and he took the key from her and opened the door. As they entered, she called out something he didn't understand. A female voice called back, and then the two blondes appeared. Nadia led him into the living room and left him with the other girls while she went to get the book and the lemonade.

The room was typical of the *palazzi* of once wealthy families who could no longer afford their upkeep and had divided them into apartments and furnished them with what was left after they moved to smaller places, many of the pieces large and dark, some of them very nice, all of them old. But overlaid were indications of another kind of material ease—a new stereo and a collection of LP's next to it, a Nikon camera with a leather case on the table, an expensive leather jacket tossed over the back of a chair. The girls themselves wore new clothes, everything squeaky clean. Even their skin was fine-textured and pale. They were almost like dolls rather than people. Bruno began to wonder what he was doing here. One of the girls, the one with straight hair and a longer face, asked him in very careful Italian what he did but she didn't understand his answer. He repeated it several times, while she drew her brows together in valiant but futile concentration. Now the other girl pointed to herself and said in fractured Italian, "Me Heather."

"A pleasure to meet you. I'm Bruno."

"Bruno," she said.

He nodded.

"You say Heather," she said now, with a coy look.

He knew he couldn't pronounce a name whose sound his ear was not even vaguely attuned to, and he didn't want to try, but she insisted. "Ehzah," he said. Both girls laughed and repeated, "Ehzah, Ehzah," over and over, laughing each time they said it. He smiled politely and insincerely.

He minded having his pronunciation laughed at, of course, though he would have laughed at it himself if he had been with friends. He also thought it was rude of them not to be more polite with someone they barely knew. But more than that it was their self-assurance that grated on him, their careless material wealth and the sense they projected that just because they were American they owned the world and made the rules however they wanted, without self-consciousness or self-questioning.

Finally, Nadia returned to the room, a book under her arm and in her hands a tray with a pitcher of lemonade and four glasses. She set the tray down and poured the lemonade. Now the two blondes stood up, as if on cue. As they left the room, carrying their drinks, Heather said something in English to Nadia that Bruno didn't understand and, nodding towards Bruno, flicked her eyebrows up in a suggestive way. Bruno's discomfort suddenly passed into anger. He stood up. "I need to go." He didn't look at Nadia. "I'll be late for lunch."

She followed him to the door. When he shook her hand good-by, she looked at him, her face flushed, her eyes searching, troubled, not trying to hide it. He turned away and left.

As he walked home, he tried to sort it out. Nadia's two friends were intensely irritating to him, but it went deeper. It seemed to him that when they looked at him they saw *Foreign, Second Class* stamped all over him. It didn't matter that his culture was older and had made more important contributions to civilization. There was no getting past the fact that Italy was without political importance, without significant power in the world. And he felt, irrationally or not, that this lack of status reflected in some way on him.

And there was more. There was that moment when Heather gestured to Nadia as though they had planned together to bring him back to the house. Her expression had not been unlike that of a man in a whorehouse smiling to a friend as he went upstairs with a prostitute. For a moment, Bruno saw in his imagination the girls talking together beforehand, Nadia gleefully planning with her friends how she would lure the Latin lover to the apartment and then they would disappear. She would tell them all about it afterwards, of course.

*What a fool I am*, he thought. *She was playing with me. An American girl leaving an Italian man heartbroken, instead of the other way around. She's not who I thought at all. She's just a foreign femme fatale.*

The phrase *femme fatale* stopped him, though. There were many things he didn't know about Nadia, many, he was sure, that would be strange and difficult for him if he did, but he was quite certain that *femme fatale* was not the right description for her. She had been friendly, her responses to him showing a possible interest but certainly not seductive. And that look in her eyes when he left. That had been honest, and there had been genuine distress in it. He sighed. This openness of hers intrigued him, even while it disturbed him. He had been raised to believe that you must always present a public face, that making a *bella figura*, a good impression, was vitally important, but she appeared comfortable just letting him know who she was. And she seemed to be looking for the same from him. It wasn't that she was brash like her friends. That would have made him dismiss her immediately. But she so often seemed to speak to some rarely explored part of him.

He thought about the pain she had let him see those last few minutes before he left. He wasn't sure what had happened. Had she felt his anger? Was she hurt that he had left so quickly? Or was she embarrassed, maybe just as appalled by that Heather person's gesture as he was? By the time he got home he had decided that he just didn't know what happened. Nadia was American, and he was on unknown territory with her. But all that evening he was haunted by the thought that he might have been too quick to be offended, might have misread the situation and unfairly hurt Nadia's feelings. When he relived the look she had given him, as he did frequently throughout the evening, he wanted to rush back to her apartment and apologize. She would say it was all right and he would take her in his arms.

The next day he went to the stationery shop in Piazza Nazario Sauro and bought a sheet of white paper and an envelope and carried them over to the wall of the riverside to write a note to Nadia. It took some time to think exactly what he wanted to say, and the rough stone of the wall made some of his letters look like spider legs, but he was satisfied with what he finally produced.

*Dear Nadia,*

*Thank you for inviting me yesterday. I am sorry I had to leave so suddenly. I am looking forward to seeing you next Sunday.*

*Your friend,*
*Bruno*

He sealed the letter, put a stamp on it—but, after some thought, no return address—and mailed it. He then braced himself for the long wait until next Sunday, the first Sunday that his family would be gone.

All that week the house bustled with preparations. Ivana was impatient with everybody, his mother was flustered and nervous and Graziella was difficult and cried at the slightest provocation. When they finally left on Saturday morning, Bruno was glad to see them off.

# 6

Bruno had always lived in a household of relatives. Until tonight, the only time he had slept alone in a house was the night Graziella was born. He usually enjoyed the small amount of solitude that came his way, and he was looking forward now to an uninterrupted evening with a book, eating supper a little late if he wanted and stretching his long legs out in the matrimonial bed. But the hours before the evening meal passed slowly, and, when he finally sat down to eat, the food seemed insipid without the presence and conversation of his family.

After dinner he tried to read, but the sounds of the empty apartment picked at his concentration. He got up, poured himself a glass of wine and sat back down at the kitchen table with his book, but it was useless. He pushed the book away, stood up and lit a cigarette.

It had been like this the night Ivana was in the hospital giving birth to Graziella. His grandmother, although she complained that she didn't trust hospitals and that she didn't understand why you had to go to a hospital to have a baby, stayed all night in the waiting room, along with his mother, his aunt, his sister and Ivana's mother. Bruno had gone to the hospital with them, but after several hours, when he said something about having papers to correct, the women had sent him home.

"You don't need to come back," his aunt said. "Get some sleep. You'll need it once the baby comes home." And the other women laughed, as though they knew something he didn't.

He was relieved. Surrounded by those women who all seemed to know what was going on, talking about labor, afterbirths, and swapping stories of births gone wrong with the perverse excitement of old men exchanging war stories, he had felt left out at first and then fearful. But he wasn't able to settle down at home either and was glad when Annamaria arrived to fix his supper.

"I don't know why you need someone to cook for you."

"I don't. I'm fine. I didn't expect you to come."

"*Mamma* wanted me to, and it wasn't worth fighting about. Besides," she said, putting her arm around him, "I thought you needed some care."

"Well, I'm glad you're here. How is Ivana?"

"Don't worry. She's doing fine. You'll have a beautiful, healthy son by tomorrow morning."

And so it was, only it was a daughter and not a son, and, although Graziella was pronounced healthy, he could not, on that first day, see any beauty in the wrinkled-skinned, red-faced, eyes-squinched, little thing that was presented to him. Beautiful or not, though, the hair on his neck stood on end when he saw her, and he was filled with a desire to protect her, to make sure her life was good in every way, to do anything, even die for her if necessary.

But it had been a long, lonely night waiting for Graziella to be born, and tonight promised to be the same. Bruno put his cigarette out, went into the living room, and, without turning the lights on, so as not to alert the mosquitoes, opened the shutters to the window.

The evening sounds of the neighborhood, amplified by the stone confines of the narrow street, filled the air. The voices on the television at the café next door collided with the ruckus of several motorcycles below, their young owners opening the throttles with the clear intention of making as much noise as possible. Bruno leaned on the window sill, the night air warm and alive on his skin. In the street below, two lovers walked by slowly. The man's arm encircled the woman's shoulders, her body swaying as she leaned against him. Further down, the small patch of sky visible above the tile rooftops was the deep blue that marks the first edge of night. The color of Nadia's eyes, he thought now.

He gave himself up to images of Nadia. Her graceful movements, the flesh on her arms so round and firm, the way she had of meeting his eyes. She was so open to the world, so unafraid. He decided that tomorrow he would invite her to have lunch. He had promised to check on his grandmother's house once a day, and he could take Nadia with him. The patio there was private and had a view of the hills. *Nonna* was sure to have left a roast for him, and they could pick up some bread. There would be tomatoes and fruit from the garden.

But he soon tired of planning. He wanted to see Nadia. He wanted to dispel the last remaining doubt about who she really was, but mainly he just wanted to be with her. Tomorrow, however, would come when it came, and the only thing he could do to hurry it was to sleep. Unfortunately that didn't feel possible right now.

He left the window, took his key and went down to the street. He headed north, veering east when he hit the river, as though he were going to Nadia's building, but then, unwilling to behave like some adolescent, he crossed the Ponte alla Carraia. He turned down via della Vigna Nuova which would lead him downtown. The sticky heat of the day was gone, this part of town was nearly deserted, and, as Bruno walked down the dark, narrow street flanked by tall stone buildings, he felt free and confident. Being able to walk the streets any time of night, without wartime curfews, still had the power to amaze him.

When he emerged into Piazza Repubblica, he was suddenly bombarded by tourists, the Germans and Americans particularly noticeable, tall, robust and blonde, wearing sporty clothes, as though they were at the beach instead of in town. Bruno had heard that there were fewer than usual this year, but, if that was true, they must all be out tonight. They had commandeered the center of the city.

He was fourteen when the Americans first came to Florence, the age Nadia was when he met her. He had been impressed with the relaxed, casual way the officers spoke with their subordinates, so self-assured they didn't have to strut and berate anyone under them the way the fascist officers did. And they were all so friendly. They seemed grown up to him then, but he realized now that they had been only boys. There were black ones, too, the first black people he had ever seen outside the newsreels of the campaigns in Africa. And they were still here these Americans, still friendly, still self-assured, and right now he wished there were some way he could get across the Ponte Vecchio without having to make his way through them.

But he didn't want to turn around and go back the way he had come, so he crossed the Piazza and headed east towards the bridge. The Ponte Vecchio had been closed to traffic some years before, leaving the bridge free for pedestrians, mostly tourists. Shops lined the narrow sidewalks, except in the center where the bridge opened up on both sides into porticos overlooking the river. Bruno stopped at the portico on the east side of the bridge.

He lit a cigarette and, leaning on the railing, looked upriver to the Ponte alle Grazie, the bridge closest to Nadia's apartment. He wondered what she would be doing now. Would she be asleep? He imagined her long thick hair spread out across the pillow. He took a last drag of his cigarette and threw it over the ledge. He watched the orange glow fall until it hit the water and sizzled out in the shallow, sluggish stream that was all that was left of the Arno this time of year, so different from the wild fury that had torn the city to pieces less than a year ago. It had been like this in 1944, low and narrow, a third of its full winter width, when the bridges had been blown up. He had never understood why the Germans had to destroy the bridges when the Allies could have waded across in places, if they had wanted to. And anyway, it had taken them no time to throw up Bailey bridges.

He could still see the profile of Ponte alle Grazie after the Germans had mined it, the twisted trolley car tracks curling up over the rubble of broken stone. The trolleys were all gone now, replaced by buses, and the current generation would never know the forbidden fun of riding on the steps outside the open cars, daring to hang on by one hand. There had still been trolleys when Nadia was here as a girl. Would she have hung outside? Italian girls didn't do things like that, especially not in those times, but Nadia was American. She had different rules.

And even here things were changing. Bruno was disturbed by some of these changes, but there was much from the years when he was growing up that he was glad Graziella would never have to see. Still she needed to know. All the young people did. It was the only hope.

Bruno continued across the bridge and stopped in the little café on the corner for an ice cream. He chatted for a while with the waiter, who had been a schoolmate, and then set off down Borgo San Jacopo, his back towards Nadia's apartment, heading home. But the ghosts of the war were abroad tonight. This was the area the Germans demolished when they retreated from the city, blocking access to the only bridge they had spared. Bruno passed by the ruins on a daily basis during the years of recovery. Now, crossing Piazza Frescobaldi to the riverside, he was at the spot he had been standing as an adolescent just days after the Germans left, when he saw three men injured by a mine. They were climbing over the rubble down river, and one of them tripped the mine. When Bruno heard the explosion, he thought at first that the Ponte Vecchio was joining the other bridges. But when he ran to the riverside, he saw the sprawled men near Ponte alle Grazie and heard their screams. It was only minutes before a group of bystanders picked their way to the injured men, but it seemed like hours to Bruno, and he wanted to yell at them to hurry, wanted to run out himself, but he was on the other side of the river and several bridges down and it would have taken him a long time and anyway he wouldn't have known what to do when he reached them.

He had been planning to explore the rubble himself, drawn by the debris of what had once been people's lives. The buildings were gone, only the outlines of the separate ground floor rooms remained, with piles of stone and plaster and here and there a recognizable object such as a shoe or a hat or some fragment of furniture. Everywhere there was paper, in wads or loose sheets or even halves of books. His stomach tightened now as he thought about how this venture might have gone for him. Well, the war was long over, and he was still alive, but at least one of those men wasn't. He had never heard whether the other two survived, but he would not forget those screams.

It always happens so quickly, he thought now as he continued down the *lungarno*. One wrong step and you can never go back. And now the Russians and the Americans are just a push of a button away from blowing the whole world up. He felt the bite of anger. Why couldn't they just blow each other up without involving everybody else?

It was almost eleven now. Maybe he would be able to sleep. He was yawning when he entered his building, and it was with optimism that he undressed and lay down. But the clock tick-tocked through the room, boorish and loud. His pillow was hot no matter how many times he turned it, and his body found lumps in the mattress that had never been there before. He got up and tried to read, but he was too sleepy to pay attention. He lay back down but again could find no comfortable position. Finally, sometime between four and four-thirty am, he fell into a groggy slumber.

He woke late the next morning and cut himself shaving. He went to the kitchen, but ragged from lack of sleep and too many cigarettes, he wanted nothing to do with breakfast. So, with a scab on his chin and no caffeine to sustain him, he set out for the theater, ready to be especially attentive to Nadia to make up for last time, but cautious, too, ready to throw his defenses up if necessary. He arrived early, and she was not yet there. As the time approached for the film to start, she still had not come. He went in at the last minute and sat on the aisle in the back so that he wouldn't miss her if she came late. But she didn't come.

Bruno walked home from the theater, too tired and disappointed to try to understand why she hadn't come. He stopped and bought fresh bread in the piazza below his home. Once he arrived in the apartment, he put water on for pasta and rummaged around until he found a couple of tomatoes and a slab of Fontina cheese. He placed these and the bread on the table. When the water began to boil, he swirled the pasta in and then set a single place at the table. He lit a cigarette and paced the kitchen while he waited for the pasta to cook. When it was done, he drained it, mixed it with *pancetta* and eggs and parmesan, placed it alongside the other food, poured a glass of wine and sat down. He was hungry and ate rapidly since there was no one to talk to. When he finished the meal, he peeled and ate an apricot. Full and sleepy, he was ready for a siesta.

He woke around three-thirty, refreshed but confused and discouraged. He went into the kitchen to make coffee and found the sink filled with dishes from last night and this morning. He had never washed dishes before. Ivana had arranged for someone to come in on Monday to do some cleaning, but he was afraid that if he left them piled up in the sink they would begin to smell. He rolled up his sleeves and tackled the job. He was surprised to find that there was a certain satisfaction in getting them all scrubbed and clean. Ivana always dried them and put them up, but he didn't see any advantage to that so he left them on the drain to dry. Then he filled the little espresso pot with water and coffee, placed it on the range and sat down at the kitchen table to think things over.

There was no way of knowing if Nadia had stayed away because her feelings were hurt, or if it was for some other reason that had nothing to do with him. The only way to find out was to go to her house, which meant risking having to deal with the two blondes. Or else to wait another week. But she might not come even then.

He considered letting the whole thing go. Nadia probably had no interest in him. She was a nice girl. What would she want from an older married man? She had probably been out with her friends. On the other hand she had met him at the movie and invited him to her house. She was a grown woman. How could she not know where something like that would go? And there had certainly been some romantic static. But why hadn't she come this morning? Maybe it was just that, maybe she had only seen him as a teacher until that day, and when she understood the possibility of something more, she didn't want anything to do with it. Maybe she had a boyfriend, someone her own age. And even supposing she was interested, was this what he wanted? An affair was bound to bring complications to his life just when everything was going well. An affair with an American might be even more problematic, especially when the American was also part of this new generation. Who knows what crazy expectations she might have?

The coffee began to gurgle, its aroma filling the room. He got up, poured himself a cup, took it over to the table and sat down. All this talk was stupid, he thought, as he spooned sugar into the cup. If his family had been home, maybe it would have been different. But whatever doubts he might have, he knew he was not going to stay here, alone in the house for two weeks, knowing Nadia was just on the other side of town, not knowing why she hadn't come, with nothing to distract him but his dull, sulky student who would rather write her boyfriend's name a hundred different ways than do one simple algebra problem. Besides, some things might be different, but when you got right down to it, he was a man and Nadia was a woman. The rest could be figured out. And, he realized now as he sat thinking, there was something appealing about the challenge. *"Forza,"* he said aloud, encouraging himself.

He got up, washed his face and hands, checked his beard, decided he had better shave again, and once that was done he set off for Nadia's apartment. As he arrived at the door of her palazzo, he saw that the number on the door was thirty-seven. He had sent the note to fifty-seven. How could he have made such a stupid mistake? He stood outside for a moment, trying to order his feelings. It was all clear now. She had been hurt by the way he treated her last week, she hadn't gotten his note, and hadn't come to the movie because she was offended and didn't want to see him.

It was Sunday. The *portiere* wasn't there and the outside door was closed. Nadia was only a short term tenant, so her name wasn't on the brass plate of doorbells outside the door. Bruno stood a moment and then rang a bell randomly. There was no answer so he rang another. Now he heard the click as the lock on the big door was released from inside one of the apartments and he entered. Just as he pushed the button for the light, a voice called down the stairwell asking who it was.

"I'm sorry. I rang the wrong name," he called back.

He waited until he heard the door above close and then climbed the steps quickly. He rang the bell outside Nadia's apartment, prepared to deal with the blondes, but Nadia answered. Her hair was pulled back in a ponytail, and she wore a simple, straight shift with a blue pattern that matched her eyes. She looked surprised to see him and a little uncomfortable.

"You didn't come to the movie?" he said.

"I thought you were mad at me."

"No. I was really sorry about last week. I sent you a note explaining, but I think I sent it to the wrong address."

"I didn't get a note" She looked confused.

"I know. I sent it to the wrong address," he said again. "That's why I came now."

The light in the hall, on an automatic timer, went off now. "Come on in," she said, her voice hesitant.

He didn't want to go into the apartment. He pushed the button to turn the light back on. "Let's take a walk. I'll explain it all to you. We can go up to the Piazzale." The back way to the Piazzale Michelangelo was just down the street, and, at the top, there was a little café.

She hesitated.

"Come on. I'll buy you a coffee."

She smiled, but didn't answer.

"Come on. I want to make it up to you."

She nodded now.

She stepped back inside to get her purse, and they walked down the steps and out of the building together. It wasn't yet four, and the narrow street was quiet and deserted except for a scrawny black and white cat who sat washing its face outside the doorway of the building. The sidewalk was barely wide enough for one, so they walked in the street, strolling slowly, side by side. Nadia was long-legged and her head came up to his chin. He enjoyed walking next to her.

They came into the area where via San Niccolo' widened, and the buildings were now pink- and orange-colored stucco instead of the heavy grey stone of the older *palazzi*. Ahead two schoolboys, still in their Sunday clothes, were kicking a soccer ball around. Their clear, boyish voices resonated in the quiet of the afternoon as Bruno and Nadia approached, and now, with a wild kick, one of them shot the ball towards them. Bruno quickly steered Nadia further to the center of the street, and the ball went harmlessly by. It was just as well that they had moved, because several yards further down a stream of water suddenly cascaded from above, splashing noisily on the pavement below, leaving the smell of damp in the air and splattering Bruno's trousers with tiny dark spots that he hoped wouldn't stain. They looked up to see a woman watering her flowers on the tiny balcony above.

Nadia laughed. "It's so warm, it would have felt good to get wet."

"The water's not clean. And besides you would look a mess."

"I don't care," she said, her head slightly tilted as she looked up at him, her eyes full of laughter and challenge. Bruno had never heard anyone say that they didn't care about looking their best, had never known anyone who didn't care about making a *bella figura*. He started to ask her what she thought the world would be like if nobody cared how they looked, but the water hadn't fallen on her and she looked so nice, her creamy skin glowing in the sun, that he said nothing.

They turned south, passed through the old city gate and into the square below via San Miniato al Monte. There were more people here—a few groups of tourists, several couples walking with their arms around each other and a family with a small girl dressed all in pink and white. Bruno and Nadia followed them up the broad steps shaded by the row of cypresses on the right. A low wall ran in front of the cypresses, and every ten meters loomed one of the stark wooden crosses that represented the fourteen Stations of the Cross. On the left wild herbs grew in the cracks of a high wall, its mossy stones a medley of size, color and texture. The steps themselves, a ramp of patchwork flagstones, had a rise of five centimeters every two meters. While Bruno's longer legs were comfortable taking three strides on each level, Nadia struggled. He shortened his steps, taking four so as to keep pace with her.

"You don't have to do that," she said, taking the unnaturally long steps that were the only way she could make it in three. "I can keep up."

Although it seemed clear to Bruno that it was his role as a man to accommodate her, not the other way around, he had had enough experience with his independent sister not to protest. Besides he found the determined look on her face attractive.

It was cooler here than it had been in the street below, but the climb was long and soon they were both beginning to breathe hard. Nadia stopped her long strides and began scurrying as she tried to do four steps in the time he was doing three. Bruno shortened his steps again.

"Thanks." She smiled at him.

"My pleasure. You looked like a little kitten hopping along next to me."

She laughed, and he was glad that he could amuse her. He soon found a rhythm that matched her steps, and they continued upward at a slower, more harmonious pace, allowing themselves to be passed by some of the tourists, as well as by a pair of nuns walking purposefully, the younger one carrying a mesh bag with several purchases wrapped in brown paper.

About halfway up a middle-aged couple in front of them stopped, obviously out of breath.

"We used to come up here sometimes on Sundays," Bruno said. "My mother would get winded and have to rest, and my father would stay with her, but my sister and I would run the whole way. I was so sure then that I would never be old, never be like them."

"You're not old."

"No, but I certainly couldn't run up." In fact, while he wasn't seriously out of breath and didn't need to stop, he could feel the climb on the back of his calves.

"Did you really run all the way?"

"Yes. I'd get there before my sister did. I'd have a chance to catch my breath. Then I'd pretend that I hadn't gotten winded."

"Did she believe you?"

"For a while. Eventually she caught on. But by then I was older and too dignified to run with her."

They reached the top, and Bruno bought a couple of *limonata's* at the little stand set up at the top of the steps. "You've got a great spot up here," Bruno said to the man selling the drinks. "You must do pretty good business."

The man shook his head. "Not many tourists. The Israeli war really screwed us. The Americans are afraid to come."

"But the war only lasted five days."

"Yeah, but you know how the Americans are. They won't go anywhere if there's anything political going on."

"Would you say that was true?" Bruno said to Nadia, partly because he wanted to know, partly to save the lemonade man the embarrassment of saying anything rude about America and partly because he wanted him to see that this attractive young woman Bruno was out with was American.

"America is pretty isolated and protected," Nadia said. "Any kind of unrest abroad feels strange and scary to them."

"You're American?" the man asked. When Nadia nodded, he said, "Well, tell your friends to come next year. Tell them our food and wine are good, and our cities are beautiful." He grinned at Nadia. "And our young men are nice, too."

"I'll tell them," Nadia said, glancing at Bruno.

Bruno led Nadia to a low wall nearby where they sat and smoked and finished their drinks. After they brought the bottles back, they walked across the big square that overlooks Florence and leaned on the stone rail at the north side of the square, looking down at the city.

"They should take the photos for the postcards from up here,"

Bruno said, "where you can see all the bridges. Most of the postcards that are supposed to show the bridges have a view where the Ponte Vecchio blocks the Ponte Santa Trinita. I can't figure out why they do it. The Ponte Santa Trinita is the most beautiful one."

"I think most tourists are just interested in the Ponte Vecchio. They like all the cute little shops on it. They can't really tell the other ones apart."

"Did you know that the Ponte alle Grazie used to have little buildings on it, too?"

"No."

And so, as they leaned on the parapet, their arms so close he could feel the heat of hers, he told her about the little houses and the cloistered nuns that lived in one of them. She asked a lot of questions: whether they had windows, how big they were, what the people in them did for plumbing. He answered her as well as he could, while the warm sun stroked his back, and below the familiar shapes and colors of his city lay hazy in the heat.

"Let's go look at San Miniato," Nadia said straightening up and stretching so that her dress was pulled tight across her breasts.

San Miniato was Bruno's favorite church. He loved the way it stood on the hill above the square, its facade of green, white and pink marble part of the Florentine landscape. In the afternoon the sun bounced off the gold background of the mosaic that decorated the front and its twinkle was visible throughout the city. Bruno met Nadia's eyes and smiled. "Let's go."

It was another hot climb to get to the church, but the interior was dark and cool and smelled of centuries of candle wax and cold stone. Several dozen tourists walked around, their footsteps echoing in the hollow of the stone building. Bruno and Nadia stopped first at the central aisle to look at the marble inlaid pavement with its signs of the zodiac. Bruno found out that Nadia was a Pisces and, according to her, he was a Gemini.

She said that Geminis were cold and intellectual and of two minds. Bruno liked the idea of being intellectual, but didn't consider himself cold, and he told Nadia so.

"It's never all true. Everybody is influenced by more things than their sign."

"Do you really believe in this nonsense?"

"I don't know that I believe in it, but it's fun."

Bruno pondered this for a while. The signs certainly lent themselves to artistic portrayal, as was obvious on the pavement of the church, but he felt no interest in the idea of random predictions about your personality and future. Still he knew that many of his female students, even some of the intelligent ones, read their horoscopes, giggling as they did. Both his sister and his wife did, too.

After Bruno and Nadia made the rounds of the chapels in the nave, they went down into the crypt, the oldest part of the church, and sat in one of the pews. It was a small space, with little light and a low wooden beamed ceiling. They could still hear people moving around above, but the sound was muted now.

"It's so quiet and peaceful here I can almost imagine why someone would want to be a monk, staying here your whole life, not worrying about the rest of the world," Nadia said.

Bruno could imagine taking her behind one of the columns and kissing her, but he said, "When I was about seven or eight years old they took me to the Duomo for the first time, and I was so impressed with the space and how the place seemed silent even though there was a priest saying Mass, that I told my mother I thought this would be a good place to do my homework. I couldn't understand why she laughed, but I felt very clever when she told all my family what I had said."

"That's sort of the same thing," Nadia said, smiling. "Did you ever climb up to the top?"

"No."

"I did the first time I was here. When you get to the top you have to walk around on the inside before you get to the door to go outside. It's pretty narrow, and the cupola curves over you so you feel like you are leaning inward. The railing is thin and low, and you are up really high. The time I went there was a large woman, a tourist, who panicked and refused to move either forward or back. She just stood there, making horrible moans. We had to wait while a custodian squeezed around us to reach her, and then we had to back all the way down to make way for him to lead her out."

"It doesn't sound like much fun."

"It was pretty scary, but it was exciting, too."

"Do you like excitement?'

"Yes."

"I can be exciting." He glanced at her.

She lowered her head, but he could see that her mouth softened as though she were going to smile, and then she looked up at him, her eyes making contact with his. "I believe it." Before he could answer, she stood up and said, "Come on. Let's go."

As they left the church, Nadia took his hand and pulled him towards the cemetery. "Let's look around." Once they were inside, she released his hand, but as they wandered around the family plots, the white marble chips of the path crunching beneath their feet, he could feel the warmth and the weight of her hand as though it were still in his.

They moved through the cemetery slowly, while she stopped to read the names and dates on the tombstones, piecing together the tragedy of childhood deaths in some places, marveling at the span of long lives in others and noting how many young people had died in the years of the war. Bruno politely kept up his end of the conversation, while resolutely pushing back thoughts of his daughter, dead now for four years, dead in the cold ground.

"Look, it's shady over here." Nadia pointed to a stone bench under a poplar tree. "Let's sit down."

Bruno waited for Nadia to be seated and then sat down beside her. He was intensely aware of her presence next to him, the curve of her shoulder, the smoothness of her white throat, the rise and fall of her breathing. A pair of starlings scuttered around near their feet. Nadia flicked a small rock with her foot, and one of them jumped straight up, four or five inches off the ground. Nadia laughed. "I like cemeteries," she said. "They remind me of my mother."

"Your mother?"

"She died when I was five."

Bruno's throat spasmed and he closed his eyes. Graziella was five now. He didn't want to think about how losing her mother would affect her. She was so soft and vulnerable in her brief experience of the world. Nadia must have been like that. He turned to look at her. "I'm sorry," he said.

"It was a long time ago." She shrugged, but he noticed that she looked away.

They sat a while in silence. Bruno felt deeply sad for the little girl who had been Nadia, but the woman she was now took on a new reality for him. She was no longer just an American who had everything she wanted or needed. Something inside him shifted and softened.

"I was with my grandmother," Nadia said now. "They left me there when my mother first got sick. My grandmother told me my mother had gone away and wasn't coming back. I thought my mother had left because she didn't love me anymore." She looked down as she spoke, and her voice was distant, as though she were talking to herself. "Eventually, after a week or so, I guess, but what seemed like forever to me, my father came and took me to see her grave. We sat in the grass by her tombstone, and he explained it all. He told me that my mother was in heaven, that she didn't want to go away, that she still loved us and that she was looking down on us and taking care of us." Now she looked at Bruno. Her face was soft and peaceful. "Ever since then cemeteries have seemed like places where everything's all right."

Bruno was touched that Nadia had shared this with him, and, although he didn't believe in God or heaven, he was glad that Nadia's father had told her this and thought that under the circumstances he might have said something like that to Graziella. "Your father sounds like a good man."

"When I was growing up, I thought he was perfect. I still love him, but it's not the same. He doesn't understand me at all."

It had never occurred to Bruno that his own father might or could or should understand him, or for that matter that he would have even wanted him to. When Bruno was five years old and his father first came back from the war in Abyssinia, Bruno had resented him. Later, as a schoolboy he had admired him, had feared him, had felt protected by him. There had been times, too, when Bruno had hated him. And, throughout it all, of course, he had loved him and wanted his approval. But expecting to be understood by him—that was a novel thought.

"What doesn't he understand?"

"After my mother died, my father's job took him out of the country a lot, so I lived with my grandparents on a farm in Oregon. It was lonely, and I spent most of my time waiting for visits from my father. When I was twelve he let me come live with him." She looked at Bruno and smiled. "It was wonderful. We lived together, just the two of us. We played chess in the evenings. I got to travel with him. I helped pass refreshments when he had parties, and when I was older I played hostess for him. I was completely happy. I never thought about politics. I just believed what he told me."

She pulled her hair behind her ears, hunched her shoulders a little and drew her brows together. "But when I went away to college and began to learn about what was going on in the world—civil rights issues, Vietnam, things like that—I found out how different we were." She hesitated and then said, "I was angry that he wasn't who I wanted him to be, and I could tell he was disappointed in me, too. We had a big argument one day. It was terrible. He had never been angry with me before. I didn't like that. I'm all he's got, and I love him, and I don't want us to be mad at each other, so I don't talk about serious things any more. But I feel like I can't be who I really am when I'm with him." She paused and then looked at Bruno, tilted her chin up and grinned. "So I'm a coward, and I deal with him by staying away a lot."

"He must love you very much."

"He does. That's the problem."

Bruno's chest tightened. If only Adelina had had that problem. And then, even as he was deliberating whether to tell Nadia, he heard himself saying, "My oldest daughter never knew me." His heart thudded in his ears. He had grieved for more than four years now, but had never said the words out loud before. He looked at Nadia, feeling as vulnerable as if he were a small child.

"Tell me." Her voice was gentle.

Bruno let his breath out slowly. "I didn't know about her until she was dead. The worst part for me is that she never knew how much I would have loved her if I had known. I envy your father."

"Why didn't you know about her?"

"It was during the war. Her mother left town. I didn't even know she was pregnant."

"Were you in love with her?"

Bruno shrugged and spread his hands. "What can I say? I was fourteen. She was my first."

"Why did she leave?"

"She thought she would be safer. Everyone was afraid. People were moving from place to place, trying to get away from the fighting."

"Did you ever try to find her?"

"It wasn't like it is today. Most people didn't have phones, and the Germans had cut the lines for the few that did. Trains weren't running. Nobody had cars and, there wasn't any gas even if you did. There were no tires for the few bicycles people managed to hide. The mail was unreliable, and anyway inflation was so bad and food so scarce that finding money for a stamp wasn't even thinkable." He stopped, feeling like there was no way she could understand. It was hard sometimes even for him to remember how it was. "I don't know how to describe it."

"I know that it was bad. I've seen some of the movies."

He nodded. "People were separated all over Europe. It took years for life to settle down and families to get back together. By the time I could have looked for her, I was almost seventeen." He paused. "I thought about it sometimes, of course, but there is so much distance between a seventeen-year-old and a fourteen-year-old."

"How did you find out then?"

"I saw an obituary in the paper."

He had been standing on the corner by the news kiosk in Piazza Repubblica, reading the paper, when the name caught his attention, and he looked down at the small, black-bordered notice on the bottom of the page. It was an obituary for an eighteen-year-old, Adelina Cassini, who had been killed when her Lambretta was hit by a car. Bruno didn't know anyone named Adelina, and Cassini was a common name. Something else had caught his eye. He read on. *Survived by her mother, Silvana Giudici, and her grandfather, Giancarlo Pastori, both of Empoli.* His stomach fluttered. Silvana Pastori. After all these years. It was her. It had to be. She must have married someone named Giudici. Silvana had lived in Empoli. How many Silvana Pastori's could there be in Empoli? When she got pregnant she must have used his name so her people would think she was married. She would have told them he died during the war. There were so many quick marriages and lost records at that time that it was easy for women who found themselves pregnant to explain it that way.

After much internal debate, driven by curiosity and maybe some need to tie up a loose end, he had asked for the day off at school and driven to Empoli for the funeral. He arrived early and slipped into one of the back pews, not wanting to intrude on Silvana's grief, just wanting to see her. As he waited for the service to begin, he looked at the memorial card that the usher had handed him at the door. His own face stared back at him. Younger, a female version, but there was no doubt about the shape of the dark eyes, the aquiline nose, the thick shock of hair. Born April 29, 1945. He counted backwards, a cold chill running through his body. How could it be, he had only been fourteen? But there it was. And Silvana had never told him. He fled the church and sat in his car for a long time before he drove home.

"I'm sorry," Nadia said now.

"I hate thinking of her gone and never knowing she had a father who loved her," Bruno said and then was silent, afraid he would not be able to control his voice if he said any more.

"What do you think her mother told her about you?"

"Probably that I was a war hero." He laughed at the irony. It came out like a dry bark.

"At least she didn't think you had abandoned her."

Bruno nodded.

Nadia reached out for his hand, gave it a little squeeze and then let it go. Her eyes were soft and concerned. Bruno felt overwhelmed with gratitude. The only thing he could think of to say was, "Thank you."

"For what?"

He smiled. "For existing."

She laughed. "I love the way you Italians are so romantic."

A breeze rustled the leaves in the tree above them and moved lightly over Bruno's skin, bringing a fresh, clean scent. Nadia was right, he thought, the cemetery was very peaceful. To the left of where they sat stretched long corridors with name plaques on the walls to mark the people in the common graves below. Many of the plaques had photographs, and some had eternal lights that glowed red. A grey-haired woman, her short, lumpy body dressed all in black, stood in front of one of the plaques, rosary beads in her hand. Her lips moved as the beads passed through her fingers, and at regular intervals she stopped to kiss the cold marble where the name of someone dear to her was engraved. Bruno felt a sudden kinship with her and with everyone else visiting the cemetery today. Life was so full of tragedy, but they were still here. This was their time, to feel and enjoy and be alive. And he could not imagine any better way to do it, than to sit here next to Nadia, who looked as beautiful and fresh as the early morning and who, miracle of miracles, seemed to care about him.

"My back gets tired sitting on these benches," Nadia said now and stood up. Together they left the shade of their tree and completed the circuit of the cemetery, coming back out on the piazza.

"I want to see what's in there." Nadia pointed to the gift shop next to the church. The little store was stocked with postcards, guide books and other tourist items. A tiny man, bent with age, sat on a tall stool behind the cash register, grinning toothlessly as he swayed and jerked in time to the rock and roll music that was playing on the radio. Nadia picked out a postcard of the church and a jar of face cream made by the monks. As Bruno was paying for them the storekeeper looked at his watch and changed the station to one with church music. A few seconds later, a tall young monk, vigorous and healthy looking, his bare feet in sandals, his creamy white robes swishing behind him, entered the shop. He collected money from the till, spoke a few minutes with the old man and left. As soon as he was gone the old man turned the radio back to the rock station. Nadia hurried out the door, catching Bruno's eye, her own eyes sparkling with delight as she invited him to share her amusement. Outside she burst into laughter.

"Did you see that?" she said to Bruno who had followed her. Her throaty laugh bubbled unrestrained and happy across the open space, light bounced white and intense off stone and marble and everything else, and Bruno laughed with her, a full, happy laugh.

# 7

*I'm in love.* The phrase echoed in Bruno's head as he walked home after leaving Nadia at her door. It was not what he had expected and it troubled him, even as he felt like singing it out to the world. An affair was one thing. To fall in love was another. It brought Ivana into the situation. There was no going back, however. He was not going to let Nadia go. He would just have to find a way to protect Ivana.

But it was difficult to keep his attention on Ivana. His thoughts kept going back to Nadia, as he remembered each detail of the afternoon.

After they left the cemetery, they had crossed the square in front of the church and walked down the broad, marble steps towards the Viale.

"I hear music," Nadia said.

"There's a place just down the road where they dance," he said. "Do you like to dance?"

"Yes, but I'm not very good. They tell me I try to lead."

"You just need the right partner. I'll teach you if you want."

The walk was downhill and easy. Soon, as they rounded a bend in the broad avenue, they came up on the little outdoor café where a juke box was playing. An area defined by potted cypresses was reserved for the dancers. Bruno led Nadia through an opening on the side and immediately onto the wooden dance floor, avoiding the surrounding tables where they would be expected to order something. If they wanted a drink later, they could get it at the counter and pay a lot less.

A Tommy Steele song was playing. The words were in English and Bruno couldn't understand them, but the rock and roll beat was strong and inviting. Nadia was already swaying to the music by the time Bruno found an open spot. He fancied himself able to do a pretty good jitterbug, but she began a free dance, paying little attention to what he was doing except for allowing him to occasionally twirl her. Her long pony tail swung with her movements. When her eyes met his, they were shining with fun. Bruno was somewhat at a loss as how to keep up with her. He had really wanted a slow dance, but there was a crowd next to the jukebox, and in the meantime he found he was enjoying watching her move, the curves of her body both visible and elusive under her straight shift, her slim arms and legs carelessly graceful. So he did the steps he knew and watched.

Eventually "Notte de Luna Calante," a slow romantic song, came on. Now Bruno put his right hand firmly on Nadia's back and with his other clasped her hand so close to his chest that he could feel his heart thumping through her fingers. Her body was thin and more muscular than any woman he had held before. The feel of it next to his, the smell of her hair and the touch of her warm breath on his skin were intoxicating. And, yes, she did try to lead. He held her closer and whispered, his lips close to her ear. "Close your eyes." She became lighter in his arms then. "Pretend that you don't have any feet, that you're floating," he whispered now, as an excuse to touch her ear again with his lips. She seemed comfortable when they danced cheek to cheek, so he brought his lips down to her neck. She did not protest or move away, but he sensed a tightening. "Are you all right?" he asked.

"Yes," she said, but her body was no longer connected to him or to the music. He was confused. It obviously wasn't a matter of modesty or virtue, as there was nothing of the nice, old-fashioned girl about her. Alone in a foreign country, she went where she wanted when she wanted, including being alone with him. Was it because she didn't like him then? He moved a little away, but now she snuggled into him.

Just at that moment the song ended, and now the faster music started again. The younger couples were doing the twist, and Bruno and Nadia joined in. Neither of them was very good, but they kept at it, laughing at themselves, while Bruno waited for another slow song. After several more fast songs, another romantic Italian tune came on. Bruno held his arms out to Nadia, inviting, but she looked at her watch and said that she had to go.

"Stay a little longer," he cajoled. "One more dance."

"I can't. I'm already late."

"Come on, please."

She shook her head and started towards the road. He had no choice but to leave with her. She chatted away as they walked down to her place, while he was silent, wondering if she was meeting another man, someone her own age maybe or even another American. He didn't think so, but he just didn't know Nadia well enough to be sure. And if there was someone else, would he be able to compete successfully? The thought was both irritating and energizing.

When they reached her front door, as she was searching around in her purse for her key, he said, "I'm going up to my grandmother's tomorrow to take care of things. She has a house out near San Domenico. It's beautiful up there and cooler, too. I could take you, if you like."

She looked down and then looked up at him, meeting his eyes, and now he saw clearly that she acknowledged the pull between them. His pulse raced.

She looked down again, as she handed him the key to open the door. "It sounds great."

"I'll pick you up around noon. We can have lunch."

She nodded. "I'll see you tomorrow, but I have to run now. My dad calls on Sundays, and he gets worried if I'm not home." Then she was gone.

That evening he took a long walk, heading east along the river down to Ponte alle Grazie and then coming back along the other side. The sun was setting and the shreds of red and orange and pink that stretched across the sky were reflected in the Arno, the movement of the water making it seem almost like the river itself was on fire. Bruno stopped and leaned on the wall of the riverside to watch.

He thought about how, when he was a student, on the night before final exams he would become intensely aware that today anything could still happen but that after tomorrow what was now the future would be an immutable part of his past, one that might affect him for the rest of his life. He had the same feeling now. And it was not only what might happen with Nadia, but in six more weeks he would have started his new job. Soon his whole life would be different in ways he could not know until they unfolded.

He expected there to be pain in these changes. Love affairs are rarely without pain, and he knew that he was entering the public school system at a time of student unrest. But he would not think about it now. He watched as the sunset faded into dusk and walked back home.

He went to bed soon after he came back and slept deep and well. The next morning he rose early. His feeling of well-being lasted as he dressed and went down to the neighborhood café for coffee. He chatted with the bartender about the recent sorrows of the *Viola*, the Florentine soccer team, until it was time to get the car and pick Nadia up.

He drove to her neighborhood, parked the car and walked to her building. He rang the bell on the outside door, and she called down to him from her window that she would be out in a few minutes. She arrived soon afterwards, looking cool and fresh in a white blouse, short skirt and sandals. He held the car door for her and then got in on his side. The interior was small, and their elbows almost touched.

The windows were open because of the heat, but a whiff of some light, floral fragrance she was wearing reached him briefly before it faded. He made a little small talk, but soon gave up trying to compete with the blaring sounds of the city. She seemed comfortable with his silence. Bruno was glad because, like all Italians, he took his driving seriously, and the closeness of her presence was distraction enough from the demands of the road, packed with cars, bicycles, motor scooters and pedestrians, all out for as many chances to show off their skill as they could possibly find, or, for that matter, as they could possibly create.

Soon they reached the broad avenues that circle the city, and Bruno stopped to buy bread, so that he wouldn't have to stop in the square in San Domenico, where his aunt worked and would, if she hadn't already gone to the sea, be furious if she saw Nadia in the car.

He drove faster now that they were out of the city. The road wound between the high walls of private properties, where flowers and wild herbs grew in the cracks between the muted colors of the stones. An occasional branch of wisteria, escaped from the hidden gardens above, draped its purple flowers over the stone. Here and there were brief stretches where the walls were lower and the hillside beyond was revealed. Cream- and apricot-colored villas, surrounded by the low growth of tended vineyards and the silvery patches of olive groves, decorated the green background of chestnut and pine and oak and cypress. The scent of sun-heated resin drifted through the car, and the warm air, rushing through the window, tossed Nadia's hair across her face.

When they reached San Domenico, Bruno turned up the narrow via Vecchia Fiesolana and then onto via Fonte Lucente until he came to the turnoff for his grandmother's house. A few kilometers further down a side road that cut through an area of cultivated land, he reached her place. He pulled up by the front door of the small house, parked the car and got out.

Wheat fields, bleached this time of year a pale tawny color, contrasted harmoniously with the dark green of the cypresses and the deep blue of the sky. The ochre-colored walls, green blinds and red tiled roof of the house seemed to grow out of the land. A man's voice giving orders to his ox carried from a neighboring field, while *Nonna's* chickens clucked softly as they scratched for bugs beside the driveway. Far below, the sound of the Mugnone River, splashing across its rocky banks, made for a peaceful backdrop. But as Bruno came around to open Nadia's door, the house seemed suddenly small and unadorned. He became aware of the cracks in the plaster walls, the chicken droppings by the front step and the smell of the steamy pile of manure behind the stable. Maybe it would not be good enough for Nadia's taste.

"Well, here we are," he said.

She got out of the car and looked around. "This is beautiful," she said turning to smile at him.

"More beautiful with you here." Now he was happy.

He led her around to the patio off the kitchen where he found the iron key hidden, along with several spiders, under a flower pot outside the door. He jiggled the key in the lock the way he knew and got the back door open. It was cool and dark inside. The blinds on the one small upper window were closed, and the strips of beads that hung across the back door to keep out the flies muted the light that came from outside.

"It's really dark in here." Nadia said, standing in the door, holding the beads on either side of her so that she was framed in light.

"It's cooler, and it discourages flies."

"It *is* cooler," Nadia said and came into the kitchen now.

She wandered around the room while he put water on to boil. She ran her hand over the smooth surface of the marble countertop, examined the jars of preserved vegetables on the shelves and sniffed the swathes of peppers and garlic hanging from the open beams.

"Do you approve," he asked.

"Absolutely."

They went back outside then, and he took her to the garden where they picked tomatoes and basil. In the orchard around the side of the house they found ripe peaches. They brought their full basket back to the kitchen, and Nadia washed the tomatoes and cut them in wedges while Bruno put oil in a pan with a handful of basil and a couple of cloves of garlic. While it sizzled on the stove, he poked in the oven to see what his grandmother had left. He found a small roast beef and held it out to show Nadia.

"How long has it been there?" She wrinkled her nose. He was surprised at her reaction. He had grown up in a time when meat was a luxury, and he knew that *Nonna* had intended it as a special treat.

"Since Saturday, I imagine." He emptied a jar of tomatoes into the hot oil and turned the heat down. "My grandmother probably cooked it right before she left for the sea. What's the matter?"

"I've never eaten meat that wasn't refrigerated."

"It's not good after it's been refrigerated. It gets tough."

"But it'll go bad."

"Come on. It's covered with rosemary, inside and out, the kitchen is cool and the flies can't get to it in the oven."

"Rosemary?"

"It slows bacteria down," he answered, and then, after a pause, "What do you think people do who don't have refrigerators?"

She thought a while. "We always had a refrigerator. I think my parents always had refrigerators, but I've heard my grandmother talking about the ice man. And I guess some people smoked meat. You're sure this is all right?"

"I'm sure," he answered, but he was fascinated by her reply.

Refrigerators were still objects of marvel to him. He couldn't imagine having always had one. Of course, Nadia would have been a baby during the war, and anyway there had been no fighting and destruction in America. Her whole life would have been easy. It was hard to imagine, but interesting, too. Well, the world was better now for everyone, and he hoped it would stay that way—for Nadia, for himself, for Graziella, for everybody.

Nadia set the plates on the big stone table in the patio, and Bruno brought out a bottle of mineral water, a flask of wine and a loaf of unsalted Tuscan bread. He poured them each a glass of wine, and they sat in the shade of the arbor that covered the patio while they waited for the sauce to cook. Nadia was quiet and avoided eye contact, but Bruno felt wonderful. The hot, lazy air rustled gently through the leaves of the trees and was soft against his skin. Bees buzzed from flower to flower, the earthy smells of farmland—wild fennel, freshly mown hay and sun baked earth—were everywhere, and across the table sat a beautiful woman he was in love with, while four full hours stretched out invitingly before he would have to go back to town.

As they sat drinking wine, he tried to put her at ease. He told her stories of roaming the countryside when he was small and hunting in the nearby woods when he was older. He glossed over the war years. The wine and the talk seemed to work because she became more relaxed, laughing at his stories and telling him about her childhood, riding her horse, picking blackberries and the time she got into a clump of poison oak.

"Like nettles?" he asked.

"Much worse."

Bruno had walked through a stand of nettles when he was about six years old and remembered the sting. It was hard to imagine something much worse. "But it's not very common?"

"It's pretty common in many parts of the country."

"Why doesn't anybody ever get it in the movies then?"

She laughed and said that it wasn't very romantic, didn't make a very interesting story and that most people got it when they were kids and then learned to look out for it. He made her promise to draw a picture of it for him, because he wanted to make sure that if he ever got to America he would be able to recognize it.

Eventually the sauce was done, and they went back in the kitchen. Bruno put the pasta in the water and gave Nadia the bowl of tomatoes, a cruet of olive oil, the meat and the peaches to carry out. He found a jar of wild artichokes, thumbnail sized, that his grandmother had put up in oil. He brought these out, too. Then he drained the pasta, mixed the sauce into it and brought it out to the table. "*Buon appetito*," he said, in the traditional way, as he sat down.

Nadia ate with a good appetite and talked as she ate, moving her slim arms, not in specific, meaningful gestures like an Italian, but in swooping loose movements, her wrists rotating freely and grace-fully. But once they finished the pasta and moved onto the meat and salad, she held her knife and fork in a way that seemed all wrong to him and wasn't able to handle her food with the same grace. Bruno had seen this way of holding your utensils in the movies, but he hadn't realized how clumsy it was until now. He tried not to stare as he watched her struggle to cut the meat, change hands and then try to scoop up her tomatoes on her fork. But when she picked up the peach and bit into it, juice dripping down her chin and hands and ready any minute, he was sure, to spill down her blouse, he inter-vened.

"You're going to ruin your clothes."

"Yeah, peaches are messy."

"Americans really do eat with their hands."

"Just fruit."

"What about chicken? I've seen them in the movies."

"Well, how else are you going to eat it?"

"But your fingers get all greasy."

"And you lick them off like this." She looked up at him and smiled as she licked the peach juice from her fingers.

Although there was a certain sensual suggestiveness in her gesture, Bruno was shocked. He had certainly licked chocolate off his fingers when he was a boy, but even then he had been too fastidious to do it in front of anyone except maybe his sister. He could imagine how his parents would have scolded if they had seen him.

"It bothers you when I do that?"

He nodded, but smiled to soften his comment. "It's barbaric."

"Then I won't do it." She tried to cut the peach now, and a piece of it flew off the plate. She looked at him, her expression something between distress and amusement. He laughed.

"Look." He showed her how to hold the knife, so that it was more maneuverable. "See how much easier this is." And he demonstrated with his peach, holding it with the fork while he peeled it and cut it in small pieces. "You don't need to use your hands at all." She peeled what was left of her peach, if not gracefully, fairly competently considering she had just learned.

"You Americans are so strange. You're going to put a man in space, but you don't know how to use a knife and fork."

"And you Italians make so many beautiful things, beautiful clothes, beautiful leather, and then you wear pointed shoes." Her tone was teasing.

He looked down at his shoes. The toes were pointed, and they looked quite elegant to him.

"You don't like my shoes?"

"There are things about you that I like better."

"And there'll be more before the afternoon is over," he said holding eye contact with her.

This time she looked back, a long look that acknowledged his intent and accepted it.

They finished eating and she carried the plates in, while Bruno went to the stove to make coffee. She came up behind him and put her arms around his waist, leaning against his back. He froze, uncomfortable. The first move should have been his.

He wasn't sure what to do now, so he turned around and kissed Nadia. He had intended a gentle kiss on the lips and then a plea to let him finish the coffee, but the touch of her warm lips changed his plans. He kissed her again, a longer kiss. Now she began unbuttoning her blouse.

He took her hands in his and held them still. "Easy."

"Don't you want to sleep with me?"

"Of course, but we don't have to be in such a hurry."

"Okay," she said, her voice small. He couldn't tell from her face if she was embarrassed or doubtful or maybe just surprised. He didn't want to make her feel uncomfortable, but he was thrown off balance by her switch in roles.

"Why don't you go back out and sit down," he said, making his voice gentle. "I'll bring your coffee out to you."

"I'll stay here and keep you company." She sat down at the kitchen table. He put the coffee on and then went into the living room, telling her he would be right back. The little day bed he used to sleep on when he was a boy was piled high with magazines, coats and a tangle of his grandmother's knitting. He removed it all, placing it carefully on the chest by the front door. As he did this, he wondered about Nadia. Did she just jump in bed with anyone? Everybody knew American girls were loose, but she had seemed different.

He came back in the kitchen, took the coffee off the stove, poured two cups and brought them to the kitchen table. He drank his fast, tossing it to the back of his mouth so that it wouldn't burn his tongue, but she sipped hers slowly, blowing on it to cool it. Finally she finished.

"Now," he said, his voice husky as he stood up and reached his hand out to her. She got out of her chair and came to where he stood, lifting her face to him. The flesh under her chin was full and smooth and creamy white. He touched it with the back of his fingers, something he had wanted to do for some time. Then he kissed her. She seemed to enjoy that, and he certainly did, so he kissed her some more, his hands beginning to explore her body, and again was surprised by her response. She was neither resistant nor responsive. The women he had known had been more or less shy, depending on their experience, and concerned with protecting their virtue, or, if they had already lost that, concerned with protecting whatever reputation they did have, but they had all been unabashedly passionate. Nadia seemed to have no concern either about morals or about what people thought, and she was obviously comfortable with the idea of making love with him but there was something guarded in her body, a tensing when he touched her as though she were bracing herself for this rather than wanting it.

"Are you a virgin?" he asked.

"No."

He nodded and led her to the little bed in the next room where he permitted himself to become lost in the taste and the scent of her skin, in the swells and the warmth of her body, in the needs of his own. He came before he entered her with a pleasure so sharp he cried out. Then he lay beside her, stroking her hair, her warm breath on his skin, the pat-pat of her heart under his other hand. "Don't worry," he said. "Just give me a few minutes, and it will be your turn."

Now as his interest slowly built again, he focused on her, taking his time, finding out what she liked, staying with it until he felt she was ready to move on. It was a long, slow business, but he felt patient and confident. Then she grabbed his arm and cried out, and the fear in her voice told him what he had suspected, that this was her first orgasm.

After it was over, they lay on the narrow bed, naked and sweaty and spent, her head on his shoulder and her dark hair spilling all over his chest, the warm smells of their bodies mingling with the slightly musty odor of the rarely used bed. Eventually he wanted a cigarette, and as he reached over her to get them from his shirt pocket, she kissed his arm.

Later that evening, after he had taken Nadia home, after he had gone back to his apartment and eaten, Bruno went into the living room and sat in the dark a long time. Memories enveloped him—the scent of Nadia's hair, the smooth whiteness of her skin, the American way she pronounced her r's. She was different from any woman he had known.

In his youth Bruno had played the field in the traditional Italian way, making advances to all women and expecting rejection. It had been that way with Ivana. He met her when he was a third year student at the University and she was first year. During their long courtship and longer engagement, she had been the custodian of her virtue, setting the limits on their amorous behavior. This was what he expected. After their marriage, their life together had continued predictable. He was comfortable in his role and usually knew what to expect from her. He assumed she was equally comfortable in her role, and there was no question she knew what to expect from him. She had, in fact, an uncanny way of knowing what he was going to do almost before he did. Her predictability had been a balm to Bruno in the crazy years after the war and an anchor in the fifties and sixties when everything was changing so fast.

With Nadia it was different. Being with her wasn't restful or safe. She continually threw him off balance. She was from America, that faraway mythical land, and she was also part of these new times. He was intrigued and wanted to know and understand her, every intimate detail. And, more than that, her mixture of fearlessness and vulnerability awakened a long dormant sense of adventure in him.

He lit a cigarette, stretched his legs and thought of how she had been so bold about wanting to make love and then so unsure of herself when they had actually been in bed. With Ivana he felt that her passion could match his, and it did. But with Nadia, who seemed so free and comfortable with the idea of making love, he found an unexpected modesty, a shyness and even a lack of confidence in her sexuality. What kind of men had she known?

He stood and went to the window. He felt alive in every atom of his being. He would treat Nadia the way she deserved to be treated. He would make every moment with her good. And when it ended, he would find a way to end it well. Not like it had ended with Silvana.

# 8

*Florence, Italy, 1944*

The siren blared the all clear. Bruno pushed open the wooden shutters, leaned on the window sill and squinted against the late morning sun. As he watched the piazza come to life, he kept a lookout to see if Silvana would appear. And she did. Within minutes she slipped around the far corner, crossed the square and stopped to talk with the butcher while he clanged open the steel shutters of his shop.

Bruno was fourteen, and Silvana had arrived in his neighborhood a few months before. She had long, dark hair with red highlights, and when she walked her hips swayed and her dress clung to her thighs. She was the maid, and, it was understood, also the mistress of Dr. Agnelli. Dr. Agnelli's black market trade often took him out of town, and Bruno knew that during those times she was available to the local men for a little change.

She entered the shop now. The plate glass window was empty except for two skinned cats hanging by their feet. A handwritten sign below advertised them as rabbits, but everyone knew. The butcher shooed the flies off one of the carcasses, wrapped it in brown paper and handed it to Silvana. As she emerged with her parcel, she looked up and caught Bruno's eye. He looked away, not wanting her to think that he was watching her, but she came over and called up.

"Come on down," she said. "Walk me home." Accents of her local dialect roughened her speech. She was not someone Bruno's parents or peers would approve of. He glanced around.

"What are you afraid of?" she asked, laughing.

Since the fall of Mussolini, the Germans had been taking men for their work camps and there was a rumor that they were now taking teenage boys. Bruno, who looked older than his age, wasn't supposed to leave the house any more than absolutely necessary. This danger added another edge to his excitement. He mustered his courage and called back, "Sure, baby," in the way he thought a man of the world would. She gave him a look that told him that she was not impressed with this approach, but she gestured invitingly with her hand.

He struggled with the laces of his outdoor shoes, quickly rubbed his finger over his teeth (tooth paste was as scarce now as soap, and water was carefully rationed) and then slipped out the door of his apartment. The lights in the stairway had burned out months ago and new bulbs were nowhere to be found in the city, but the massive *portone* of his building was open and gave off enough light for him to do the steps two at a time. He stumbled once but grabbed onto the iron rail and managed not to fall. Halfway down the last flight he slowed to a casual pace.

She was waiting outside the main door, the afternoon light framing her. His breath caught, but he kept his face calm as he approached and greeted her.

"Come on," she said, and he fell in beside her. "This heat is a killer." She raised her arms to lift her hair from her neck, and her dress pulled tight across her breasts. He could smell her sweat. She twirled the thick mass of her hair into a loose rope and drew it down the front of her shoulder. He wanted to touch it, to smell it, to bury his face in it.

As they left the piazza heading towards Via del Leone, they passed two small boys playing marbles inside the doorway of their building. "They make me miss my little brothers," she said, indicating the boys with her chin.

"How many do you have?" he asked, glad of something to say.

"Four. Four little ones and one older one." Tears shone in her eyes.

"Where are they now?"

"My family lives in a little village south of Empoli." Her face was sad. And then she brightened. "Come on. Let's go along the riverside. The air is fresher." A stench had pervaded the city for days, mainly of uncollected garbage, but carrying, too, whiffs of things burning and things dead. Once they reached to river, it did smell better, but Bruno felt exposed and vulnerable here in the open.

"Why did you leave?" he asked, keeping a sharp lookout both for German soldiers and the fascist *squadristi*, the Black Shirts.

"My father's in Russia—if he's even alive—and they want to put my older brother in the army, too, but he's hiding and can't work, and things are so expensive. There wasn't enough food. When Dr. Agnelli offered me a job as a maid I took it." She looked down at the ground. "I didn't know what else to do. I'm glad I can send money home, but I miss them." She paused. "What about you? You have a sister. I've seen her. And I've seen your mother, too."

He nodded.

"Where's your father? Is he in the army?"

Bruno nodded again, though in fact his father was hidden up in the hills with the partisans, but that was not something you told anyone. "We haven't heard from him in a long time."

They walked a while in silence. "Do you like going to the movies?" she asked suddenly.

"I love the movies."

"Can you imagine being a movie star?" And then, her voice shy, "Sometimes when I'm alone, I pretend that I'm a movie star."

She glanced at him. "That's stupid, isn't it?"

"You look like a movie star."

"You're nice." She smiled. He was surprised at how young her face looked now.

They had reached her *palazzo*. "It was fun talking to you." She disappeared inside before he could answer.

They met almost daily after that. Silvana's reputation had given her an aura of danger that played into Bruno's initial attraction. At first he was disappointed when he discovered that she was just a girl his own age, but he soon found a companion in her, as confused and scared about what was going on as he was. He longed to touch her but contented himself with fantasies of becoming rich enough to support her and her family, and, in the meantime, until that became possible, of arriving just in time to rescue her from the advances of some drunken German soldier.

About a month after their first meeting, when Silvana had not appeared in the piazza at her usual time, Bruno walked over to her *palazzo*. He was afraid to ring the bell in case Dr. Agnelli was there, so he leaned, in what he hoped was a nonchalant way, against the doorway of the building across the street where he could see if she came out. He tried to look confident, but he was alert for the sound of heavy boots, ready to duck inside at any danger. Silvana must have been watching from her apartment, because soon she opened the blinds to her third story window and called out, "Wait. I'm coming down."

A few minutes later, the big door of her *palazzo* opened, she poked her head out and beckoned him in. "Come on," she said and ran ahead of him to the back steps and up to the top story, where she had left the door of the servants' entrance open. They entered and crossed the hall to her bedroom, a small room furnished with an iron bedstead, a marble top table by the bed, a straight chair and a wardrobe missing the hinge on one of its doors. The headboard of the bed had just enough flecks of paint remaining to show that it had once been decorated with roses and lilacs. On the walls hung several pictures of saints. One square window set high let in a little light. Silvana turned towards him now, and he could see that her face was pale and dark shadows deepened her eyes.

"What's wrong?" he asked.

"I'm afraid."

"Tell me."

"Dr. Agnelli is gone."

"But he goes all the time,"

"Yes, but he's taken his things—pictures, silver, things like that."

Bruno understood immediately. Dr. Agnelli's business could not have been so prosperous without some connection to the Fascist authorities. "He's gone north then, afraid of what will happen when the Allies arrive."

She nodded.

"What will you do? Can you stay here?"

She held out her arms. "Hold me."

He put his arms around her and held her tight, trying to still her trembling. The earthy, oily scent of her hair filled his nostrils. He kissed her hair, then her face, then her lips. After that there was a tangle of sensations—the warm mingling of their breath and saliva, the intricacies of her clothing, the revelation of her breasts, stolen glimpses of the dark triangle below, the moist softness of her hidden parts, and then the almost unbearable moment of release.

He lay beside her once it was over, feeling suddenly empty and private, but she turned on her side, propped herself up on one elbow, her head resting in her hand, and asked, "Do you think it's safe for me to go home? They say the Allies are almost here."

His stomach tightened. "Isn't there some way you can stay here? I don't want you to go."

"The *portiere* is closing the apartment here. There's no other place."

Bruno thought frantically. "Maybe you could hide in the *cantina* here."

"It would never work." Her voice broke.

"Is there someone who can go with you?" Images flooded his mind of her fighting and screaming as German soldiers held her down.

"I'm not afraid of going by myself. It's just if they're bombing, or the way the English strafe from the planes."

"Will you be all right even if you get home?"

Tears were pouring down her face. "I don't know. I haven't heard from my family in weeks."

"The mail's not getting through very well now. Or maybe they went somewhere else to be safe."

"And even if I find them, what if they discover what I've been doing? My brother would kill me."

"Why did you do it?" he asked, feeling suddenly angry, partly because he was scared for her and partly because he hated what she was, hated the disgrace of it.

"He said he needed a maid. But he offered me extra food. And money to send home. I was afraid he would send me away." She was having trouble talking through her sobs. "I couldn't go home. My mother was barely feeding the little ones. After the first, it wasn't so bad. He was kind, most of the time."

"But all those other men? Don't you hate being, you know—a prostitute?"

"What difference did it make? I was already ruined. No one was going to marry me." She took a few deep breaths and composed her face. "It meant a little more money. So I'd just pretend it wasn't happening and concentrate on medicine, soap, a little meat, all the things my mother could get with the money. Maybe even a piece

of chocolate for me. And at least I never did it with a German."
She looked off into the distance for a while. "It's lonely, though.
Everybody hates me. Except the men when they want something."

It was hard to stay mad at her. They talked some more, and he
promised to think about it that evening and come up with a plan
for her. Soon his hands began reaching for her, and they made love
again. This time she made him go more slowly, showing him what
she liked, intensifying his own pleasure as well. He lay beside her
afterwards, his body so deeply relaxed it seemed like he was glued
to the bed, and then something in the slant of the light alerted him
to the hour. It must be almost seven.

"I'll see you tomorrow in the piazza," He hurried into his
clothes, making her turn away so she wouldn't see the ragged state
of his underwear. "We'll figure something out."

"Actually," she said, "I do have . . . well, there is this man who
lives on the other side of the Arno. He said I could come stay with
him anytime I wanted to."

"What would he want from you?"

"It wouldn't be so bad. He was pretty nice."

"Don't. Please don't. We'll think of something else." He was
dressed now and turned towards her. She was smiling, and he could
see that she was pleased with this new idea. He wanted to argue,
but it was late and he was afraid. "Wait until tomorrow. Please,"
he said, as he went out the door. He ran all the way home, barely
getting inside before the curfew.

All that evening he felt separate from his family. It seemed
impossible that they could not see that he was not the same person
he had been that morning. He was a man now. And he had to find
some way to take care of Silvana. Maybe he could go with her to
her family, protect her on the way.

The next day, Silvana didn't come to the piazza. It was after five
before he could get out of the house. When he got to her building

everything was closed up.

"She's gone," the *portiere* said.

"Gone? Where? When did she leave?"

"Let it go, son. A nice boy like you doesn't need to get mixed up with a *puttana* like her."

A whore. That's what they all think. "Please, I need to know."

But the *portiere* either didn't know or wouldn't tell.

Bruno tried the butcher and then the man at the newsstand. Nobody knew anything.

When he finally got home, five minutes after the seven o'clock curfew, his grandfather, his mother, his aunt and his cousin were all waiting for him at the door. His little sister, Annamaria, hovered behind them. "What the devil do you think you're doing out at this hour?" his grandfather asked.

"It's that *puttana* he's been hanging out with," his aunt said, her voice shrill.

"Dottor Agnelli's gone and . . ." Bruno tried to explain.

"You put yourself at risk for that *puttana*?" his grandfather bellowed. He raised his hand and swung, hitting Bruno hard above his left ear and knocking him off balance. They were all around him now, his aunt yelling, his mother crying and his grandfather trembling and red in the face. Annamaria, stood in the far corner of the room, her back against the wall, her eyes wide.

Bruno put his hand to his hot, stinging face. "You can't keep me away from her," he yelled, and ran to the bathroom for refuge, the only private place in the home.

He was sullen the rest of the evening, hating them all, refusing to speak to anyone, even Annamaria. He vowed to himself that he would find Silvana and help her.

The next day the Germans posted pamphlets ordering the evacuation of the area around the river. Bruno's building was just outside the evacuation area, but Silvana's was in it. He went down to the river to watch as lines of people carrying their possessions straggled down the streets. Some had children in their arms, others carried elderly relatives on their backs. A lucky few dragged wooden carts behind them, horses and donkeys having long ago been confiscated. Many of the women were crying, their wails rising and falling in a communal rhythm. Bruno watched carefully, looking to see if Silvana was among the refugees, but he did not find her.

Everyone he talked to had a brother or a cousin or a friend with first-hand knowledge about how close the Allies were, but every report was different. Artillery boomed increasingly louder from the south, making the sky was hazy with smoke. The smell of gunpowder drifted through the open spaces of the city. It was clear that it would not be safe, if even possible, to go south.

Bruno no idea what part of town Silvana might be in, but he crossed the river and wandered the streets for hours. He knew it was useless, but he hoped to run into her. Finally he gave up. There was nothing to do but wait for the Allies to arrive. It would be safe for her to go home then and he would follow.

Two days later new fliers ordered everyone to stay inside, blinds closed, warning that if they even looked out their windows they would be shot. The word that circulated was that the Germans were going to retreat, destroying the bridges behind them. Bruno had heard so much talk and so little reliable information during the last year that he didn't know what to believe, but that night he felt the explosions move through the very earth his building sat on. They continued all night, their force so impressive it seemed that the whole city was being leveled.

The next morning the streets were full of the cry, "They're gone. They're gone." Bruno dressed quickly and ran out of the building. The air, heavy with smoke and dust, stung his eyes and scratched his throat. When he reached the river and saw the rubble that was all that was left of the bridges, of via de' Bardi and of via Guicciardini, he struggled to grasp that something so present one day before could be so completely demolished. His city, his home, the birthright he had taken for granted was now unrecognizable.

But the Allies had arrived. The Germans were still on the other side of the river, fighting with the partisans, but this side was liberated. Everyone was outside, laughing and crowding around the soldiers, the women thanking them, the men shaking their hands, the few partisans on this side bumming cigarettes with the air of one soldier to another. Crowds of Florentines surrounded the few military vehicles heading south. They plied the soldiers with cards for friends and families they had been separated from. Bruno pushed his way through and pressed a note with Silvana's name and the name of her village into the hand of the driver of a British jeep, just in case she had decided to go that way.

But as the Germans slowly retreated from the other side of the river, it became clear that the damage was far more than downed bridges and dusty piles of stone and plaster. What railroads, telephone and telegraph lines the Allies had not destroyed in their advance, the Germans demolished as they retreated. They dynamited the water treatment plant and the power plants. They left land mines and booby traps everywhere. They deliberately and effectively shut down the whole region. The challenge of finding the most basic food, water and sanitation overrode all other endeavors. Travel was unthinkable. As Bruno struggled through the days and weeks and months that followed, his feeling of impotence grew, mocking him, so that he wanted to yell, to pound on something, to break something. But everything was already broken.

# 9

Each day for the rest of the week, Bruno took Nadia to his grand-mother's. He picked her up in the morning, around eleven, and they had lunch and spent the afternoon together. At five o'clock he drove back down to the city, dropped Nadia off at her house, and then went to his lesson, where he wrestled for an hour with the dull, resistant mind of his student.

Most days Nadia brought her camera. The first day she brought color film to take pictures of the countryside, but after that she brought black and white film and took picture after picture of Bruno. She said that black and white was better for showing the play of light on the contours of people's features. She wanted him to talk, to look natural, so he asked about the two American girls he'd seen her with, and he was pleased when she said that they were room-mates, not friends. He asked her other questions. Nadia revealed she had a diaphragm, and Bruno felt relieved that he needn't worry about birth control.

As they sat on the patio one day with their after lunch coffee, she picked up her camera. He knew the routine so he asked her what she thought about Viet Nam.

"It's a terrible mistake," she said, putting down the camera. "It makes me ashamed of our government."

"America has too much power." He was relieved that they would not disagree over this.

"Lots of Americans are against the war. Especially young people. People like my father aren't really bad. They are just afraid." Nadia's voice trailed off.

"What is your father like?"

"He's always been good to me but he thinks that we shouldn't criticize the war. He says our government has reasons we don't know. He just . . ." She was silent a moment. "He says that people need to respect their government and obey the law or they will become barbarians."

"And you think . . . ?"

"If the government is wrong, somebody needs to say so and do something about it."

"If the Germans hadn't been a nation of followers, the holocaust might not have happened. Europeans don't ever want that to happen again, and so we have to be on guard. Dictatorships seduce people with nationalistic pride, at first, then once they have the power, they throw dissenters in jail or silence them in other ways. There's not a lot you can do then except get yourself killed."

"I think about it sometimes," Nadia said. "All over the world there are people who risk their lives by saying what they think. If I were in that kind of situation, I'm not sure I would have the courage." She picked the camera up. "But life is about more than just staying alive, being safe."

Bruno laughed. "Don't discount just staying alive."

Nadia stood and came to his side. "Don't turn around. I want to get a profile."

He stared ahead, feeling anything but natural talking to empty space.

"And keep on talking."

He began to recite the alphabet.

She laughed and clicked away. After a few shots she sat laid the camera on the table and sat down again. "I wonder how I would live with myself if I had kept quiet about people being hurt just because I was afraid."

"A lot of people in Italy are struggling to find an answer to that. Fascism is gone, but we still carry our past, and it isn't always easy to live with." He shrugged. "We weren't all heroes. Often it wasn't even yourself you were protecting—it was family, or anyone you cared about."

"I'm glad I grew up in a democracy," Nadia said, "where I could say anything I wanted."

"Well, we have democracy, too, now, even if it's disorganized and corrupt. I'm sure there's more freedom in America than many places, but even Americans aren't completely free to say whatever they want. You can have all the protections by law in the world, but life is what it is. Government means power, and power is always dangerous. Not to mention the need to compromise and be discreet on a personal level, just to get along with the people around you."

"It's true. I don't always tell my father everything I believe. I hate hurting him."

"There you are. Freedom is relative, at best."

"How did you get to be such a cynic?"

"The point is, there aren't any easy answers. My mother came home from Mass a few weeks ago. The priest at her church is a sweet, lovable old man. During the war, he hid some people who were in trouble with the authorities. I think he also let the partisans meet at the church and keep some of their pamphlets there, or something. I forget the details. And of course he had to lie when he was questioned. Anyway, my mother said that his sermon was about how lying was a sin, no matter what the circumstances, but that sometimes you had to sin if you wanted to be a good Christian." Bruno shook his head. "The poor devil did the brave thing and is still worrying about it."

"That's terrible. It makes me want to go tell him that it's all right to lie if you are helping people."

Bruno was touched by her caring. "It's good to understand, but he thinks it was a sin, and there's nothing you could say to change that or to change how he feels."

She picked the camera up. "Do you think it's always wrong to lie?"

"No, of course not. Lying can protect people. It can keep the peace. It can get you what you want."

She lowered the camera. "You would lie just to get what you want?"

"You have to make your way in this the world. Nobody is going to do it for you. Sometimes the only way to is to make yourself seem whatever is needed at the moment."

"But you must think some lies are wrong?"

He thought a moment. "I wouldn't lie without a reason."

"Would you lie to me?"

"I haven't."

"But would you?"

"Would you want me to tell you the truth even if it would hurt you?"

"Yes," she said emphatically. "How can you have any kind of relationship if you aren't honest?"

Bruno didn't know how you could keep a relationship together if you were always honest.

"It's very important to me," Nadia said. "Promise you will always tell me the truth. And don't say you will unless you really mean it."

Bruno's hesitated. His skin tingled with a sense of danger. He had spent most of his life trying to keep people from knowing too much about him. Even with Ivana he had withheld some part of himself. So far, his time with Nadia had been uncomplicated, but would it always be that way? He did not want to talk to her about Ivana, but not talking was different from lying. He had told her about Adelina, something he had never been able to tell anyone, and the experience had been liberating. More than liberating. It had changed the color of the world. He knew suddenly that he didn't want to lie to her. "I promise," he said.

Another time, she said, "I hate it when people ask me where I'm from because I don't know what to say. It's even worse than when they ask what I intend to do."

It was that lazy time of day when the world goes quiet. Bruno had no complaints at the moment and Nadia's didn't resonate with him. "You're from America," he replied, idly. "And, you're a woman, so you'll get married and have children."

Nadia was silent. She looked down and ran her finger round and round the crumbs beside her plate. Eventually, when her silence persisted, Bruno began to understand that she had spoken from a real concern that deserved more than his flippant answer. He tried to think of something helpful to say, but all he could come up with was something Ivana had said after Graziella was born. "Everything will make sense when you have a baby."

"I would like to have children," Nadia said, "that's important. But I want to do something, be somebody."

"You are somebody. You're American."

"Not really. Not all the way."

He raised an eyebrow.

"When you've lived outside America as long as I have, you know how America looks to other people. It makes you feel different. Anyway being American isn't being something."

"You're good at math. You could be a bookkeeper."

"A bookkeeper?" Her voice was cool. "That's not being somebody."

"Well, what do you want then?"

"I want to do something to make the world a better place. Something that matters."

Bruno hesitated. These were the dreams of young people. He, too, had had them once, but they were long lost. He felt suddenly very distant from Nadia. Life just didn't go that way.

She looked at him, her eyes serious. Then, as if reading his thoughts, she said, "I don't mean anything big. I just want to do something I can feel good about."

Bruno wasn't sure how to help her. "What were you studying?"

"I was studying comparative literature, mainly because I already spoke several languages. I'm supposed to be doing research for a dissertation. But I don't want to."

"What's wrong with continuing with what you have prepared for? Doesn't it pay well?"

"I hate the idea of teaching university students esoteric theories about literature that they will take seriously when I don't really. If I were going to teach, I think I would enjoy teaching high school students."

Bruno raised an eyebrow. "Not all of them, I promise you."

"I just wish I could make up my mind and then focus on something."

"How can you afford to change what you have been studying?"

"My father would help me, I'm sure."

"You Americans are amazing. You're fretting because you have a plateful of choices, when most of the world would be happy to have one."

"I know. I feel ridiculous."

"Don't feel ridiculous. Take advantage of your situation."

"But I don't know what I want to do."

"What do you like?"

"I like animals. Especially horses. I've thought about being a veterinarian, maybe."

He grinned. "Maybe you could be a cowboy." He used the feminine article, making *cowboy* a feminine noun.

She smiled.

"What's so funny?"

"You said, *'una cowboy.'*" But *'cowboy'* can only be a man. You can't make it a woman by just changing the article."

He laughed, too, when she explained. "So how do you say a lady cowboy?"

"Cowgirl."

"Cowgehrl."

"Cowgirl," she corrected. They spent several minutes then with Bruno unsuccessfully trying to imitate Nadia's pronunciation of the short "i", eventually, tiring of this, he said, "Tell me more about America."

Nadia told him of the things she missed in America—the grassy lawns in Oregon where her grandparents lived, the trees along the side of the streets, the frame houses painted white. "There's so much open space in America."

"Like in *The Giant*?"

"Well, that's Texas. Flat and dry. Where I lived there are more hills. It's greener. But compared to here, there's much more space."

"Those acres and acres of land with nothing on it were amazing," he said. "I liked the movie, though the makeup crew wasn't very successful in making James Dean look old."

"I know. But I loved the scene when he had his feet up on the rail and looked through them."

"I was surprised he didn't get hurt. I would have thought with all those armed cowboys out west, he would have been shot for such a disrespectful gesture."

"It was more cocky than disrespectful. Not enough to get shot for."

"The bottoms of his feet in their face?"

"That's not considered disrespectful in America the way it is here."

"But the bottoms of your feet—all the places they've been—spit and dog *cacca* and who knows what else?"

"I never thought about it that way. I thought it was just something that wasn't done in Italy."

"You Americans put your feet on your furniture, too."

"I don't when I'm here, at least," she answered. And he was glad of that, but still he wasn't able to persuade her not to walk around barefoot. The first day, when she had gotten up from the bed and swished through the house naked, watching the beauty of her slim body had given him a pleasure so sharp it was almost painful, but he was not comfortable with seeing her bare feet on the cold tile floor. He had bought her a pair of the wooden clogs peasants wear.

"But I like to be barefoot," she had said.

"You'll get sick." He had been told that all his life.

"In this weather?"

She had a point about that, still. "It's dirty, and it makes people think you're not nice."

"Nobody's looking. I don't do it where they can see."

"I'm nobody?" He smiled.

"I like feeling free."

"There are other ways of feeling free."

"My feet like to feel free." She grinned.

He hadn't wanted to argue with something as silly as her feet feeling free, but he kept after her and eventually she agreed to wear the clogs, though in fact she never put them on unless he reminded her and somehow they always seemed to come back off five minutes later. Even now, sitting beside her on the patio, he could see her bare feet under the table.

As he lay in bed that night, drifting off to sleep, he thought about Nadia, so serious about trying to decide what she wanted to be. He remembered wondering, when he was a child, what he would grow up to be. When grown-ups asked, he told them that he wanted to be fighter pilot, but, looking back now, he couldn't find the feeling that had prompted his reply. He couldn't remember if it was because he loved the romance of planes, or because he fantasized about being a hero or because he knew he would be praised as a good fascist boy for saying that. In any case, the war came and he was too young to join the military. In the years that followed the need for survival swallowed all other ambition. There had been no choices.

The next day, after they made love and lay relaxed, side by side, she turned to him and said, "I love you." A part of him had wanted to tell her his feelings for some time, but he had been afraid of where it might lead. If it had been in the heat of passion he might have responded without thinking. He had certainly told her how much he loved the whiteness of her throat, the smell of her hair, the round firmness of her breasts. But her voice was shy, she looked open and vulnerable and he knew that these were big words. She was talking about something more than just a summer romance. He felt a rushing of blood in his ears. She searched his eyes as he wavered.

She looked away. "You don't love me then?" she said in a little voice.

His world collapsed in on him. He reached over and turned her face back towards him. He seemed to be slipping away into some anchorless space, but, looking into her unguarded eyes, he knew that something very important was happening to him and if he didn't tell her the exact truth now he would lose it.

"I love you," he said. Her whole face lit up, and, even though he knew that his life had suddenly become much more dangerous, something in him lit up, too, with excitement and relief and pride in declaring himself.

"I love you," he said again. "And that's the problem."

"Your wife?"

He nodded.

She was silent a moment. Then she held out her arms. "Hold me."

He held her, and, for the time, at least, Ivana faded away.

The days unfolded, long and lazy, until Sunday came around when Bruno didn't have a lesson. He brought Nadia back to town later than usual and then, as they sat in his car in front of her building, he asked if she would like for him to come by later and take her out for a movie and dinner.

"Why don't you come up with me now? I'm the only one here tonight. I'll fix you an American dinner."

He agreed. They went up to the apartment together, and, now, knowing that the other girls weren't there, that they didn't count anyway, he was comfortable. She left to use the bathroom, and he sat in the living room, his arms stretched along the back of the sofa, pleased with himself, as he waited for her to come back. Her father's call came in soon afterwards. Nadia took it, sitting next to him on the sofa. Because she was speaking English, Bruno couldn't understand what she was saying, and, eventually, thinking that she and her father had talked long enough, he began kissing her neck. She pushed him away, suppressing a giggle.

"You're so beautiful. I can't help it," he whispered in her free ear.

She put her hand over the receiver. "Stop. He'll hear you."

Bruno continued to kiss behind her ear and in the little hollow of her collar bone and the inside of her wrist until she finally hung up.

"You're terrible," she said, giggling. "He wanted to know what I was laughing about."

"What did you say?"

"I said I was coughing. Hee wanted would be furious if he knew about you."

"But he doesn't. Was he calling from America?"

"Yes."

"He must be very rich to be able to talk for such a long time."

"No. He worries a lot about money. He has to dress well and have parties and things like that for his job."

"What does he do?"

"He works for the State Department."

"An ambassador?"

She laughed. "No. It changes. He's been a vice consul but never an ambassador. But wherever he is, he keeps in touch with me. It's important to him." She sighed.

"And you're not happy about it."

She was silent a while, her finger tracing the piping on the edge of the sofa. "I want to be who I am, and I don't know how to do that without hurting him."

"To be who you are?"

"I think people like my father care too much about their own security and not enough about what other people need. And he thinks appearances are more important than what's real." Her voice wavered. "I hate feeling like I'm disappointing him."

"But appearances are important."

"I know. I traveled a lot with him and learned how disrespectful you can seem if you don't think about how other people see you. I don't want to do that, but sometimes I just want to do things my way."

"Like walking around barefoot?"

She grinned and nodded.

Bruno thought about his father, how often they had fought and how much he missed him now that he was dead. "He's your father. Probably not the best person to argue with. But you don't have to agree with him to love him. And he'll love you no matter how mad he is. You're his family, after all."

"But it's hard to talk to him." She hesitated, then grinned again and said, "He thinks I'm still a virgin."

Bruno hadn't wanted to ask her directly about her sexual history, but now he asked, "How old were you the first time?"

"I had just turned twenty-two. It was my first year in graduate school. His name was Joe." She looked at Bruno now, her eyes amused, her voice teasing. "You should be grateful to him. He's really the reason I'm here."

Bruno raised an eyebrow, inviting her to continue.

"I knew him at school, and I went with him for a year. My father didn't like him. He had long hair and marched in protests against the war. My father wanted to break it up, so he offered to send me to Paris for a year, and I accepted. That's where I was when I heard about the flood. It was easy to come here."

"Well, I don't know about your boyfriend, but I'm grateful to your father at least."

"The truth is we had already broken up. Joe was going to Canada to get out of the draft and he wanted me to come with him. I didn't want to. I had almost finished the course work for my degree, and I didn't see why I couldn't follow him a semester later, but he didn't want me to wait." She was silent a moment. "If he had been nicer about it, I probably would have given in. But he got mad and said if I didn't stay with him, it was over." She looked away a moment and then turned back to Bruno and smiled. "So I told him it was over."

"Were you engaged?"

"No."

"Do most American girls sleep with men they aren't engaged to?"

"A lot of them don't. But a lot of them like me believe in—I don't know how to say it in Italian—free love." She thought a while.

"It means making love when you want to, not having to follow old fashioned ideas. Being free about it."

Bruno was confused. "You mean you do anything you want? Like orgies?"

"No, of course not. I guess it means that it's okay to sleep with anyone you are in love with, or at least very attracted to."

"Even married men?"

"Well, if they loved their wives they wouldn't betray them."

Bruno caught his breath. Did she think that he didn't love Ivana? He didn't know what to say. Finally he asked, "Do you really think it's that simple?"

"People who love each other want to be faithful."

"Women, yes. They are monogamous, and that's good. But men are polygamous by nature."

Nadia snorted. "That's just an excuse. Commitment is commitment. Men or women."

"You sound like my sister. She says there shouldn't be any difference between men and women."

"I agree."

"It's not a matter of agree or not agree. It's a question of how things are."

"They need to change, then. I grew up being told that boys had to sow wild oats, but women had to be virgins when they married. But I think that if I'm in love with someone I want to be faithful, but if I'm not, who I sleep with isn't anybody's business but mine."

Bruno was shocked. "You talk a lot about freedom," he said slowly. "You want to say anything you want, do anything you want. You want your feet to be free. You want your love to be free."

"Well, freedom is very important to Americans."

"It is to Italians, too. We wanted to be free when the Fascists were in control, and we wanted to be free when the Germans were occupying our country. We don't like authority of any kind telling us how to run our lives. But that's a reasonable sort of freedom."

"And my feet aren't reasonable when they want to be free?" Her eyes were teasing.

"Your feet are beautiful no matter what they do." He raised her hand to his lips.

"So it's beautiful for them to be free then." She tilted her chin up and grinned.

He put his arm around her and pulled her closer to him. "But restraint is part of what makes things beautiful."

"Why?"

"Without restraint you don't have anything." He traced the shape of her cheek with his free hand.

"Why?"

"Think about a river. Without riverbanks, you would just have a big muddy marsh. If people didn't follow certain proprieties, they would be just a bunch of animals."

"Grr," she said and nuzzled his shoulder. "What kind of animal am I?"

"You're not an animal." Then, as he found better things to do, the conversation ended.

Later, when Nadia got up to go to the kitchen, Bruno started to follow her but she stopped him. "Stay here. I want to surprise you."

He sat down in one of the massive straight chairs in the living room, its ancient brocade upholstery tattered and stiff against his back, and lit a cigarette. The two windows in the room faced north, towards the river, and from the one immediately to his right a shaft of light was angled so as to cross in front of him. Bruno blew smoke rings and watched them turn blue as they floated into the light. Outside the pigeons murmured as they began to roost on the ledges, and he could hear a woman calling from a nearby apartment to someone in the street. In the kitchen Nadia moved about with a clatter of metal and glass. He wondered what she would cook for him. He had always heard that American food was terrible. The powdered eggs and powdered milk that had arrived from America after the war supported this opinion. Although no one he knew had actually eaten these things, they had fed them to the chickens, and the chickens grew fat and fertile, and the eggs and meat that they gave were fine. He'd also heard that Americans ate corn right on the cob like you give to animals. But Nadia seemed to have good taste in food, and the aroma from the kitchen carried the scent of tomatoes and onions and pork, all promising, though they were mixed with something else he couldn't identify.

When she brought the food to the table, Nadia explained that the pork was cooked in a sauce she called *barbeque*. It was the most American thing she could think of that he might like. The sweetness of it surprised Bruno, though he had eaten sweet and sour sauces on wild boar. Nadia served the meat with a plate of cornbread, similar to polenta but coarser and crustier. There was also a potato salad and glasses of Pilsner beer. The beer was ice cold, which muted the flavor, but he liked the way it tasted with the barbeque. Nadia served everything at the same time, no separate courses. For dessert there was an apple pie, a bit sweet for Bruno's liking, but the cinnamon in it filled the room with a delicious smell.

He enjoyed the meal, although it sat a little heavy in his stomach. There had been nothing served as a digestive afterwards, no cheese course or salad course, not even a glass of grappa or liqueur. He suggested a walk to Nadia, thinking the exercise would be good, but she said she would rather get the dishes washed before her friends came back and it would be easier if he left. He decided to leave his car outside her building and go home on foot.

The evening air had a rustle of breeze, and, as Bruno walked, the heaviness he had felt after dinner left him. He felt content, physically and emotionally. He had another week of free time with Nadia, and after that they could still meet. He was sure they could manage several times a week, which would work out well once his family was back and school started.

When he reached Piazza Frescobaldi, he stopped by the river and leaned against the stone wall. The sun was almost down, but it was still light enough to see the statues and giant urns adorning the terraces on top of Palazzo Corsini. He marveled, not for the first time, at how the building could sprawl over such a large area and still be so harmonious, almost feminine in its grace. But, artistic subtlety or not, Palazzo Corsini did not speak to him in the same way as the Palazzo Spini Feroni, facing him on the other side of Piazza Santa Trinita. A stark, fortified medieval building, intended to keep a family safe in times of danger, it sometimes appeared in his dreams, where he wandered the dark passageways, discovering new rooms that delighted him. Other times he hurried by terrifying closed doors. But the thought of those nighttime terrors did not detract from the affection he felt for the building. Ivana loved art, and Bruno often accompanied her to the museums, but his real love was the architecture of Florence, the bones of the city.

The thought of Ivana evoked Nadia's strange statement that he would not be having an affair with her if he loved Ivana. He disliked Ivana coming up in his conversations with Nadia. He reasoned that whatever happened between him and Nadia could not hurt Ivana, if she didn't know, and he found that he didn't want it to touch her in any way, not even in conversation. It was a two-way concern. He didn't want to hurt Nadia by sharing his feelings for Ivana. He could protect Ivana, but no matter what he did Nadia was going to be hurt, and he didn't know how to prevent it.

He walked along the riverside, waiting for the sunset. He expected a dramatic display of color, but the sun slipped below the horizon without fanfare, leaving the sky dull and colorless. There would be rain tomorrow, a break in the heat. He left the riverside and went home to bed soon after arriving at his apartment. He fell asleep easily, but awoke several times to the sound of distant thunder.

# 10

When Bruno woke the next morning the wind was blowing strong from the southwest, and there was the smell of rain in the air. A *libeccio*. It would bring a storm. After a hasty breakfast, he grabbed an umbrella and left on foot to get the car before the rain came. By the time he reached Nadia's building the sky was dark and low and his skin tingled with the charge in the air. It was earlier than they had agreed on, but he rang Nadia's bell, and, when she let him in, he asked her if they could leave right away so they could get to his grandmother's before the storm hit.

They hadn't been in the car more than a minute before a streak of lightening lit up the sky, followed by a sharp crack of thunder, and then the rain began. Great bullets of water pelted the roof of the car, and on the street pedestrians ran for the eaves, newspapers and purses over their heads. The car lurched its way through puddles and fought to escape control as the wind battered it. Bruno tightened his grip on the wheel and leaned forward to peer through the brief openings the wipers provided as water sheeted down the windshield.

"Porcini," he said, chuckling.

"What?" she yelled. His little Fiat 500 was noisy at the best of times, and now the pounding of the rain, the squeak of the wipers and the slapping of water on the tires combined with the roar of the engine to drown out her voice.

"Porcini," he yelled back. "Mushrooms. This rain will bring them out."

She pointed to her ears, shrugged and shook her head. Clearly conversation was impossible under the circumstances, and anyway he needed to keep his attention on the road. But hot weather and heavy rain—another few days and the mushrooms would be out. Bruno could almost taste them. Ivana might be back by then, and they would go to their favorite spots, but he would find time to take Nadia, too.

Finally they arrived at his grandmother's house. The driveway was flooded, leaves and plant matter clung to the side of the house, and the tall cypresses in front swayed and dipped wildly. Bruno parked as close to the doorway as he could, then reached in the back seat for his umbrella, got out and rushed to Nadia's side of the car. Nadia slipped as she got out, and he grabbed her arm. She leaned into him, laughing. They ran huddled together towards the house, as the rain blew sideways and bounced up from the ground under the umbrella. By the time they made it to the house and Bruno got the back door open, their clothes were wet and clinging to their skin. Bruno closed the door, and the sound of the storm was suddenly muted, but now in the dark, cool kitchen his socks and pants legs felt clammy against his skin. He turned the single light on, found towels and, as they dried off, he told Nadia again about the mushrooms.

"Porcini are the best," he said. "Have you ever had them?"

She shook her head.

"We'll go get some. I know a great place, and I'll cook them for you." Although Bruno expected his mother or his wife to provide him with three good meals a day, he also liked to cook himself. During the war in Abyssinia, when his father and uncle were away, his grandmother, his mother and his aunt all lived together, and the kitchen was the center of the household. Watching the women prepare food, he became interested and they let him help. His father made fun of him when he came back. Since Bruno at five years old had enjoyed being the only male in the house and was none too pleased with his father's return, his father's disapproval provided further incentive, and over the years he had become quite a good cook. Now he pondered how to prepare the mushrooms for Nadia. Usually his favorite way to eat them was grilled with a little garlic so that you could focus on their rich earthy taste, but today he was visited by the memory of how they tasted sautéed and diced into a white sauce and served on tagliatelle. He had never made them this way himself, but he was sure he knew how it was done.

"One of the best foods in Italy," he said now. "You'll see."

"Aren't you afraid of poisonous ones?"

He smiled. "Not if you know what you're doing. Don't you pick mushrooms in America?"

"We usually buy them at the stores. And I don't think they're wild. I think they're raised in some kind of mushroom farm or something."

"What a waste with all that land and all those forests."

"Well I guess some people gather them, but I grew up being told not to touch them, that it was too easy to mistake the poisonous ones for the non-poisonous ones. But I would love to learn."

Bruno couldn't imagine not picking mushrooms just because there were some poisonous ones. Everyone he knew hunted for mushrooms and knew which ones were good and which ones weren't. Of course, every now and then some poor fool did something stupid and got sick or died, but accidents happen everywhere, and picking mushrooms was one of the great pleasures of life, almost as good as eating them.

"I'll teach you," he said. "I know several good places. Lots of chanterelles, and you always find some porcini."

"You're sure it's safe?"

"With me? Of course."

Nadia had dried vigorously while they were talking, and now she wrapped the small thin towel around her like a shawl. She began to shiver. She had slipped off her sandals, and Bruno could see that they were sodden. Her blouse and her skirt were, too.

"Come on. Let's see if we can find you something warm to wear," he said. He hadn't taken her upstairs before, feeling a little uncomfortable about her being in the more private parts of his grandmother's house, but now he led her through the arched opening to the narrow stairs and up the steep red tiled steps. There was a big chest against the wall on the landing, and he opened it. The smell of camphor and wool rose as he rummaged through old clothes. He held up a pair of green shorts, shaking his head. "The things she keeps. These are from elementary school, when I was a fascist youth boy."

"You were a fascist?"

He handed her a pair of black, old fashioned wool stockings, and she sat on the steps to put them on.

"We all were," he said, continuing to go through the trunk. "It was good in the beginning, you know. At least we thought it was. Wearing uniforms, doing things together and thinking our leader was strong and our country was great." He smiled and shrugged. "Not so very great as it turned out. We Italians just can't do anything right when it comes to politics—not since the Roman Empire. And, if you think about it, not even then." He found a faded blue-green men's sweater and held it up for her to see. "It's big enough for a dress for you."

"It'll work." She slipped it over her head. It came down almost to the hem of her skirt. She rolled the sleeves up and posed, one hand on her cocked hip. The knit sweater draped over her breasts in a way that quickened the blood in his veins. "See," she said. "It's a mini skirt, the latest fashion."

He put the other clothes back and then came up behind her where she was looking at a picture on the wall. "That's my uncle Michele," he said, folding his arms around her and cupping her breasts. She leaned back against him. He was flooded with the earthy smell of her wet hair mixed with the floral shampoo he was now familiar with. He nodded towards the sepia-colored photograph of a strong-jawed young man in uniform. "It's hard to believe he was ever so good looking. When I was a boy, he was my favorite uncle, always laughing. He has a big stomach now, grey hair, and he limps around with a cane, complaining about his liver."

"A cane?"

"He was in the Russian campaign and came back minus three toes on one foot and all the toes on the other," he said. Her body was cold against his. He wrapped his arms around her, pulling her closer.

"How did that happen?" She crossed her arms so her hands were on his. "Did he step on a mine?"

"No, frostbite." He could feel the thump of her heart.

"Frostbite?"

"Our soldiers went off to Russia on a stupid war that had nothing to do with us. They weren't prepared in any way. They didn't even have thick socks. Hundreds of thousands died." He was ready to go back downstairs, but he didn't want to hurry her. "Michele was one of the lucky ones."

"What's that plant behind the picture?" she asked.

"The olive branch? We do it on Palm Sunday and then keep it all year. It's a religious thing."

"We have Palm Sunday, too, but we have palm leaves."

"Where do you get palm leaves?"

She laughed. "I never thought about it. I don't have the slightest idea."

They moved together, comfortably awkward as his arms remained wrapped around her, to the next picture, a faded photograph of Bruno when he was six. He was standing beside an old fashioned cane carriage with a baby in it. He had just lost his front teeth.

"Is that you?"

"Yes. And my sister." He kissed the back of Nadia's neck.

"It's hard to imagine you as a child. And a fascist." She tilted her head back so that she could give him a kiss. Her lips were cool on his.

"I think things here were very different from how they were in your country."

"And who's that?" She pointed to the picture of his grandparents, standing stiffly beside each other as they stared solemnly into the camera.

"My grandparents. It was their wedding day."

"How beautiful she is," Nadia leaned forward to look more closely. "What a strong face."

"She was a strong woman. Still is."

Nadia peered closer. "That's a gorgeous dress."

"She made it. Even the lace."

"Wow."

"She's making my daughter's first communion dress."

"Is it here? Can I see it?"

Bruno was hoping to head downstairs to their bed, but he nodded and led her up the second flight of stairs to the small dark room *Nonna* used as a sewing room. He turned on the light and went over to the massive cherry wood wardrobe that took up over half of one wall. He took the dress out of the drawer on the bottom, brought it over to the table under the window, pulled away the tissue it was wrapped in and stood back for Nadia to see. The dress was made of a light organza, the bodice and sleeves intricately decorated with tucks and embroidery and ribbons and inset lace. Nadia ran her fingers over it lightly.

"This is amazing," she said, her voice muted. "And your grandmother did it all."

"Yes."

"I would like to meet her."

It didn't occur to Bruno to think she meant anything more than it would be nice to live in a world in which it would be possible for her to meet his grandmother, but even so her words made him uneasy. He wrapped the dress back up and put his arm around Nadia. "Let's go back downstairs and get you warm."

"Maybe when she gets back from vacation, you could ask her to invite me for dinner."

Bruno froze. Nadia must have felt it because her body next to his also stiffened. The room was suddenly very silent. It seemed to Bruno that neither he nor Nadia even breathed. Outside the rumble of the storm rose and subsided like a convoy of tanks approaching from the distance. Now a gust of wind assailed the house, rattling the wooden shutters. Bruno carefully let out his breath, composed himself, checking that his voice had no emotion and then turned to her, saying, "But Nadia . . ." Then he saw her face. She was white and her eyes were shiny and she wouldn't look at him fully.

"I see," she said, in a low voice.

"Nadi," he said. "Come on," a cajoling tone in his voice now. "You don't need to meet my grandmother."

"You mean you don't want me to meet your grandmother." The skin around her mouth had a chapped, red look. She ran her tongue across her teeth, and he could see that she was trying not to cry.

"Be reasonable, Nadi," he said, his voice gentle. He touched her cheek. "*Amor mio.*" He tried to look into her eyes, but she turned away. "I can't say, '*Nonna*, this is my mistress.'"

"Your mistress, huh?"

"You make it sound like something horrible."

"*You* make it sound like something horrible."

Her eyes met his, the pupils like pinpoints. "Just because I love you," she said, her voice high-pitched and tight. "I'm some sort of outcast who can't meet people."

Bruno was confused. "Would you introduce me to your father?"

She was silent a moment. Then she said slowly, "If you weren't married, I would, of course." Then she paused. "I'm sorry. I'm being unreasonable. But what are we going to do?"

"What do you mean?"

"Do you love me?"

"Yes, you know I do."

"You can get divorced and marry me, and then I could meet her."

He had of course fantasized about running off to some remote place with her, abandoning his whole world, but bringing her into it? The idea had never occurred to him. It was impossible. It would be bad enough for him to leave his wife and betray his whole family, not to mention Graziella, but to expect people to accept her. "We don't have divorce in Italy," he said. "And besides what would my family do?"

"So you're just going to go back to your wife like nothing happened?"

"What do you want me to do?"

"I don't know." There were tears on her face. "It's never been like this for me before. I don't want to lose you, but I feel like something dirty and ugly."

"There's nothing dirty and ugly about love," he said, reaching his arms out to hold her. She stiffened. "I don't know what you want me to do."

"If we're enough in love there's got to be something, some way we can be together."

This made no sense to Bruno. He had always associated great love with tragedy. What about Anthony and Cleopatra, and Romeo and Juliet, and Violetta in *La Traviata*? Even Humphrey Bogart and Ingrid Bergman didn't get to be together in *Casablanca*.

"We could run away," she said.

"Where would we go?"

"You could come to America with me."

"I love you. I love you so much, but it's not possible. Isn't it enough that we can see each other?"

"We'll figure something out" She moved forward and put her arms around him. "I know we will," she said, her voice muffled in his shoulder. He stroked her hair. Then she raised her head, "But I don't want to be somebody's mistress."

They made love then with the intensity that comes after a fight, but he was not able to put the conversation out of his mind. He had always known that he would lose her eventually, known there would be pain for both of them, but he was stunned by her naiveté. He worried that even now she didn't understand what she was doing and he didn't know how to protect her

Later after they had lazed in bed, Bruno went into the kitchen to make coffee. When he brought it into the front room, Nadia had gotten dressed, made up the day bed and was sitting cross-legged on it, reading a little book.

"Is it rude if I keep on reading?" she asked, reaching for the cup he was handing her. "I'm almost finished, and I love reading when it's raining outside." She looked up at him. "It will be like we married. Like we live together and do ordinary things."

"Of course," he answered.

Earlier on he had noticed an article in one of his grandmother's magazines. He had planned on taking it home, but he picked up the magazine and went to the straight back chair next to the bed. The shutters were closed and the room was dim, lit only by the wall lamp over the day bed where Nadia sat. Nadia was right, Bruno thought, there was a kind of intimacy in sitting here together, silently, each involved in their own thing. He shifted the chair to catch a shaft of light from the kitchen, and he began reading about how NASA was mapping the far side of the moon. They were looking for possible landing sites for a manned flight. It was going to be soon now, and he was reading everything he could find about it. But before he had finished the article his inner sense of time began to nag at him. He closed the magazine and looked at his watch. "We have to leave soon if I want to make my lesson."

"It's still raining," Nadia said. "It's going to be miserable out, and it's so cozy here. Can't you cancel?"

She was right. It was miserable out. It was comfortable here, and he wanted to finish the article. "I'll phone." He went into the kitchen, found the number in the phone book, but when he put the receiver to his ear the line was dead, as it often was during a storm

He came back in the room and sat on the bed next to Nadia. "I can't get through, but I'm not going to go anyway."

"Oh, good," Nadia smiled and leaned against him. "She'll figure out that you couldn't make it."

"She'll be delighted that I didn't make it. It's her mother who cares, but I can explain tomorrow."

Nadia lay her book down beside her and then leaned back stretching. "Umm . . ." Her eyes were squinched closed, her hands balled into fists, as she pushed her elbows back, graceful even in this movement. Bruno smiled and reached his hand out to touch her cheek with his fingers. He never tired of feeling how soft her skin was.

"What are you reading?" He leaned over to see the title. It was *Letters to a Teacher* from the school at Barbiana. The book had just come out and was making a stir in Florence. "The School at Barbiana? How did you know about it?"

"One of my co-teachers," she said.

"I knew him you know."

"Who?"

"Don Milani. The man who started the school at Barbiana. He was a priest here in Florence, actually he was a communist before he converted, but he was a trouble maker, complaining that the Christian Democrats weren't concerned about the poor, so the bishop sent him out to Barbiana—a little dead end town. When he got there he started a school for drop outs." Bruno laughed. "And then the students wrote a book about it, and now he's even more of a thorn in the bishop's side."

"What's he like?"

"Was. He died. Just a few months ago."

"Well, what was he like?"

"Passionate about education. He thought you couldn't have good government without a good educational system. It's easy to dupe people who haven't been taught to think. He wanted the people who didn't have anything to have a voice. And, like all of us, he didn't want anything like the war or fascism to ever happen again. Ever."

She nodded.

"I'd like to read it when you're finished," he said.

"Sure. It's short, and I'm almost done." She put her hand on his. "I'm sorry I was stupid about your grandmother. I sometimes forget you're married. I don't actually forget, I think about it all the time in one way, but when I'm with you sometimes it's like time stops or something, like every minute is forever and there's nothing else out there. Like there's no way anything can hurt us." She shook her head. "I'm not explaining very well."

"No, I understand."

There had been times when he was young, when the war was finally over and he and Ivana were falling in love and he would sit beside her on one of the stone benches in the square of San Marco, his knee close to hers, wanting her so badly and yet in some way content to just to be with her, and later when they were first married and he would wake up with the smell and warmth of her in bed next to him, times when he felt that every moment was enough, that the world was his. But this was different. Although being with Nadia made him feel vibrant and alive, and though the world made more sense than it ever had, he knew that at some point there would be some kind of reckoning, and he felt more vulnerable, not less.

"What would happen if your wife found out?"

"She would cry for weeks and throw things at me whenever she saw me and then finally forgive me." His stomach clenched at the image of how her face would look. But he would not let it happen.

"Does she love you?"

Bruno was surprised. "Of course."

Nadia was silent. Then she said, "She would be hurt if she knew that you love me."

"It would hurt a lot of people."

"A lot of people?"

"My mother would cry, too, and tell Ivana that was just the way men are and women have to learn to live with it. My grandmother would yell at me and probably hit me, maybe with the broom, maybe even hard enough to make me bleed, and then cry when she saw the blood and go to church and pray for me. And my sister, I don't know, she'd threaten to kill me. She'd probably do it, too, but my mother wouldn't let her. And for the rest of my life, any time she was mad about something she would bring it back up again."

"Just like the Italian families in the movies."

He smiled a little at the drama of the picture he was painting, but he remembered scenes between his parents, remembered how his stomach knotted.

"Your wife?"

"My wife?"

"Your wife would keep bringing it back up or your sister?"

"My sister." He laughed. "Ivana would eventually forgive me, but Annamaria is more of a fireball, and she thinks women don't get treated fairly in the first place."

"You sound like you're afraid of your sister."

"Of course not." And he wasn't. He was five years older and the boy in the family and so had always had the advantage and always would. No, he admired Annamaria's feistiness and was sympathetic to her complaints. Still, being in her bad graces was not one of his favorite things.

"But you're the boss in your family." Nadia went on, an edge in her voice. "Italian men are always the boss, aren't they?"

"Of course. You have to be the boss about certain things or you won't feel like a man. But women need to feel like women, too. They need to feel desired, not rejected. And I don't want to hurt my wife that way."

"So you're going to hurt me instead?"

He didn't know what to say. It was obvious that he and Nadia were caught in a tide that could only end up in pain for both of them, and he would have given anything to know how to protect her, but he had no intention of adding Ivana to the list of casualties.

"Nadi, my love," he said. "I don't want to hurt you. I just want to love you."

"I know." Her voice was softer now and sad. "I lost my mother when I was about the age of your daughter. I don't want to take her father away. I know how that felt. I don't want to hurt anybody. I just want . . . I don't know. I just wish it was different."

"Come on. Let's don't waste what we have," he said. He leaned over to kiss the back of her neck and she nuzzled her face into his shoulder. He put his arm around her and with the free hand reached over for her pack of Marlboros that lay on the bed. He shook out two cigarettes, lit them one-handed and gave one to her. They smoked in silence for a while, and then she picked up her book and went back to reading. He sat beside her, enjoying the American tobacco, wishing that time would not move forward, knowing that it would.

When he finished the cigarette, he opened the magazine again. He stopped reading from time to time, trying to imagine what it would be like to go to the moon. There would be the excitement of actually having achieved such a momentous endeavor as well as a string of new experiences that no human had had before. There would probably be fear, too, especially at night when you didn't have anything to do. And a sense of finality. Here you were, almost four hundred thousand kilometers from the earth, alone, away from your family and nothing you could do to change it. The crew were all Americans. They had already started training. Soon, the Russians would go, too. But the Italians would never make it, not that they weren't good scientists. Look at Fermi and Marconi. Galileo, for that matter. Most of the American scientists weren't even American, just people like Einstein and von Braun. But America had the money. That's the way it was. He finished the article and put the magazine down intending to go to the table by the door and rummage through the scraps of old newspapers his grandmother kept, but as he stood up it seemed to him there was an increase in light outside. Now, he could no longer hear the pounding of the rain.

He went into the kitchen, lifted the iron latch, and swung open the heavy oak door. The rain had stopped. He stepped onto the gravel driveway. Clouds still covered the sun, but there was a clear sky to the north, and the air was full of ozone and the quiet light of late afternoon and the talking of birds as they came out from wherever they hide during a storm. Bruno breathed in deeply, trying not to think about how black his lungs must be from the pollution in the city. It would be better after this rain. Nadia came up behind him, put her arms around his waist, and leaned against him. "Since you're not going to your lesson, let's go to the movies. *To Sir, with Love* is playing at the Aurora."

*To Sir, with Love* was supposed to be good and the Aurora was just off Viale dei Mille, where Bruno's friend Dario's family owned a pizzeria. They could eat there. "We can go to dinner afterwards." Bruno said, glancing at his watch. "If we leave now we can make it."

But the warmth of Nadia's body against his suggested something else. "Or we can go to a later show," he said, tracing the shape of her neck.

"Mm. That sounds good."

# 11

He was standing on the big square of the Piazzale looking down at the city. He knew something was wrong even before he heard the first faint drone, distant, barely audible but immediately recognizable. His stomach tightened. He looked up and scanned the cloudy sky, unable to see them but knowing they were there, knowing where they were heading. The sound intensified, and now the bombers broke through the clouds, their dull green bodies almost graceful as they swooped down, wings outspread. Lower and lower they came until finally the hatches opened and the bombs spilled out like the trail of manure that carriage horses leave as they trot down the street. Their target, as always, was the cathedral.

Bruno clenched his fists, his breath tight in his chest, willing the bombs to miss, and then suddenly he was awake in his bed, the taste of adrenalin in his mouth, the light of an almost full moon on his face. He lay there, his body cold with evaporating sweat, trying to stay with the dream in his half-awake state, needing to compose a different ending, to make those deadly, mindless objects turn away from his city.

It had been years since he had had the dream. It had started towards the end of the war. During the early stages of the war, the bombing in Florence had not been intense, and he had been more worried in those days about finding something to eat or being rounded up by the fascists. But afterwards, after the bridges had been blown up and the city mined, after he had seen the newsreels of Monte Cassino and Naples and Dresden and Hiroshima, the dreams began.

In the first one he was standing in via Cavour, just a block away, while he watched the bombs hit the cathedral. The whole building exploded, stone flying through the air in all directions. Variations of the dream continued to haunt him for several years. Sometimes he was in the nearby streets, other times he was watching from the hills or from a high window. At first there was always the deep buzz of the approaching planes, then the bombs littering the sky like some flock of heavy-bellied, metallic birds zeroing in on their target. After that maybe a big crack in the dome that slowly widened until the whole cupola collapsed, or a trembling of the ground until the building imploded, falling in on itself. Occasionally, like the first time, an explosion, debris flying everywhere. But always there was that sense of unbelievable finality. The Duomo was gone. The engineering miracle of Brunelleschi, the defining skyline of Florence, gone. In its place only dust and rubble.

He turned over onto his back now, untangled his hand from the twisted sheet and laid it on his chest. The beat of his heart was quiet and regular. The feeling that his blood was racing must have been part of the dream, but he felt as breathless as if it had been real. He lay there for a while, imagining what it would be like to have this center of your whole city destroyed. They would rebuild, of course, like they had with the bridges, using the original plans, but then a horrible thought occurred. He didn't know where the plans were kept, but both the National Library and the Cathedral archives had suffered enormous losses during the flood. Were the plans for the cathedral, especially the cupola even available now? Then he caught himself. It was only a dream. The Duomo was intact. Still things like that did happen, would happen someday, though hopefully thousands of years in the future. And what would Florence be without its massive cathedral crouching in the center of the town? He tried to imagine it and couldn't, though he knew that the Duomo hadn't yet been built in Dante's time, and Dante still managed to be Florentine. People would adjust. They always did. Things were lost, cities, even whole civilizations. The Etruscans, who were probably direct ancestors of his, were totally gone, leaving barely a trace, not even their language.

Outside the window now it was still fully dark. He turned to look at the clock. Four-fifteen. There was still time to go back to sleep. He rolled over onto his stomach and stretched his legs out diagonally in the matrimonial bed that was all his tonight. The pressure of the mattress was comforting against the length of his body. He rearranged his pillow, snuggling his face into it. The scent of the lavender that Ivana always kept with the linen was familiar and restful, and he sank into sleep.

Most of the memory and all the feel of the dream was gone by the time he woke the next morning. It was Tuesday and his family would be back on Saturday. As he dressed he went over his plans. He would talk to his friend, Paolo, who had a small apartment on the other side of town. Paolo was single, his mother had recently died and now he lived alone. The café where he worked stayed open during siesta, so the apartment would be empty that time of day. Bruno would ask him if he could have a key. It was a good area, near the stadium, easy access but not somewhere Ivana or Annamaria would often have reason to be. He would be home from school a little after one and could invent a student at three to explain why he was gone. Or if he met Nadia later there would be no need for explanations. He was often out in the afternoon.

The rain had broken the heat and cleansed much of the pollution from the valley, and, when Bruno stepped outside to get his coffee at the corner café, the air was light and fresh. He took the back street of via San Frediano, weaving his way between the mini delivery trucks that parked with two wheels on the narrow sidewalk and the cars, motor scooters and bikes that gave you a bare centimeter clearance if you stepped off. Although his whole life these days was measured by the time he was with Nadia or the time remaining before he would be with her again, the world around him was in sharper focus, too, and this morning he felt a deep connection to the bustle around him, as though in the middle of honking horns and voices calling out, today, at least, everything was in place, the way it should be. This feeling persisted as he had his coffee, read the paper, went back to the apartment where he did a few household chores, shaved, went down the block to get the car and left to pick Nadia up.

She was waiting downstairs when he arrived at her building. She wore the same blue shift she had worn the day they went dancing. It matched her eyes, he knew, although he couldn't see them, as she stood with her back to him talking to the *portiere*. He pulled the car up to the curb and got out. The sun picked out glossy, reddish highlights from her black hair, hanging loose today, and for a moment his brain supplied him with the scent of her shampoo. He greeted Nadia and the *portiere* and then held the door for Nadia. She slid into the car, sitting down first, then swinging her knees in and finally tucking her sandaled feet in, a tidy little movement that he always enjoyed watching and that left her sitting with her knees a little towards the driver's seat—towards his seat. He closed her door, went around to his side of the car and got in.

"Did you sleep well, *amore*," he asked.

"I stayed up reading." As he turned the ignition on, she showed him the little book she had been reading the day before. "I'm finished. I brought it for you."

"Thanks. Can you put it in the back?"

She leaned over and tossed it onto the back seat. "It really made me think," she said. "These boys want to learn so badly, but they don't want to learn a bunch of stupid stuff. They want to understand the world around them, history and science and politics and how to express themselves so people will listen. And then the movie last night—it was the same thing. People do want to learn. They just need to be treated with respect."

Bruno laughed. "My teachers seemed to think that the way to make you learn was to scare you half to death. I don't know if it worked or not, but I didn't want to teach that way. I just wanted to be tough enough so they would learn but . . ." He shrugged. "Who knows what they learn? Or why?"

"I learned from you," she said, "but I think students who haven't had the advantages I had need to start with things that are more immediate."

"More immediate?"

"You know. To do with their own lives." She took a deep breath. "I've often thought I would like to do that. Go into the poor areas and teach people to understand what's going on in the world, to ask questions and to really think about things."

Bruno glanced at her out of the side of his eye. He loved the little furrow she got in her brow when she was being serious. "The powers that be are never going to let you seriously educate the poor."

"Why would anybody be against education?"

"It's much easier to control ignorant people than educated ones."

"But if your people aren't educated how can your country be successful?"

Bruno shrugged. "All politicians want is to get elected and stay elected. Down south in Sicily where all the old women are religious and most of them don't read, the communists put pictures of St. Joseph on their posters, calling him a worker. By the time the Christian Democrats caught on and put holy pictures on their posters, the people thought the Christian Democrats were the ones lying and now they all vote communist thinking that the hammer and sickle are some sort of religious symbol."

She laughed. "Really?"

"Really. And it suits the politicians."

"Most of my friends think the only way to change things is to have a revolution. That it's necessary to be violent, or nobody is going to change. Like Castro. Sometimes I think that, too—that it's the only way to get the job done. But it bothers me. I saw how things were here after the war. It doesn't make sense to tear everything up. But teaching people is always a good thing."

"It's not easy for young people to understand," he said. "I was thirteen when the partisans started organizing seriously, when things got really bad here. Fourteen when Florence was liberated. I didn't join the partisans. I was too young and I was afraid and I was tied up with my first girlfriend and anyway my father wouldn't have let me, but I was ready. If the war had lasted another month or two, I would have been right there with them. At least I would have been on the right side—I knew the fascists were bad—but even that is just luck at that age. Who knows how I would have felt if my family had been fascist?"

He was silent a moment thinking. "I was bothered by seeing beautiful things destroyed, but I didn't really understand about people's lives. Not really. Mainly I was afraid." When he thought back on that time everyone around him seemed to be covered with a veil of gray—their faces, their clothes, their voices, their smells. Even when he looked back at himself, he seemed to have been gray and unformed. Only his memories of Silvana had any color.

"It was worse for the older people who understood more. And they felt so much shame," he said.

"Shame?"

"They were taken in by Mussolini, pushed around by the fascists and then occupied by the Germans. And there was shame, too, at being treated like the enemy when the Allies arrived. We had kicked Mussolini out and lost lives fighting the fascists, but we were still the enemy."

"I guess the Americans were lucky they didn't have anything to feel ashamed about."

"Nothing to feel ashamed about?" Was it possible that she really thought this? "You aren't ashamed about Hiroshima and Nagasaki?"

She was silent.

"You need to think about that. Never forget it."

She nodded.

He hesitated a moment. "Here, after it was over, there were some incidents of retaliation against the fascists." He spoke more slowly now, trying to find exact words—this was something he wanted Nadia to understand. "There was so much anger. There had been so much brutality. Anyway the partisans lined a group of fascists up in Piazza Santa Maria Novella and shot them. One of them, one of the fascists, was a boy I knew slightly. He went to the same school I did, two years ahead of me." Again he hesitated. "If I had been with that group of partisans I think that if I had been ordered by the leader to fire I might have done it. I'm pretty sure I would have. In fact I know I would have. And I would be a different person today." He turned to look at her, to see her reaction.

Her forehead was furrowed, and she looked at him seriously. "What a horrible position to be put in."

"That's war. And it wasn't a question of whether I wanted to do it. In fact the harder it was the more I would have felt like I had to prove myself somehow."

"What happened to all the fascists?"

"They are around. Half the people you see on the street were fascists."

"And nobody hates them."

"One of the hardest lessons we had to learn after the war was that if we wanted peace we had to have peace with people we didn't agree with, or didn't like or who had hurt us or our family."

She was silent. "And everybody on both sides learned that?"

"Not all, but most. When you live through a war, it is so bad you would do anything, even forgive, to make sure it never happens again."

"But, how . . . ?"

"It takes some time. For years people needed to tell their stories over and over, but eventually you let it go, as much as you can, and you pretend the rest. We're not angels. We are just tired of war."

"My father says that some wars are necessary, but that everyone loses, even the winners."

"Was your father in the war?"

"He was in Italy actually. Sicily and then Rome."

"Well, he's right. Nobody wins. But I've often wondered what it would take to make a boy that age understand. There's so much pride and need and urgency when you're young, so little awareness of how things impact other people. There can also be something seductive about fighting in a war. You put everything on the line." He smiled a little. "My father and my uncle were both soldiers."

"My father says it's something you do when you have to if you want to be a man."

They were nearing San Domenico now, and he realized that he had forgotten to stop and get bread. He would have to get it in the piazza. He pulled over onto the little side street before the square, well out of sight of his aunt. She would almost certainly be back from the sea by now, and he didn't want her to see the car.

"I'll be just a moment," he said to Nadia, as he got out of the car. "Wait here."

He bought bread and some packaged cookies, the little chocolate ones he knew Nadia liked, but when he got back to the car Nadia wasn't there. He stood waiting a moment, and then, as he started walking towards the square, he saw her. She was coming towards him, but something about her face was all wrong. As she got closer he could see that she was crying.

He went towards her, took her in his arms. "What's the matter? What happened?"

She said something, but her face was buried against his chest and the words were muffled.

"What?" He took her by the shoulders and held her away from him so that he could see her face.

Her mouth was trembling, her voice was shaky and squeaky, but now he could make out what she was saying.

"They called me a whore."

"Who? Tell me."

She looked at him, her eyes red and moist, then took several deep breaths and said, "I went to the newsstand to see if the new Time magazine was out. There was another lady there. After I left I heard them saying something about me—'l'americana.' Then I heard them say, 'puttana.'"

Of course, Bruno thought. It didn't have to be his aunt. They had driven by every day, and the whole village probably knew who he was. He held her now, his stomach tight with anger as he whispered into her hair, "Piccola mia. I'm so sorry."

"I don't want to go to your grandmother's house," she mumbled.

"It's all right. We don't have to go there."

"I don't want to go back to Florence either. Can we go somewhere else?"

"Of course."

Back at the car, he opened the door for her and then slid in on his side. "Where do you want to go?" he asked as he put the key in the ignition.

"Can we go to the sea?"

The sea? Where his family was. He looked over at her. Her eyes were still swollen, and her face was blotchy. "Of course," he said, needing to do anything to make her happy again. But as they drove down from San Domenico, the idea began to appeal to him on its own merits. It would be nice to get away from the heat and humidity of Florence, to breathe the clean air at the sea and to have a cool swim. The water this time of year would be a perfect temperature.

"Do you swim?" he asked Nadia.

She nodded.

The *autostrada* would take them to *Migliarino*, and from there they could head down the coast towards Pisa. He didn't know any good beaches in that direction. He usually went up to Viareggio where his family was staying, but it would be fun to explore new places with Nadia.

"There's a beach at Pisa," he said, as they turned onto Viale dei Mille on the outskirts of town. "I've never been there but we can go look at it, and if we don't like it we can go further south."

"What about the caves at Carrara, where they quarry the marble? I've always wanted to see them."

The only way to Carrara was through Viareggio, exactly what he was trying to avoid. He looked at his watch. It was a little after ten. His family would be crossing the main road at around one, going from the beach to the *pensione* for lunch. If he and Nadia hurried they could be through there by twelve-thirty, and, unless for some reason Ivana decided to leave the beach early, he could drive right through without being seen.

"We can do that," he said, grateful to be able to please her. He pulled into the Agip station for gas. "The moon is almost full, and the caves are supposed to be spectacular by moonlight. We could spend the night at the sea if you want." He felt a twinge of danger, as he said this. But it would be fine. Ivana had called last night and almost surely wouldn't call tonight.

"Will we be able to get a place in August?"

"I think so. It's late in the season, and we'll have the whole afternoon to look."

"Let's do that." Her voice was more alive now. "We've never spent a night together."

Bruno paid the attendant and turned south, over the Ponte al Pino and towards Nadia's apartment.

He let Nadia out at her building and waited downstairs in the car. He was relieved when she appeared with her small bag five minutes later, as he had been a little concerned about time. They still had to go by his house, but, even so, if they did the *autostrada* in an hour and a half, they could get past Viareggio with thirty or forty minutes to spare. They should be all right.

He crossed the Ponte alla Carraia and found a parking spot on the Lungarno Vespucci. It was the closest place he could think of outside his neighborhood. It meant a bit of a walk, but he couldn't leave her in the car in front of his building, especially not if he would be coming out with his bag. "I'll be about twenty minutes," he said to Nadia as he got out of the car.

She made a face. "Can't let the mistress be seen, huh?"

He stopped and turned to look at her.

She smiled, but her eyes were troubled. "Go on. It's all right," she said.

He passed through Piazza Nazario Sauro, where the juke box in the local café blared a song in English, and headed down via San Frediano, past the wall where, when he was eleven, he had watched a group of *squadristi* tear down the poster of Joan Fontaine.

He had been in love with Joan Fontaine then. He stopped every day in front of the poster advertising *Rebecca* and silently declared his feelings to her as she looked down with sad eyes. But when Italy entered the war in 1941, there were to be no more American movies. On the way home from school one day, Bruno saw them, three *squadristi*, the black tassels on their hats bouncing as they jumped up to reach the poster. They had already ripped it halfway off and the one eye left on the wall seemed to beg him to stop them. He watched, powerless, hot feelings swelling inside him, as they pulled the last of her down. He had hated himself for not protesting, but they were big and there were three of them and he could not imagine at that time disobeying an edict from Mussolini.

But that was years ago. He walked quickly to his building, packed his things and returned to the car. Nadia was leaning on the wall of the riverbank, looking down at the water. He came up behind her and put his arm around her. Her body was rigid. He took his arm back and leaned beside her on the wall. A group of boys, ten or eleven years old, were playing in the water by the thin strip of land below the dam. "Watching the boys?" he asked.

"I was thinking."

"And . . ." He was anxious to get on the road, but she was clearly still upset and he didn't want to seem to be hurrying her.

"What really makes me mad is that I care. I didn't think I cared what other people thought."

Bruno was surprised. "Everybody cares what other people think. If people don't have a good opinion then what are you?"

"You care about what that woman thinks?" Nadia asked.

"Well . . ."

"Are you afraid she'll tell your wife?"

The thought made him clench his jaw, but he knew she wouldn't. "Why would she do that? That would be mean."

Nadia turned and looked at him, her eyes angry. "You don't have anything to care about. Nobody thinks you're doing anything wrong if you have an affair with me. But you're the one who's married. You're the one who's betraying someone. Why am I the one who's done something wrong?"

He was taken aback by her vehemence, but intrigued by the question. He didn't really know how to answer it. People make love with each other. That's the way they are. And sometimes the one you get together with isn't the one you're supposed to be with, but it happens. It always has. And everybody knows it. So why is it such a scandal? "In Italy it has a lot to do with the Church and the Vatican," he said finally. "They have always thought anything to do with sex was bad, and they control much of our lives, or at least try to."

"But it should be worse for the one who's married. Instead it's always the woman."

He hesitated. He had always lived in a house full of women and was familiar with their voices, their smells, their emotional ups and downs, but he was still aware of a mysterious core to them, something to do with the miracle of motherhood and the way they seemed to know things in an almost otherworldly way. He had been raised to believe that this was sacred and had to be protected, or women, with their softer nature, would become something valueless thrown about by the rougher side of men. And then there was the matter of family honor. His job was to protect the reputations of the women in his family. Any transgression would reflect on him. It had never occurred to him to question these things. Nadia might as well have asked him why the Arno was a river.

"Men and women are different," he said, and heard how inadequate this was and tried again. "Women can have children."

"Not without the help of men."

The voices of the boys on the bank carried up to where Bruno and Nadia stood. He looked down at their graceful, preadolescent bodies as they romped in the water. A few wore bathing suits, but most were in their underwear. Not so long ago they would have been naked, but the tourists had complained and now they had to be covered. It seemed strange that anyone would care whether boys that young wore anything or not, but something about their nakedness threatened the tourists. "Men have no way of telling whether they're the father or not," he said. And then he added, "Maybe men are a little afraid of women."

She put her hand on his. "I'm sorry. I'm taking it out on you, when it's really the system I'm mad at."

He hooked his arm into hers. She didn't move away this time. "Come on. We have each other. Why waste your thoughts on some old spinster who's probably never been touched by a man. She's just jealous."

Nadia gave a shaky little laugh.

"Forget about her. Let's have a wonderful day."

"I'll try," she said, as they walked together, arm and arm, back to the car. He pulled her close and kissed her on the neck. Her hair, crushed against his face, smelled of the floral shampoo he loved. He tore himself away and reached around and opened the car door for her.

Now on the *autostrada* they drove in silence. The windows were open making it difficult to talk against the rush of wind and impossible to hear anything that might be said. Bruno thought about what Nadia had said, that she didn't think she had done anything wrong. What a strange way to phrase it. It wasn't a question of right or wrong. Certain things have certain consequences. If you let people find out you're having an affair, especially with a married man, they are going to think certain things. That was the way it was. But he should have been more careful, not have gone up to San Domenico where people knew him, or at least have driven through during siesta time when no one would have been looking. Why did she get out of the car?

He glanced at the speedometer. Ninety kilometers per hour and the car was still handling well. When his 600 had been destroyed by the flood, Fiat had replaced it with a 500. Until now he hadn't had a chance to see how it handled at higher speeds. It had more pep than the 600 and was a pleasure to drive. He eased back to eighty kilometers. There was no point in using any more gas than he had to. He was confident that they could be in Viareggio before his family left the beach.

Nadia rolled her window up and said something he couldn't hear. He rolled his up, too. "What?"

"Would you marry me if you weren't already married?"

"Of course," he said. Yes, he thought, I would, if everything was different. But he was already married and he had a child. There was no point in even thinking about these things.

He looked over at Nadia. She was looking straight ahead, but he could make out the little furrow in her forehead. He was curious about what she was thinking, but it was too difficult to try to carry on a conversation over the noise of the car. He turned back to the road.

The familiar drone of the car, the slow unfolding of the land around them and his automatic responses to the demands of traffic left his thoughts to range. What Nadia had said was true. She was vulnerable in a way he wasn't. His friends would all think it was great that he had a lover, and even the women would shake their heads and say something about how men are. The men wouldn't be hostile or mean towards Nadia, but they wouldn't see her the same way they would see a nice Italian girl. And the women, the older ones, would look on her with dark thoughts and disapproval.

They would never treat him that way. The rules were different for him. Like with Annamaria and him. During the war his mother always made sure he got the biggest helping of whatever there was to eat, and he was glad to get it but sometimes he shared with Annamaria, because he knew she was just as hungry as he was. As she got older, Annamaria made sure he knew how she felt about being as smart as he was and far more driven but never given the same opportunities. Nadia was right. None of it was fair. And yet that's the way it was, and how do you change it?

It was a little after noon when they reached Viareggio, out of the farm country with its defined spaces, its colors of earth and vegetation, and into the openness of the coast where the sky always seemed bluer and wider. They drove down the broad viale Regina Margherita that lay between the town and the sea. All around them people in brightly colored beach clothes walked or rode bicycles or motor scooters. The air was full of the smell of salt and iodine, of strains of music from the jukeboxes along the way and of the sparkling light that flashed off the stone pavement of the sidewalk. Art nouveau hotels and bright cafes with stainless steel counters lined the street to their right. To the left, beyond the arched entrances of the individuals beaches and the colorful beach cabanas and the long stretch of sand crowded with people and deck chairs and umbrellas, beyond a strip of green water ruffled in white by the gentle surf lay the sea, almost as vast and blue as the sky.

Soon the tiled domes of the Caffe' Margherita rose up on the right, the last landmark before the arch of the entrance to the Cassandra beach, where his family rented chairs and an umbrella. Bruno's heart began to thump. He looked at his watch. Twelve-twenty. Ivana would be taking Graziella in the water for her last dip. As he got close enough to make out the sign of the beach up ahead, a child, her head of dark curly hair so familiar, ran out onto the sidewalk. Ripples of terror ran up and down his spine. Then the child turned, and she didn't look at all like Graziella. Now they were even with the beach entrance. He glanced to the left, his heart still beating wildly. His family was somewhere over there, so close. Then it was over. The beach was behind them, getting smaller and smaller. He hadn't seen them, and he didn't see how they could have seen him.

"I love the sea," Nadia said next to him.

He turned to look at her. Her head was back against the seat, her eyes were closed, and strands of her hair that had escaped from her scarf were blowing about her face. She had never seemed so desirable.

# 12

Bruno drove north, past the little villages, past Forte dei Marmi, past the stretches of undeveloped beaches where the water was strewn with seaweed and fishing boats. He pointed out the white marble quarries visible in the Apennines that rose up to the east.

"I thought it was snow," Nadia said.

"From here they're beautiful. Up close they're big gashes in the mountains. You'll see when we go tonight."

"I've always been curious about them." Her voice was serene. Coming to the sea had been a good idea.

Several years ago, Bruno and Ivana had eaten at a restaurant high on a promontory near Lerici. Their table was on the terrace, and he remembered seeing a little cove below, with clear, calm water and no people. He thought he could find it again in time for a swim before lunch.

The restaurant was on the main highway, just as he remembered, and he could see the cove nestled between two of the high crags common on that part of the coast. The side closest to the highway was relatively flat and seemed easily accessible. He parked the car at the restaurant, and they hiked down. There was no beach, only a strip of rock and pebbles at the water's edge. He looked at Nadia to see if this would suit her.

"It's beautiful," she said. "I wonder why there isn't anybody here."

"It's noon now. The sun is overhead. But look at how high those rocks around us are. It's probably in the shade most of the day."

Nadia had her bikini on under her clothes. By the time Bruno had changed behind a towel, she had found a relatively flat place on one of the larger boulders and was sitting on a towel, putting suntan lotion on her arms. He sat down, took the bottle from her, and spread the lotion on her back.

"Mm," she said, rolling over to face him.

Moving to her feet, Bruno carefully applied lotion between each toe, taking his time. He continued up her legs and belly and reached under the bra of her bathing suit, where her nipples were hard and tight. She put her arms around his neck and pulled him down for a kiss, but when he tried to remove her bra she stilled his hand and protested, "They can see from the highway." She kissed his hand and sat up. "Now it's your turn. Let me put some on you."

He lay down obediently, but when she squeezed the bottle nothing came out. She shook it a couple of times, but it was empty. "You've used it up."

"That's all right. I don't burn. I just get dark."

Nadia tossed the bottle aside and lay face down with her head on his stomach. She seemed to have forgotten their conversation earlier that morning. Bruno he knew he would never forget this moment. How it felt to lie here with the heat of the sun on his body, the smell of Nadia's sun tan lotion lingering in the air and the sound of the water lapping against the shore. He felt, as he often did with Nadia, that he had stepped outside the flow of his daily life, outside the flow of normal time. He laid his hand gently on her back, feeling the rise and fall of her breathing.

"I can't do it," she said.

"Can't do what?" But he knew, and the world around went a shade dimmer.

"Can't be some sort of *puttana* that everybody looks down on"

He was silenced for a moment by the starkness of her words.

"You're not a *puttana*," he said after a moment. "But people have ways of judging things. Especially the older ones."

"But I love you. It doesn't make sense for that to be wrong." She sat up and faced him.

He turned onto his side and raised himself on one elbow. "It's not because you love me. It's because we are having an affair." He shifted his body so that a bump in the rock pressed into a different part of his hip. "We're not married," he said gently. "The world says that women are not supposed to make love to people they're not married to. And they're especially not supposed to get caught."

"It's just that I love you more than anything in the world, but you love your family more than me. It makes me feel ridiculous."

"I love you totally, beyond words," Bruno said. "But they're my responsibility."

She was silent. "The thing is, I don't even want to be the cause of your leaving your wife, and especially not your daughter." She paused. "I didn't know it would be so complicated. I always thought if people loved each other, they should just be together. I guess I've been really stupid."

"No, you haven't," he said. But he saw how their getting involved had been a mistake. Nadia hadn't known what she was getting into, and there was no way of undoing it now. "Come on," he said, "It's really hot. Let's go in the water. This is our day. Let's have a good time."

"You're right," she said. She stood, and though her voice was still tight she took his hand when he held it out to her.

They picked their way over the rocks to the water. There was a sharp drop several feet from the shore. Bruno looked to see if Nadia was comfortable in the deeper water. She was smiling as she swam forward with a slow breast stroke. "It's so cool and clear," she said. He slowed to match her speed.

Ivana hadn't learned to swim until she was grown, and she rarely ventured in over her head. Bruno enjoyed swimming side by side with Nadia. The water, salty and buoyant, formed crystals on his eyelashes that made everything around him sparkle. They made their way to where the sheltered area met the open sea and the water became rough. He pointed across the bay to the blue and red and green fishing boats lined up in the port of La Spezia. "That's where Byron swam from here to La Spezia."

"I think I could do that," Nadia said.

"Distances always look shorter over the water, and who knows what currents there are. Besides you would miss lunch."

"I really think I could do it."

They were treading water now, but having to take a few strokes backwards every few minutes as the current pulled them towards the gulf. "You don't like limitations." He splashed water in her direction.

"I don't like meaningless bourgeois values, and I feel like I'm surrounded by them." She splashed him back.

"There are reasons for them," he said gently.

"Like what?"

He turned onto his back and looked at the sky. He shaded his eyes with his hand. "Like if everybody made love with everyone they wanted there would be many fatherless children."

"There's birth control."

"It wasn't available here in Italy, not legally at least, until recently." He took two big strokes backward against the current.

"You think they're right. You think I shouldn't have slept with you." There was an edge to her voice, and she was treading water furiously.

"No, I think they're wrong." He turned over to face her. "The difference between us is that I don't think I can change the way things are."

"The difference between us is that nobody calls you a *puttana*."

Bruno considered his words carefully. "I'm a man. I have different needs. I can't get pregnant." As he spoke he heard the echoes of his father's voice. He didn't want to be like his father, didn't think he was, but he was tired of feeling blamed for the situation. "I don't make the rules."

"What do you think should have happened? Would I have been a better person if I hadn't let you screw me?" She used the vulgar Florentine verb, *scopare*.

He was surprised by her use of such coarse language. He modulated his voice carefully. "I don't think you're a *puttana*. But there's nothing I can say that's going to make you feel any better. Let's go back. I'm hungry." He held out his hand towards the shore, inviting her. When she started back, he followed. He dug his arms into the water, swimming fast and strong, and passed her. He reached the shore, climbed out and found his towel. As he dried himself, he watched Nadia approach with her slow breast stroke. She seemed so little, just her head showing, as it bobbed out there in the water. She was so young and alone here in a foreign country. She was right. They were in this together, and she was carrying most of the burden.

When he and his cousin Renato were boys and visiting one day with their families at their grandparents' home, they had turned on the hose behind the house. Bruno knew they weren't supposed to be playing with the water, but Renato, who was a year older, urged him on, telling him not to be a baby. Bruno couldn't remember exactly how it had come about, but at some point they had discovered that, when they held the nozzle against the ground, the hose began burying itself. They watched in fascination as a meter, two meters, three meters of hose dug itself into the earth. They tried to pull it back out, but they couldn't. Even after they turned the water off, the hose remained stuck. Eventually they had to tell their parents. Renato's father laughed, but Bruno's father twisted his ear and called him fool. Now, standing at the edge of the water and watching Nadia, Bruno remembered how angry he had been at the unfairness, and he thought he understood how Nadia must be feeling.

When Nadia stepped out of the water, he came towards her, holding out her towel. "I am sorry that woman hurt you," he said. "If I knew how to make it go away, I would. I love you. I know that." He wrapped the towel around her. "Americans do things differently from Italians, and even here the people that grew up before the war do things differently from the younger ones, and the older ones fight the changes. You got caught in the middle." She was silent, but she let him dry her shoulders and arms and back and didn't protest when he ended with a kiss on her neck. "We can't change it, but we can be good to each other."

She leaned against him, smelling of salt water and sun-warmed skin. "It's so beautiful here, the water, the sky, the little villages we passed, being with you." She reached behind and touched his hip as she said this. "I don't want to lose it, but I don't know how to be part of it."

Their lunch smelled of the sea—pasta with a sauce of clams, mussels, octopi and just a touch of tomato. It was accompanied by a carafe of local white wine, light and clean. Afterwards they found a sandy beach, rented chairs and an umbrella and slept. Bruno woke up hot and sticky and with a dry mouth. He had been dreaming, but he couldn't hold onto anything that happened in the dream. He only knew it had been about Silvana. He lay there, his eyes closed. It was such a natural thing, he thought, for men and women to make love, yet it led to such trouble.

"Are you awake?" Nadia asked.

"Uhm. Did I snore?"

She laughed. "I don't know. I was asleep." She stretched, her bare belly taut as she arched her back. He wanted to bury his face in it, bury his whole self in it. "I'm ready to go back in," she said. "What about you?"

After a drink from the water fountain by the showers, they walked across the beach towards the sea. He had on a pair of rubber flip flops, but she was barefoot and soon began hopping in the hot sand. She ran the last few yards. When Bruno caught up with her he smiled, raised an eyebrow and asked if her feet felt free enough now. She grinned, kicked wet sand at him and ran into the surf. He followed. This time they stayed close to the shore, laughing and playing. The cool water was refreshing, and Nadia seemed to have forgotten her cares of the morning, or at least put them aside. When they came out Bruno felt he should offer her his flip flops, but he knew he could never cross the sand barefoot without hopping and running and making a spectacle of himself. "Here," he said, removing the right one. "Take this." And they walked back, the one shoe each one had giving them enough relief from the hot sand to make it bearable.

"This is the way it should be," she said. "Sharing bad things, not just good ones." She sat down on her chair and handed him back his shoe. "When we're together I feel like we're lovers and friends and part of each other, but we aren't really."

Bruno sighed. She wanted so much. Life wasn't like that, but they were part of this moment together. Wasn't that worth something? A vendor came by with cold drinks, and Bruno bought one for each of them. The cool liquid was good against the salt in his mouth.

"What scares me," Nadia said, "is that I think our separate lives are the real ones, and this isn't. And I don't want that to be true. I want to be with you forever."

Bruno had always known there would be no forever for them. He remembered the lines from Leopardi he had learned in school.

*O natura o natura, perche' di tanto inganni i figli tuoi,*
*Perche' prometti allor quel che non rendi poi?*

It was true. Life fills you with desires and promises and then doesn't fulfill them. But he was determined to enjoy what they had. There were no other choices.

That evening, after dinner, they drove up into the mountains. "Did you always want to be a teacher?" Nadia asked, as they sat outside one of the smaller caves where marble was quarried. A *Do Not Enter* sign roped off the entrance to the cave. A truck and a large crane were parked in front. The area was strewn with marble—large slabs, small chunks, tiny chips, and fine dust. The moonlight reflected white off their hard-edged facets and off the great slashes in the mountain where the marble was exposed. Where the pale light didn't reach black, jagged shadows loomed. Bruno and Nadia sat side by side on a big slab, his arm around her. Bruno, who had always been drawn to the night, to its mystery, to the way it seemed to promise something more, something different from his everyday life, drew her closer and bent to kiss her.

She drew away. "No, really. I want to talk. Tell me why you decided to become a teacher."

"I stayed in school because I was a good student, and I studied physics because I liked it. I teach because what else can you do with it, if you're not a Fermi?"

"Didn't you want to help your students?"

"I didn't think of it that way at first. It was a job I could do. Later there were a few who gave me real satisfaction." He glanced at her. Her throat shone as white as the marble. "You were one of those." He let his fingers run down the side of her arm and then smiled. "Look at where it got me."

"Were you attracted to me then?"

Bruno thought for a while. It was a hard thing to find words for. "Not that way. You were a child. But I noticed you. There was something."

"I had a crush on you," she said, her eyes teasing.

"Really?" He was surprised.

"Uh-huh." She chuckled. And then after a pause, "I've decided. I'm going to be a teacher. I like the idea of helping children who don't have much of a chance, showing them there's something better. Like Sidney Poitier in *To Sir with Love*."

Bruno tried to imagine Nadia, an attractive young woman, influencing a group of rowdy, underprivileged adolescents and failed. "Are you sure? I suspect it's not as simple in real life."

"Don Milani did it. And besides it's what I want to do. I just need to get started."

"But you are teaching already."

"That's just something I was doing to pay the bills, so I could stay here. This is about what I'm going to do with my life."

Bruno was confused. Life was for living, surviving, enjoying what you could. Jobs were what men did to pay the bills and to get respect. Or what women did to help out, when they weren't too busy with babies.

"I always knew I wanted to do something to make the world better," she said. "For a while I wanted to go in the Peace Corps, but my father was afraid and asked me not to."

Bruno nodded. He could understand that.

"My friends back in the states are marching to protest the war, and I feel like I should be there to do it with them. I never feel like I belong in America, but I don't belong anywhere else either. I do feel like I belong with my peers, with the things they are trying to change." She paused. "I don't agree with all of it. They are burning Detroit now." She shook her head. "I saw how it was here after the war and even worse when we were in Germany. I don't want to be part of something like that. But I can march and sign petitions and I could get a job teaching in poor areas, helping people get out of the ghettoes, live happier lives. That would make sense to me." She looked away, her face very pale in the moonlight. "My father wants me to come back."

"Are you going to?"

"I think it's time. I told him I didn't want to finish my doctorate. He said that was all right if I had something else I really wanted to do. I stalled him, but he's right. I think it really is time for me to go back."

Bruno had to clear his throat to make his voice work. "When?"

"At the school they think I'll be here all year, but I'll tell them I can stay until Christmas. That should give them time to find someone else." She put her hand on his leg and looked at him. Her eyes were shy and pleading. "You can come with me. We can live together. You can get divorced in America."

America, where everyone was rich, where he could be with Nadia for the rest of his life. What she was offering was enormous. He tried for a moment to imagine it, but there was no point. He knew it wasn't possible.

"I can't."

"Yeah, I guess I knew that. But I can't stay here."

"There are rural areas here where good teachers are needed." But he knew that she could never get licensed in Italy, and, even if she could, the problem was deeper than that.

She didn't answer. He tightened his arm around her, and she lay her head on his shoulder. They sat a while in silence.

"I just wish I belonged somewhere, to someone, to something."

He did belong somewhere and to someone, and these belongings were ties that bound him, when what he wanted was to be free to live in a world that held nothing but Nadia and him. He kissed the top of her head.

"This place is spooky," she said finally. "Let's go back to the *pensione*."

Bruno was reluctant to leave the warm night air. "How about the beach? We can take a walk by the sea."

She smiled and nodded, but when they rose to leave, she looked up at him and said, "Hold me." He took her in his arms and held her tight, as though if they could merge their bodies they could make a path together somehow. Eventually they ended up on the front seat of the miners' big truck.

Bruno woke the next day to the sounds of early morning. The German woman who owned the *pensione* was bantering with a delivery boy below his window. Somewhere further in the distance a woman was singing. Bruno slowly opened his eyes. The sun had found its way through the half open blinds, as had the smell of freshly baked bread. Beside him, Nadia was still asleep. She lay on her side, facing him, one hand under her cheek, her hair strewn across the pillow, her breath warm and moist on his arm. He lay still, watching the rise and fall of her breast, the barely visible flutter of pulse in her neck, and marveled at the miracle of her aliveness. He felt like he had found something he had been looking for all his life, something that had to do with who he was on the deepest level. But even as he breathed in the moment, tried to hold it close, he could not ignore the shadow of fear that no sunlight could chase from the room.

He got out of the bed as quietly as he could, found his robe and slippers and went across the hall to the bathroom, then came back and washed and shaved at the basin in the corner of their room. When he turned around, he saw that she was awake. She held out her arms to him, and he walked towards the bed, opening his robe.

"You weren't kidding," she said. "You do get tan."

He looked down and saw the distinctive line where the brown of his body met the white of the area that had been covered by his bathing suit. His heart missed a beat. How would he explain a tan to

Ivana? He closed the robe quickly so that Nadia would not see how his passion was waning and didn't take it off until he was in bed next to her. The warmth of her body, the touch of her fingers on his skin soon pushed all thoughts of Ivana from his mind.

When Bruno and Nadia came into the dining room for breakfast, it was empty except for a group of American girls talking noisily and an older couple, probably German, Bruno thought, certainly not Italian. Chintz curtains hung on the windows. The walls were decorated with pictures of rosy-cheeked, blonde children wearing little skirts and shorts embroidered in red and green. The room, with its low ceiling, exposed beams and flowery curtains, was attractive in what seemed to him to be a northern sort of way, the kind of room you would want to be in if the weather was bad like he imagined it was often in Germany.

Most of the tables held the remains of a meal from earlier risers, but in a corner near one of the windows Bruno and Nadia found a small table still set for breakfast. Bruno held Nadia's chair and then sat down, feeling that he had wandered into a foreign world. But this was Nadia's world, and he wanted to experience it. Even when the proprietress informed them that they could have a nice German breakfast with eggs and sausage and potatoes and Nadia enthusiastically accepted, his need to know everything about her, his joy in learning every new detail, outweighed his sense of what was proper to eat at this hour.

Nadia's meal took some time to arrive, but the waitress offered them coffee while they waited. Bruno declined, asking her to bring his with Nadia's breakfast and with the roll he had ordered, but Nadia accepted the coffee. She sat across from him with her elbows on the table, the cup held in her right hand, the fingers of her left hand curled around it, her eyes fixed on the coffee. Her head was down, and she was silent.

Bruno couldn't tell if she was unhappy or just quiet, but he was grateful for the silence. The worry about his tan and how to explain it to Ivana had resurfaced. He would have liked to talk about it with Nadia, he wanted to tell her about everything, but it wouldn't be courteous either to Nadia or to Ivana. He had to think of something to say to Ivana, though. She must not suspect what he was doing.

Nadia looked up now. "This is nice. I'm glad we had this time together."

"I'm glad, too," he said, pulling his attention back towards her. He reached across the table and touched her hand. She smiled, but he could see the sadness in her eyes, and he felt the edges of the same something brush against him. It seemed impossible that his being with her was nothing more than a swatch cut from the fabric of time, like something that you could put in your pocket and take home to keep, a treasured memory but nothing to do with the flow of every-day life. But Nadia would leave. It could be no other way. And he did not know what he would do then. His everyday life seemed so far away, so interminable and empty, without Nadia.

"What are you thinking?" Nadia asked. "You look sad."

"I'm thinking I should spend some time at the sea with my family." The words surprised him even as he said them. But his family would expect it, and maybe it wasn't such a bad idea. He could spend a day at Viareggio, and perhaps if he reconnected with his family he could make more sense out of what was happening to him. Actually, he could kill two birds with one stone. If he could figure out a way to swim before Ivana saw him without his clothes, he could explain the tan that way. The family took Graziella to the beach in the morning, and then, after siesta, they usually went to the park. He could arrive at lunchtime and say he wanted to swim in the afternoon since he missed his morning swim. It would work.

"I don't see any way around it." He squeezed Nadia's hand.

Her face was expressionless.

Their breakfast arrived. The smell of eggs and sausage was heavy and not appetizing at this early hour, but the coffee was strong, the rolls were warm and crusty, and Bruno, no longer worried about the tan, was not about to let anything bother him. "Just one day," he said, as he spread a little curl of butter on his bread and topped it with apricot jam.

Nadia cut a piece of sausage and pushed it around her plate but didn't eat it. "Tomorrow would probably be the best time. I have to meet with one of my colleagues to talk about books and curriculum, and my period is due today anyway."

"We can go to the movie tonight after my lesson, if you want," he said, relieved that she didn't seem upset, "and then I'll leave tomorrow morning, spend the night and come back on Friday. *Il Sorpasso* is playing at the Edison. I'd like to see it."

"Yeah, I saw it was on. I'd like to see it, too."

Bruno tore off another piece of his roll, smeared it with butter and jam and put it in his mouth.

"Why don't we go to the movie Friday when you get back? I have a lot of business I've been neglecting. I can probably get everything taken care of by then."

"I'll pick you up Friday afternoon then."

"I can meet you at the theater. That will be easier."

"I can make the six o'clock show after my student and we can have dinner afterwards." By Friday his friend, Paolo, would be back from vacation and they might be able to have his apartment for a few hours that evening.

Nadia had picked at her breakfast and finally, leaving most of it on the plate, put her napkin down and said she was finished. Bruno finished his coffee and wiped his mouth. He didn't have to be back in Florence until midafternoon, so he suggested they drive north, up the Amalfi coast, and look at some of the fishing villages in the area. Nadia had never been there, and it would keep them far away from

Forte dei Marmi for the rest of the morning. They could drive back during siesta, when his family would be resting.

# 13

Bruno had just arrived, a little before lunch was due to be served, and now he sat next to Ivana on the patio swing with Graziella in his lap. The area was ablaze with color—clay pots full of red geraniums, a pink rose sprawled against the warm ochre of the stucco wall, the sky the deep blue it only achieves near the sea. Bruno felt detached from it all, like a living person trying to enter a postcard.

"My *Babbo*," Graziella said, caressing Bruno's cheek. "Did you miss me?"

Bruno leaned his head down to whisper in Graziella's ear, "Yes, *amor mio*, I missed you." She smelled like sea and shampoo and her own little girl smell, but still it was as though there were a barrier between them. He tightened his arms around her.

"I can almost swim." She squirmed away so that she faced him. "Will you watch me tomorrow?"

"Of course." And now that she faced him, her childish voice so confident, he felt more connected, but instead of the usual joy she gave him, sadness enveloped him. She knew so little about the complexities of the world, and someday she, too, would have to deal with them.

"She's been working really hard," Ivana said. "She can float on her stomach and on her back."

"I'm impressed," Bruno said to Graziella. "You can show me tomorrow." Then he turned to Ivana. "I'm going to get a swim in this afternoon. I'll go while you are at the park with Graziella."

"I'll come with you. The grandmothers can take Graziella. It will be fun, just the two of us."

Bruno's stomach sank. He buried his head in Graziella's curls, so that his face wouldn't show while his mind tumbled in all directions. There was nothing for it, though, but to act pleased and try to figure out some other plan to keep Ivana from noticing his tan. He looked up and smiled at her. "That will be nice." His voice sounded like he was an actor in a play.

He was quiet during lunch, unable to shake the sense that there was too much space between him and everything around him.

"*Che bella famiglia che ha, signore,*" the proprietress said as she removed his pasta dish and brought his main meal. What a beautiful family.

"*Grazie, signora,*" he said, looking around at the women in his family—Ivana, serene, content; *Nonna*, regal-looking with her arched nose and well-defined eyebrows, still vibrant at almost eighty; his mother, *Mamma Do'*, small and round and gentle, always overshadowed by the people around her, but so special to him; and Graziella, beautiful Graziella, basking in the love of everyone around her. This was his family, his people, where he belonged, but he felt like he was seeing them all for the first time.

When the meal was over and they stood up to leave the table, he told Ivana he was going to buy cigarettes. "Get me a *Grand Hotel* while you're out," she said. *Grand Hotel* was a *fotoromanzo*, a magazine with romantic serial stories illustrated by still shots of real actors. Bruno usually teased Ivana, saying he couldn't understand why a woman as intelligent as she was would want to read such trash, but today he said nothing.

At the tobacco shop, instead of the *Nazionales* he usually bought, he asked for a pack of the more expensive Marlboros that Nadia smoked and that he was becoming accustomed to. He lit one outside the store, but they didn't taste the way they did with Nadia. He went back inside and bought a pack of *Nazionale*s. He told himself that he needed to forget about Nadia for these two days and focus on his family, but, when he passed a café with the blue and white sign of a public phone, he entered. He would just check in with her for a few minutes and then get back to his family. He bought a handful of *gettoni*, slipped them in the slot and dialed Nadia's number. The phone rang six, seven, ten, twelve times, and he finally had to accept that she wasn't home. But maybe it was better this way. Right now he needed to forget about her.

He walked slowly back to the *pensione*, stopping to get Ivana's magazine. Ivana would want to make love during siesta, of course, as they had been apart for almost two weeks. And he would muster up enough passion for her not to suspect it was the last thing in the world he wanted to do right now. He would have to be careful because of the tan, but the shutters would be closed against the afternoon heat, and he could probably manage for her not to see much of him.

But when he got back and gave her the magazine, she smiled, thanked him and buried her nose in it. She didn't put it down until four when they had their afternoon coffee and headed for the beach.

The little cabana wasn't big enough for two, and Ivana changed first, so she was already sitting in her lounge chair when he came out in his bathing suit. It had been dark in the cabana, but here in the sunlight he could see the tan line around his waist. He pulled the suit up high to cover the tan line, but now the line around his legs showed. He tried to stretch the material of the bathing suit so that it would cover more skin but then became self-conscious, afraid everyone was staring at his strange antics. He would just have to keep Ivana from seeing him. He took a long way to their umbrella so that he could come up from behind.

"What were you doing back there with your bathing suit?" she asked, when he arrived at their chairs.

"It just didn't seem to fit right."

"Hmm." She lifted her sunglasses. "Let me see."

"No, no. It's all right now. It was just twisted."

She looked at him with a thoughtful expression but didn't say anything.

When she got up to take her swim he followed, carefully staying behind her. Once they were in the water, he kept his body submerged, and when they got out he stayed behind her again and grabbed his towel as soon as they reached the chairs. When eventually she went back to the cabana to dress, he was worried that she would wait for him and see how dark he was when it was his turn to change. But when she came out, she stopped to talk to the custodian, and Bruno hurried past, pretty sure she hadn't noticed anything. By tonight he would be able to explain the tan by the afternoon spent in the sun.

That evening they all went out together for their before dinner walk. Graziella, who usually pranced around, weaving in and out among the adults, was listless and dragged behind. When they sat down for dinner she refused to pick up her fork. "I'm not hungry," she said.

"Try to eat a little," Bruno said.

"Does she have a fever?" *Nonna* asked. "Don't feed her if she has a fever. Starve a fever."

"*Poverina*. She's not hungry," *Mamma Do'* said, stroking Graziella's hair.

"A little broth, maybe," the proprietor offered. He had come to their table when he saw that Graziella wasn't well. "Go make her some nice broth," he said to his wife who had come out of the kitchen. Now they were all talking at once, each with their own theory of what to do. Graziella slid out of her chair and climbed into Ivana's lap.

"She shouldn't eat if she doesn't want to," Ivana said calmly.

Graziella began crying softly.

*"Lasciatela in pace,"* Ivana said, her voice irritated now. "Leave her alone."

The others continued to express their concern and offer their suggestions, but they gave Ivana and Graziella some space.

Bruno felt like he was watching it all from the wrong end of a telescope. The feeling persisted throughout the evening. Graziella didn't protest when Ivana decided to put her to bed before *Carosello*, her favorite TV program, was due to start. "I'm a little worried," Ivana said to Bruno. "I'd like to keep her with us tonight. Do you mind?"

And Bruno, of course, said that he understood.

The next morning, Graziella was still listless, and Ivana made an appointment to take her to the doctor. While they were gone, Bruno went down to the café and called Nadia.

"Thank God you called." Her voice was tight, its pitch all wrong. "My period still hasn't come. I'm really scared."

"It's probably just stress. My wife is always late when she's worried about something."

"I'm never late." Her voice was quavering. "It's been two days now."

"I'll leave after lunch and come straight to your house. We can talk before the movie. But I'm sure it's nothing."

"Please hurry." Now her voice broke, and he could hear her crying.

"Don't worry, *tesoro*. It's nothing. I'm sure."

"My father will kill me," she said and hung up.

Bruno was used to Ivana's period coming late, and he knew that he and Nadia had been careful. It was clear, though, that Nadia needed him, and he considered leaving before lunch, but when Ivana and Graziella came back from the doctor, Graziella climbed into his lap and he didn't have the heart to tell her he was leaving right away.

"The doctor said it might be a little virus, but it might also be the beginning of an inflamed appendix," Ivana said. "If she's not better by tonight, he wants to see her again."

They were outside on the patio. Graziella's head lay against Bruno's chest. He didn't like the quiet way she sat. "Do you think we should take her back to Florence today?"

"Let's give it some time." Ivana's voice was calm. Bruno had great trust in Ivana in these matters and relaxed somewhat. He relaxed even more when Graziella ate a couple of forkfuls of pasta for lunch.

When lunch was over and it was nap time, he sat by her bed and read to her. Once she fell asleep, he leaned over, kissed her and began packing his things to leave.

"Do you have to go?" Ivana asked.

"My student." He shrugged and spread his hands. "I have to. I'll phone tonight."

She raised an eyebrow but didn't say anything. Bruno went to say good-bye to *Nonna* and to his mamma. "You're leaving while Graziella is sick?" *Nonna* said.

"I have an appointment, *Nonna*. I can't help it."

"I don't like it." She glared at him.

"But he has to work," Bruno's mother said, accepting, as she always did, whatever Bruno said.

"You could call and cancel," Ivana said now. "I'd feel better if the car was here."

Bruno was worried about Nadia and was anxious to get back to her, but he was worried about Graziella, too. He agreed to call his student. He didn't want to talk on the phone by the front desk where the proprietor could hear him, so he went back to the café to phone. He tried Nadia first and there was no answer. He tried his student then, and there was no answer there either. He tried Nadia again. No answer.

When he went back to the *pensione* and told Ivana he hadn't been able to reach his student, she suggested he go back to Florence, do his lesson and then call. If Graziella was worse he could come back. Bruno agreed, took his bag, and went out the door and down the street to where he had parked the car, but just as he passed the window of their room, he heard a shrill scream.

It was Graziella.

Bruno ran back to the room. Graziella was sitting upright in the bed, crying. Ivana was sitting beside her with her arm around her.

"What's wrong?" Bruno asked from the doorway.

Ivana held her hand up to silence him. "I can't understand you, *amore*," she said to Graziella. "You need to stop crying so you can tell me."

"Make him go away," Graziella said between sobs.

"Who? Tell me, love," Ivana said.

"The funny little dog."

Bruno was confused. He crossed the room and sat on the foot of the bed so that he could hear better.

"It's all right," Ivana said, stroking Graziella's head. "There's no little dog. It was a bad dream."

"No, he was here," Graziella said, her voice quavery.

"Where. *amore?* What did he look like?"

"He was sitting here." Graziella touched her stomach.

"It was just a dream. There's no dog here."

"But I can still feel it." She began crying again.

Ivana laid the back of her hand on Graziella's forehead and then on her cheek. She leaned down and put her lips against Graziella's forehead. Then she looked up at Bruno. "She has a little fever."

"It hurts," Graziella said, whimpering. Bruno stroked her foot through the cover.

"Stay with her," Ivana said, helping Graziella lie back down. "I'm going to call the doctor."

Graziella lay curled on her side, her eyes closed, her right leg pulled up to her chest. Her face was pale. She was no longer crying, but her breath was coming in little shudders. "I'm here, *piccola*." Bruno moved to where he was sitting beside her.

Graziella didn't answer. Bruno brushed her hair back from her face. He didn't want to go back to Florence when she was like this. As soon as Ivana returned, he would try again to call Nadia and explain that he couldn't leave Graziella until he was sure she was all right. Nadia would be home soon. And if the doctor said there was nothing to worry about, there was still plenty of time to get back to Florence.

Ivana came back, followed by the proprietor, *Nonna* and *Mamma Do'*. "The doctor wants us to bring her in," she said.

Just as Ivana reached the bed, Graziella sat bolt upright, her eyes wide, then leaned forward and threw up.

*Mamma Do'* stepped back towards the wall, clenching her hands to her breast, "*Oddio, Oddio*," she repeated again and again, her voice soft and fluttery like a dove. *Nonna* rushed to the sink, grabbed a towel and rushed back to the bed, pushing Bruno out of the way. "Get a mop," she directed the proprietor, who poked his head out in the hall and bellowed to his wife, "Tina. Bring a mop."

Ivana caught Bruno's eye. "Bring the car to the front door," she said, her voice quiet but sliding easily through the chaos in the room.

On the ride to the doctor's office, Graziella sat in Ivana's lap. Ivana's demeanor was more calm than usual, which made Bruno nervous. Ivana could be as emotional as anyone, but she had a way, when things were serious, of being very quiet and focused. Still, Bruno thought, there really wasn't anything to worry about. It was probably just an upset stomach. Children get upset stomachs. But the brush of an unseen hand across the lining of his own stomach reminded him that life was treacherous and that the unthinkable could and did happen.

The doctor's office was on the third floor. The elevator creaked as the floors slowly passed by through the open grill of the cage. Bruno glanced at his watch. It was almost three. He was supposed to meet his student at three-thirty. It was clear that he was going to miss the lesson, but there was plenty of time to call and cancel. If the doctor said it was just a little stomach ache, he could still go back to Florence, and he could spend the time he would have spent with the student with Nadia instead. And, either way, since Nadia wouldn't expect him until around four-thirty, they would probably be out of the doctor's office in time for him to phone Nadia and explain before she started worrying.

A woman who introduced herself as the doctor's wife let them in and led them to a large room where she told them to wait. Graziella sat on Bruno's lap, her eyes shut, her head leaning against his chest. Bruno didn't like the way she was so quiet, closed into herself, but at least she didn't seem to be in any pain. After a few minutes she opened her eyes and looked around the room, which was furnished like a living room with well-maintained antiques.

"Who's the other baby with Baby Jesus?" Graziella asked, pointing to a painting on the wall. The Virgin Mary and another woman were sitting together, and at their feet two small children were playing. All four figures had haloes.

"I think that's John the Baptist when he was a baby," Bruno answered. "And the other woman must be his mother, Anne."

"The colors are pretty," Graziella said. Mary was dressed in a brilliant sky blue, the folds of her dress carefully shaded. Anne was dressed in rose. The greens and ochers of the Tuscan landscape behind them were rich and true to nature.

"It's been restored," Ivana said. "That's why the colors are so bright."

"I like it," Graziella said

Bruno was happy to see Graziella pay attention to her surroundings. In a few days she would be back to her usual happy self.

"Did Raffaello paint it?" Graziella asked. Ivana had recently taken Graziella to the museum in the Pitti Palace, and Graziella had discovered Raffaello's paintings.

"Probably some minor Renaissance painter," Ivana said. "Maybe a student of Michelangelo's. Remember Michelangelo? He made the statue of David."

Graziella nodded. "Those ones are scary," she said, pointing to two paintings that hung on the other wall. One was of St Anthony holding the baby Jesus and one of St. Christopher carrying the infant across a river. Age had darkened the details and made the flesh tones sallow.

"The paint just got old," Ivana said. "That's why they look that way. That one is St. Anthony," she said pointing to one, "and that one is St. Christopher." She pointed to the other one. They're both really nice saints who liked children. And if you lose something and pray to St. Anthony, he'll find it for you."

Across the room, an antique clock sat on a small inlaid secretary. Its face was about ten centimeters wide, and Bruno had to squint to make out the time. It was three-twenty. The doctor still hadn't called the other family in the waiting room, and they had been there before the Cassinis. It would be after four before Bruno could phone Nadia.

But, at least, Graziella seemed better. She was still leaning against him and her voice was small, but she seemed to be enjoying looking at the paintings with Ivana.

It was ten minutes to four when they finally went into the examining room. The doctor poked and prodded and asked questions. Graziella winced as he touched her stomach and several times let out little yelps, but she didn't cry and even smiled back when he joked with her. She didn't seem that sick, and the doctor didn't look concerned.

Finally, after what seemed a very long examination, the doctor asked the nurse to stay with Graziella so he could meet with Ivana and Bruno in his office. "She has acute appendicitis," the doctor said, once he was seated behind his large mahogany desk. "We have to operate." He paused a moment, looking from Ivana to Bruno. "She didn't eat much and she threw up, but still it can be dangerous to do surgery before we're sure her stomach is empty. It is also a risk to wait. If her appendix bursts, it would be very serious." He shook his head, his face solemn. *"Molto grave."*

*Molto grave?* What did he mean by that? Bruno's mouth was suddenly dry and metallic tasting. The doctor continued, "I'll operate tonight, but I want to keep a close eye on her until then. I want her in the hospital right away." Bruno could hear Ivana, beside him, asking questions. He could see the doctor's mouth moving, see the light glinting off his glasses, see the gray strands in his thick hair, but the words seemed to be floating around the room, disconnected from any meaning.

"Are you all right?" Ivana asked, glancing at Bruno as they came out of the doctor's office.

Bruno couldn't find his voice.

"Don't worry. She'll be fine. He's a good doctor, and this is a good hospital." Ivana left Bruno in the little room with Graziella while she went to make some phone calls. Graziella was lying on the examining table, and Bruno went to her side. His little girl in the hospital. He didn't trust his voice and didn't want to scare Graziella, so he took her hand in his. The need to do something, to make her all right, was like some wild animal trying to claw its way out of a cage. But it was useless. His mind could only come up with irrational impulses—bribe the doctor, negotiate with the universe, change reality through the sheer force of his will. He stood by her bed, afraid and powerless, until, after what seemed like an interminable passage of time, Ivana came back.

They drove to the hospital. Bruno was braced for the dreary colors and smell of disinfectant and old rubber that he associated with hospitals, but this was a new building. Graziella's room, a double, was airy and light, and there was no one in the other bed. Soon after they got Graziella settled, *Nonna* and *Mamma Do'* arrived in a taxi. Then Annamaria, who was staying with friends a little further up the coast, rushed into the room. For the next hour or so, the nurses were in and out, taking blood pressure and temperature. Graziella was fussy and whining because she wanted something to drink and the doctor wouldn't allow it. *Nonna* was bustling around, trying to take care of everything. There were definitely too many people in the room. Finally the nurses had finished, for the time being at least, and Graziella, who had been given a sedative, was lying quietly. Now Ivana gave *Nonna* the task of taking Bruno's mother out to the lobby and sitting with her. "If we can keep things quiet enough in here, maybe Graziella will sleep." Then she turned to Bruno. "Did you ever get hold of your student?"

*Nadia*, Bruno thought. He felt the blood drain from his face. He looked at his watch. She would be arriving at the theater about now. Or maybe she wouldn't even go to the theater after he failed to arrive at her apartment.

"You should call her now and explain," Ivana said.

Bruno nodded. He started towards the door.

"Why don't you go with him?" Ivana said to Annamaria. "He looks like he could use some moral support."

"Come on," Annamaria said, hooking her arm into his. "Everything will be all right. I'll stick close to you."

Bruno phoned his student and told her that he wouldn't be coming, but he didn't dare call Nadia with his sister hovering nearby. "I'm all right," he told her. "You don't need to stay with me."

"You don't look all right. And besides what are sisters for if they can't care about their brothers?"

"No, really. I need quiet. Time to be alone."

"You'll just get more scared if you're alone. Come on, let's have a cup of coffee, and I'll cheer you up."

There wasn't much Bruno could do. He was afraid that if he insisted she would watch him from a distance and see him making another call. He would have coffee with her and show her he was relaxed now and then say he had to go to the restroom. Maybe he could lose her that way. But he would have to do it soon. Nadia would be waiting for him. He had no idea what Nadia had thought when he didn't come. Still, there was nothing he could do about it until he was able to get rid of Annamaria.

But there was no getting rid of Annamaria. She was waiting for him when he came out of the restroom. Bruno finally gave up. He returned with Annamaria to the room. Graziella was asleep, and Ivana sat beside the bed, distant and calm. There were only two chairs in the room, so Bruno went and stood by the window. The street outside was crowded with people on vacation, going about their business, unaware of Graziella here in the hospital. Only a few days ago he and Nadia were part of them. He let his thoughts drift back to that night with Nadia. It had been the first time they had been together all night. They had made love, talked, dozed, reached out for each other in their sleep and then made love again. Differences of age and culture slipped away in the night, as did daily responsibilities.

But daily responsibilities were back in full force. And the fear that was always with him loomed larger and darker. He closed his eyes. Graziella will be fine, he said to himself, and realized that in his mind Nadia was standing beside him and he was saying this to her. He felt a sudden sense of shame. His love for Graziella was something he shared with Ivana on the deepest level. Nadia didn't know Graziella or, for that matter, know anything about a parent's love.

Why was it Nadia he now ached to be with, Nadia he felt he could draw strength from, Nadia who wasn't even family? There was something very wrong here.

"You can have all the women you want," his father used to say. "Just don't fall in love with them. That's where the trouble starts." Bruno had grown up watching his father chase after women, women not half as nice as Bruno's mother. He knew his father took what he could get in these relationships and gave no more than was necessary to get it. To Bruno this was repugnant. But now, standing by the window in Graziella's room, as he saw what Nadia had become for him and how difficult it was going to be for her and how disastrous for everyone involved it could become, he understood the other part of what his father was saying, that falling in love had far more pitfalls. Still, it was impossible for Bruno to regret his feelings for Nadia or to regret the hours spent with her.

But, if he could go back, knowing what he knew now, he hoped, and the thought was bitter, that he would have the strength to walk away from Nadia before anything got started. He turned away from the window and left the room, Annamaria tagging along beside him.

When he reached the lobby, he lit another cigarette. His body was overloaded with adrenaline and the first puff was nauseating. He put the cigarette out. "I'm going to take a walk," he said to Annamaria. "I'd like to be alone."

"I don't think it's good for you."

"Look, I really want to be alone."

"And I really don't think you should be alone. Come on, I'm your sister. I care about you."

Bruno was familiar with Annamaria's stubbornness once she took a stand. He sighed but did not argue any further.

They left the hospital and walked out into the sunlit afternoon. "It is hard to wait, isn't it?" Annamaria said, as she walked beside him.

Bruno nodded. "I just wish there was something I could do. Some way I could help Graziella."

"That's a little egoistic, isn't it? Graziella needs Ivana and the doctors right now, not you. But you could see what Ivana needs. This is hard for her, too, you know, and I haven't heard you say a word to her since I've been here."

Bruno didn't answer. It was true. Although Ivana often didn't want to talk when she was upset, it was one thing not to talk and another to ignore someone, and he knew he had crossed the line. Ivana hadn't been on his mind at all, in fact.

"Maybe there's something you could do for her. Maybe she'd like a cup of coffee, or you could stay with Graziella while she has a cigarette. At least you could offer." She looked up at him, "If you really want to help, that is." There was an edge to her voice. Then she seemed to soften. "Besides, it would give you something to do." She snuggled her arm into his.

"You're right," Bruno said. "I've been distracted."

When they returned to the room, Graziella was still asleep. Bruno presented himself to Ivana and asked how he could help.

"I feel bad about banishing *Nonna* and *Mamma Do'*. You could go to the lobby and keep them company."

"I'll come with you," Annamaria said. "Though you're the one who cheers them up."

This was an old argument between them. Annamaria was a female and her relationship with her women relatives was warm, but it held nothing of the adulation they gave Bruno. He was the male child, the center of his mother's and his grandmother's universe. When he was present, they scurried around catering to him, hanging on his every word. He loved them, enjoyed being spoiled, and returned their fondness with affectionate teasing. He would have taken it as his due, without question, if Annamaria had not protested frequently, pointing out that she was as smart, more energetic, decidedly better looking, and that she was never given her rightful recognition.

Bruno knew the truth of this, considered it bad luck that Annamaria had been born a girl, but he didn't see the sense in fretting over what you couldn't change. As much as he loved her, he was unwilling to give Annamaria the upper hand by admitting any injustice. Still, there were times when it disturbed him.

Not that many years ago, when Annamaria wanted to become a journalist, the whole family became involved in endless discussions. His mother said journalism was for men, and Bruno had agreed with her. Being a modern woman was one thing, but Bruno was uncomfortable thinking about Annamaria in the rough place he imagined the world of journalism to be. But *Nonna* had defended her. "I wanted to be a chemist," she said. "I never understood why it was all right for Madame Curie but not for me. Let the girl do what she wants. She'll get enough trouble from the world without getting it from you." Eventually, Bruno, knowing how badly Annamaria wanted this, realized that it was unfair to deny her this opportunity and agreed to support her. Annamaria had proven herself up to the challenge and had become quite successful.

"I know, I know," she said now. "'Women always pay more attention to the men in the family. That's just how it is,'" she said, imitating his voice. "But that doesn't make it right."

He was supposed to answer that outside the family it was the other way. Men took care of women, made them feel special and let them get away with things no man would ever get away with. But he didn't feel like starting that discussion. "Come on," he said. "Let it go."

"It's not that I want them to treat me the way they do you, but they make fools of themselves acting like you're the pope or something." She tucked her arm into his. "You're a dear, but you're certainly not perfect."

They were in the lobby now, where *Nonna* and *Mamma Do'* were sitting next to the window.

"I guess I'm no use to Ivana," *Nonna* said, as they approached. "She doesn't need my experience." The tilt of her head and the hurt in her voice emphasized the offence she obviously felt at being sent from Graziella's room.

"She wanted Graziella to sleep," Bruno sat down beside the old woman and put his arm around her. "She sent me out, too."

"Hmph," *Nonna's* face relaxed a little. *Nonna* and *Mamma Do'* sat side by side on a sofa in the lobby. It had been a squeeze for Bruno to sit between them. He got up now and pulled two chairs across the room, one for him and one for Annamaria, so that the four of them sat in a kind of circle. The ladies did most of the talking, while Bruno tried to pay enough attention to nod at the appropriate moments.

Finally, at eight o'clock, one of the Sisters came and told them that Graziella was going in now. They rushed to her room in time to see the orderlies wheel her out. She was groggy but awake, holding on tightly to a stuffed bear *Mamma Do'* had brought her. The family all followed her down the corridor, Ivana on Graziella's left, holding her hand, Bruno on the right, and the other three trailing behind. Graziella's eyes were wide and solemn as she lay there—so small on the adult sized gurney—and when the door of the operating room began to close, leaving her family on the other side, her face crumpled. Bruno fought a primal need to rush in after her. His hands clenched as he listened to the doctor soothing her and her little voice answering him. She was not crying. At least there was that.

A Sister showed them a small area outside the operating room where they could wait. Ivana sat closest to the door on a long wooden bench. Bruno sat next to her and Annamaria beyond him. Across from them Bruno's grandmother and mother settled in on another bench. A crucifix hung above them, but otherwise the walls were bare. *Nonna* and *Mamma Do'* pulled out their rosaries and began fingering the beads. Bruno found the sound of their mumbled *Ave Maria's* comforting, although he placed little stock in religion. He put more stock in family, a connection that seemed to come as close as anything to providing safety. But even within that nexus there was no safety today, and Bruno found himself also praying, silently and fervently. *Hail Mary, full of grace, the Lord is with thee. Please, God, please, God. Please, please, please.*

He checked his watch over and over, waiting each time as long as he could only to find out that a minute, two or three minutes at most, had passed. He stood, paced, then sat down again. He lit cigarette after cigarette and let them burn unsmoked in his hand.

"Don't worry," Ivana said. "They are getting her appendix out before it bursts. She's going to be all right."

Bruno tried to believe her, but it was as though his body, his mind, his emotions, everything was frozen and would not thaw until he saw Graziella well and happy. Eventually one of the sisters who had been assisting the operation came out and said, "*E' andato bene. Molto bene.*" Bruno felt the muscles in his face begin to relax. Then the doctor came out. They all stood up, and the doctor shook everyone's hands.

"When can we see her?" Ivana asked.

"We'll keep her in recovery until she begins to come out of the anesthesia. It shouldn't be too long. An hour. Forty five minutes, maybe."

Everyone was smiling. Annamaria squeezed Bruno's arm. His mother and his grandmother now began prayers of thanksgiving.

Eventually the door swung open again and the gurney with Graziella appeared. She lay on her back, her eyes closed, her arms at her side, pale as a corpse.

The room went out of focus, and suddenly Bruno was back in the church in Empoli, looking at Adelina's shiny, wooden coffin, imagining her lying stiffly in it. Cold sweat swept over his body and he was having difficulty breathing. *E'andato bene*, it went well, he told himself over and over, as he struggled to keep the image at bay.

"You're white as a sheet," Annamaria said.

"Oh, my God. He's going to faint," *Nonna* said.

Annamaria grabbed his arm. Leaning onto her, he felt for the bench and sat down.

"Stay with him," Ivana said, as she hurried behind the gurney. "I'm going with Graziella." Her voice seemed to be traveling farther and farther away, like a train being swallowed by the depths of a long tunnel. Now he felt Annamaria sit down next to him.

"Put your head down—on your knees," she said gently.

He lowered his head. His skin felt cold and clammy. He continued silently repeating his mantra, *"E' andato bene, e' andato bene,"* until his chest began to loosen and his heart rate subside.

When he finally looked up, they were all standing around him, their faces solemn. Then Annamaria smiled and said, "For a minute there I thought you really were going to faint."

"It's just that she looked so . . ." He couldn't say it.

"I know," Annamaria said. *Mamma Do'* nodded.

Bruno stood up and they all made their way back to Graziella's room. She was beginning to awaken a little now. Bruno's gratitude at seeing her back in the world seemed to fill the room with light. He came to the side of the bed and kissed her forehead, warm and alive.

Eventually, Graziella was able to raise drink a few swallows of juice. She was not fully awake though, and she batted at the Sister's hand when she took her blood pressure and pulse. "Let her sleep now," the Sister said. Graziella turned over onto her side and fell asleep with her hand under her cheek, looking the way she did every night.

"Go on, get some dinner," Ivana whispered to Bruno. "I'll stay with her."

"The others can go," Bruno said to Ivana. "I'll wait and go with you when they come back."

"No, go on. You need to eat something."

"I'm fine. I can wait."

"No, go on." She waved towards the door. "I'd rather do it that way. Really." When he hesitated she looked at him, her eyes serious, "Please."

They left the room and went to a little pizzeria near the hospital. When they had finished, Annamaria went back to relieve Ivana, while Bruno drove his mother and his grandmother back to the *pensione*. Afterward he drove to the little café with the phone and dialed Nadia's number. He looked at his watch, almost eleven. He hoped she wasn't asleep, but even if she was he didn't want to wait until tomorrow to explain.

Finally he heard her voice as she answered, "*Pronto.*"

"*Ciao.* It's me."

"*Cafone,*" she said and hung up.

He stood holding the receiver. He wanted to yell that he wasn't a jerk. That he could explain, but he didn't want to make a *brutta figura*. Already he was uncomfortably aware that anyone watching might have seen how stunned he was. He considered calling her back, but he didn't want to risk being hung up on again, and, even if she was willing to listen, he was certain the call would be long and maybe loud. It wasn't the right time. He would call her in the morning when they would both be more rational. He left the café angry and hurt and tired.

Back at the hospital he found Annamaria with Graziella. Annamaria said that Ivana had gone to get something at the pizzeria. Graziella was asleep. Bruno kissed her cheek and went to find Ivana. She was sitting at a table alone with a plate of pasta and a glass of wine. As he sat across from her she looked up and smiled. She had dark circles under her eyes. "The other bed in her room is empty," she said. "They are going to let me sleep in it. But you should go back and get some rest."

"Do you want me to bring you anything? Your nightgown? Your toothbrush?"

"I'll sleep in my clothes, and they'll give me a toothbrush. You could bring me a change of clothes in the morning."

He nodded, and she told him the items she wanted.

"I was afraid," he said.

"I was, too. The doctor wants to keep her for three more days. Is there any way you can stay?" Her voice sounded tired.

His need to smooth things out with Nadia was overwhelming, and he wanted to make an excuse to leave. But seeing Ivana's tired face, he knew it wasn't fair to let her carry this alone. The other women would be there, of course, but she was asking for him. And if he took the car, they would have to take cabs back and forth from the hospital. On the other hand, he could take the train back and leave them the car. He didn't need it in Florence. He usually walked anyway. As he hesitated he saw something sad and crushed creep into Ivana's eyes. "I'll stay," he said and reached across the table and put his hand on hers. She turned hers over so that she could hold his.

"Are you sure?"

He nodded. "I'll make some calls in the morning." He would just have to explain to Nadia over the phone. And maybe he could make a quick day trip back to Florence tomorrow or the next day.

# 14

The next morning he went out before breakfast to call Nadia. Instead of going to the café close to the *pensione*, he walked towards the beach and found a café on the main *viale* where no one knew him. There were several tables outside for the tourists willing to pay the exorbitant prices it cost to use them. Inside, men and women, mostly Italian, stood shoulder to shoulder, drinking their morning coffee in front of the stainless steel counter. Bruno squeezed his way past the noisy crowd to the till. He reached over a neatly stacked pile of lemons and gave the cashier four hundred lire for telephone *gettoni*. He found the phone towards the back of the room, slipped several *gettoni* in the slot, and dialed Nadia's number. When he heard her voice, he leaned close to the mouthpiece and covered his left ear with his hand. He said, "Let me explain, at least."

"What is there to explain? I'm pregnant and you're running out on me."

"Your period didn't come?"

"No."

"It's probably nerves."

"I've never been late. Not even by a day."

He was silent. Maybe she was pregnant. He felt his stomach shrink.

"I can tell," Nadia said. "My body feels heavier, different."

Bruno felt cold. Ivana had said almost the same words when she was carrying Graziella.

"Are you there?" Nadia asked.

"Yes. I wanted to explain about yesterday. Graziella had an appendicitis attack. She had to go to the hospital."

Nadia was silent for a moment. Then, in a quiet voice, she said, "I thought you stood me up because I was pregnant. I felt so alone."

"I didn't know you were pregnant."

"I told you I was late." There was another pause. "Is your daughter all right?"

"Yes, but she's in the hospital. They had to operate."

"I'm sorry." She paused. "But you could have called."

"I tried. There was no answer."

"Why didn't you try again?"

"I tried, but they needed me."

"It's always your family first, isn't it?" Her voice was angry and sad at the same time.

"She's a child."

"And I'm going to have a child." She started crying. "But I can't. My father would die of shame."

Bruno couldn't stand to hear her tears. "It will be all right," he said desperately. "We'll think of something." But he knew that it was not going to be all right.

"When are you coming back?" He could tell she was trying to control her voice.

"I have to stay here for a few days, but maybe I can come in tomorrow afternoon for a few hours."

"You're not coming back?"

"Don't cry, *tesoro*. I'll be there tomorrow at three. We can talk. It will be all right."

"Are you sure?"

"Yes, *amore*."

"I love you."

"I love you, too."

"*Ciao.*" She hung up.

Bruno left the café, dazed. He felt like he was occupying two realities, the one he had always lived in, and this new one that had seemingly come out of nowhere and was threatening to dissolve everything he knew. He struck a match to light a cigarette, but he had to cup his hands tightly to steady them. He tried to ground himself by focusing on what he had to do right now. He brain was fuzzy, at first, but then he remembered his student. He went back in the café and called the student's home. He told her mother about Graziella and said that he didn't know when he would be coming back to Florence. He left the café again. At least he had taken care of one thing.

He walked back to the *pensione*, got his car, and drove to the hospital, keeping Nadia's pregnancy pushed to the back of his mind. When he arrived at Graziella's room, she was awake. She smiled when she saw him.

"She looks better," he said to Ivana, who was sitting by the bed.

Ivana nodded.

Bruno went around to the other side of Graziella's bed and bent to kiss her. Underneath the lingering odor of antiseptic he smelled her own familiar scent, light and uncomplicated, and his throat tightened. He brushed her hair back and kissed her forehead, then her nose, and then each cheek. She giggled. "Look at my bandage," she said pulling her hospital gown up. "It still hurts a little." She scrunched her face up for a moment to illustrate her pain. But then her dimples returned and she said, "The doctor says I can have as much ice cream as I want today." Bruno made the appropriate sounds of appreciation. He gave Ivana the bag with her things. Ivana rose to go to the rest room to wash up and dress and Bruno sat in the chair.

"Look what my bed does," Graziella said. She showed him the crank that raised and lowered the bed.

Ivana came back while they were experimenting with the bed. Bruno told her that he had agreed to return to Florence the next day for his student's lesson. "Her mother is worried. She's missed so much. I'll stay just long enough for the lesson and to check on *Nonna*'s house."

Ivana nodded. "Why don't you see if *Nonna* wants to go back with you? Maybe your mother would like to go, too, and stay a few days with *Nonna*. There isn't much for them to do with me at the hospital, and it would save the cost of their room."

"I'll ask them when I get back to the *pensione*." He could take the two women up to *Nonna*'s house and . . . Bruno felt a prickle on the back of his neck and a rising hot flush. Had he and Nadia left anything at *Nonna*'s that would give them away? His mind raced as he tried to visualize how the house had been the last time they were there. The dishes were washed. There was nothing in the kitchen to show there had been two people. The bed was rumpled, but *Nonna* would expect that since he was supposed to stay there. But as Bruno thought of the narrow day bed, he remembered the scent that the linen had taken on—a scent that carried tones of him and Nadia and their lovemaking. Would *Nonna* notice as she changed the sheets? He considered entering the house, going straight to the bed, taking the sheets off and putting them in the washing machine. But *Nonna* would think he was crazy. Laundry was women's work. He could say he was becoming a modern man. But *Nonna* would tell Ivana and Ivana would expect him to do it all the time. He'd have to take the chance that *Nonna* wouldn't notice. Maybe, now that she was getting older, her sense of smell wasn't as good. And, if she did figure it out, he could endure her wrath. She would not tell Ivana, at least. She was passionate and fiery, but not cruel.

"Did you sleep last night?" Ivana asked. "You look so tired."

"I slept all right," he lied. "And you?"

"Better than I expected, but I'm hungry. Annamaria went to stay with friends, and there was no one to leave Graziella with."

"Go have breakfast. I'll stay with her." Ivana left and Bruno turned to Graziella. "What about you, little one? Have you had your breakfast yet?"

She nodded and, wide-eyed, told him about the sweet roll in a plastic wrapper that they had brought her, "with big pieces of sugar on the top." He tried to listen as she prattled on about her experiences in the hospital. He was determined not to think about Nadia's condition until he had some time alone, but it was there, like a loose tooth, and it required effort not to dwell on it. He sat beside Graziella, her trusting voice clear like birdsong in the air, her hand light on his, admonishing him to pay attention. Yesterday had revealed just how easily he could lose this daughter and his mouth went dry at the thought. The knowledge that there was nothing he could do to prevent it was unbearable. He would have willingly crossed enemy lines, swam treacherous waters, climbed sheer slopes, but none of it would have made a difference. Just as there had been no way to intervene on behalf of Adelina. And now, he had no idea how to help Nadia and his new child. He sat, shrouded in his own impotence, struggling to listen to Graziella. Finally she yawned, rubbed her eyes, and fell asleep.

He got up and went to the open window. Outside the sky was cloudless. A light breeze brought the fresh smells of summer and the sea. Across the way, the sun glowed on a peach stucco house while bright pink roses climbed the wrought iron fence in front of it. On the street below a middle age lady with perfect hair, perfect makeup, and a small white dog on a red leash—one of those rich ladies from Milan probably—passed by. She was followed by a couple, arm in arm, and then a worried looking man in a bright blue shirt. Farther on, children played in a small park while their mothers sat on benches shaded by umbrella pines. The details were sharp and vivid but disconnected from him—it was as though he had landed in a world where everything was the same, but unfamiliar. He closed his eyes and tried to ground himself in the practical aspects of his situation. If Nadia really was pregnant, what would they do? Would she want to give their child to the nuns? If she did, the child would know it was illegitimate. He tightened his hands on the window sill. There must be some other way. Some modern girls kept their babies. Would Nadia have the courage to do this? They would have to find a way to make it seem like Nadia was married, invent a dead husband maybe. But then the child would grow up without knowing Bruno was his father, without having Bruno's name. Would the child be a son, maybe? Either way, Bruno would have to find a way to protect him.

As he was trying to get his mind around the problem, Ivana returned. Keeping their voices low, they worked out the logistics of who would visit when with Graziella and how they would take turns for meals. Then Bruno left the hospital to take *Nonna* and his mother to the beach. He stopped at a phone on the way back and dialed Nadia's number. There was no answer. His jaw tightened. He needed to be with her. It would all make more sense if he was sure, if only he could talk with her. He took a deep breath. He'd have to wait until tomorrow, though, and it would be easier for everybody if he just let it go, for now. He wouldn't try to call her again.

He went back to the *pensione* and took his mother and grandmother to the sea. In the car, on the way to the beach, Bruno brought up Ivana's suggestion that he take them back the next day, and, after some discussion, they agreed. They would leave early enough in the morning to arrive in Florence in time for lunch. Annamaria and Ivana would spell each other at the hospital, and Bruno would come back as soon as his lesson was over.

When they reached the beach Bruno accompanied the two women as they waded up to their knees in the sea. They scooped handfuls of water and poured it on their heads and shoulders, gasping as the cold hit their skin, but continuing until they were wet from head to toe. The iodine in the water would prevent goiter, and it was important to get as much on their bodies as possible. After they were satisfied with their bath, he escorted them back to their chairs under the umbrella and went for a long swim by himself.

He swam quickly through the surf, where the water was green and choppy, to the calm blue beyond. Except for a few small *patine*, the little pontoon boats you could rent by the hour, he was alone with the sound of his rhythmic breathing and the splash of his arms pushing through the water. He turned over onto his back, shaded his eyes with his hand and let himself drift. Out here, cradled by the soft buoyancy of the sea, surrounded by its vastness, he was safe. Nothing could touch him. Unfortunately, he couldn't stay out here forever. That was the way of the world. Little pockets of freedom were all you got. He floated a little longer and then turned over and headed back to the shore. The current had carried him north and when he came out of the water, he saw it was a long way back. As he walked slowly, keeping on the wet sand of the shoreline, he felt a kind of serenity. He would have a son. He was sure it would be a son. He would find a way to protect him. He just needed to look at the situation like a mathematical problem which would reveal a solution if you set it up right. When he returned to Florence, and could be with Nadia, his mind would clear and he would figure it out.

He passed a little boy, about Graziella's age, building a sand castle. His hair was thick and dark, and when he looked up his eyes were gray. Is that what his son would look like? He and Nadia both had thick dark hair. Would his dark eyes dominate, or would the blue of Nadia's and the brown of his compromise to make eyes like these? Either way, Bruno must find a way to protect him. They would call him Luciano, after Bruno's father. Bruno tried to imagine little Luciano when he was the age of the boy on the beach. Graziella would be ten or eleven. But she would never know her brother. The thought struck Bruno like a physical blow.

He walked back slowly, trying to come up with a scenario in which his two children would meet, but he couldn't think of one. Eventually, he caught sight of the umbrella where his mother and grandmother were waiting. After they washed the salt and sand off in the cold water of the outside shower and took turns dressing in the cabana, he drove them back to the *pensione*. Lunch was pasta with a nice seafood sauce, followed by Milanese cutlets and slices of ripe tomatoes. But Bruno had no appetite and barely touched his meal. "*Poverino*," the proprietor's wife said. "He's worried about his little girl. Do you want me to make you some nice broth?"

Bruno was unable to persuade her that he didn't want a "nice broth."

The woman brought him a bowl of yellow liquid with circles of fat floating on top. Broth had never been Bruno's favorite, and this bowl looked especially unappetizing. He forced down as much as he could, though it was an effort to swallow the greasy stuff and it set heavy in his stomach afterward.

When lunch was finally over, Bruno left the *pensione* and drove to the café and dialed Nadia's number. "Hello," he said. "How are you?" He cupped his hand over the receiver and whispered, "Has your period come?"

"No. I told you. I'm sure." She paused. "I've been thinking. I've decided that if you won't live with me I'm going to have an abortion. I can't do this alone."

"Leave my family? How can I leave them?" he whispered frantically into the receiver. "We don't even have divorce in Italy."

"You can come to America with me and get divorced there, or we can simply live together, if you want. I don't care if we're married, but I'm not having this child unless you're with me. I know what it's like to have only one parent."

"You can give him to the nuns. Or we can find someone else to raise him."

"No."

"But an abortion. You could die." He had an image of her lying on a filthy kitchen table, bleeding to death.

"I'll go back to America. I have a friend who knows a doctor who will do it. It's safe."

"Of course it's not. And the baby. You want to kill your own child? Our child?" His knuckles were white on the receiver.

"It's easy for you to say 'our child,' but I'm the one who will have to raise it all alone."

"But an abortion . . ."

"Do you think I want to have an abortion? I've wanted children all my life. But I can't do it like this."

"We'll talk about it when I come. We'll figure something out."

"There's nothing to figure out." She was crying. "That's the way it is."

Hearing any woman cry made Bruno feel panicky, and his fearful reaction to Nadia's crying was compounded by his concern for her and for the child she was carrying. His heart thudded, but he forced himself to remain calm. "I can't talk about this on the phone. I'll be there tomorrow, a little after lunch."

"Are you sure? I'll be waiting."

"I'll be there."

"Good-by. I love you."

"I love you, too."

After they hung up, he left the café stunned. The idea of an abortion had never occurred to him. It would be dangerous for Nadia and what of the child? He reached his car and leaned against it for a moment. He was supposed to relieve Ivana at the hospital, but he needed time alone. He considered calling and asking Annamaria to go for him, but it would take her at least twenty minutes to get there and it was already past lunchtime for Ivana. He sighed, got in the car, and set off to relieve Ivana.

He was glad to find Graziella asleep. At least he wouldn't have to talk.

He and Ivana exchanged a few words, and she left. Bruno took her place by Graziella's bed, but he was restless. He stood up and went to the window. After a few minutes he went back to Graziella's bedside and sat down. He tried to relax and enjoy this time with Graziella. He told himself that whatever was coming, at least he didn't have to deal with it now. But he couldn't ignore the shadows that flitted in the back corners of his mind, the danger to this new child, the urgency he felt to help him. He had let one child die without knowing she had a father, and now this child's life was in his hands. He had to persuade Nadia, but what if leaving his family was the only way?

He watched the gentle rise and fall of Graziella's chest, her hair a mass of curls on the white linens, her dark lashes splayed against the rosy flush of her cheek, the soft flesh of her hand on the pillow beside her face, her fingers slightly curled, and he couldn't bear to think that his days with her might be numbered. He tried to drink in everything about her, to memorize each detail so that he could carry it with him always, but his mind kept skittering away. What would happen if he left? How often would he see Graziella? Maybe he could call every week like Nadia's father did. How much would it cost to call from America to Italy? Of course, if he went to America he would probably get rich like people did. Then he could support them all and even afford to come visit.

How would he tell Ivana? He would wait until Graziella was well, but eventually he would have to. Ivana would be hurt. He closed his eyes at the thought. And how would Graziella take it? She wouldn't understand now, but later when she was older he would explain how it was the only way to save her brother. Maybe she would understand then. But his mother, always so good to him, would be heartbroken. He felt his shoulders tighten. Then there were Annamaria and *Nonna*—he didn't want to be around when they found out.

"Are you listening?"

Bruno turned around. Ivana had returned and was talking to him.

"I'm sorry. I was distracted."

She looked at him and gave a little shake of her head. She had dark circles under her eyes. "I asked if she slept the whole time."

He nodded.

"You can go, if you want."

Bruno did want to go. He stood and Ivana sat in the chair he had vacated. "I'll come back early so you can have dinner at the *pensione*," he said. "You need a good meal." He leaned around Ivana and kissed Graziella lightly on the cheek, and then, as he moved away, he put a hand on Ivana's shoulder and bent and kissed her on the head. "*Ciao*."

"*Ciao*," she answered softly. He hesitated at the door a moment and then slid out of the room.

He had no more obligations until dinner time. His mother and his grandmother would be playing cards with their friends and didn't need him. He walked across the marble pavement of the hospital foyer, and, like a child who has stolen a piece of candy and, finally alone, can pull it from his pocket and enjoy it, he turned to the idea that he had forbidden himself to think about until then. The idea that if he left his family he could be with Nadia. He tried to summon the feeling of joy he felt when he was with her, but, though the pull to be with Nadia was strong like a fierce river current, he was unable to evoke the same pleasure.

He left the car at the hospital and walked to the little café he had called from before. He bought five hundred lire of *gettoni*, dropped a handful in the phone and dialed Nadia's number. She answered right away.

"When are you coming?"

"I'll be there tomorrow afternoon."

"Hurry. I have a plane ticket for Friday."

"You're leaving?"

"I can't get an abortion here. I have to go back to America"

*Friday, just a few days away.* She would be gone. The baby would be gone, too. "You don't have to go," he said. "I'm going to leave my family. I've decided." He heard himself saying the words before he knew he had thought them.

"You're sure."

"I'm sure." It was difficult to breathe.

"Thank goodness. I've been so afraid. I felt so alone."

"I'll have to take care of some things first."

"I can wait as long as I have to, if I know you'll be with me." She laughed, her voice shaky.

"I'll see you tomorrow then."

"Tomorrow."

He hung up and stood by the phone for a minute, trying to ground himself in the moment, in time which seemed to have slipped away. After a few moments, still disoriented, he left the café and walked. He had no idea where he was going. He passed a news kiosk at the corner of a small park and stopped and bought a paper. There was no one in the park, and he sat down on a stone bench, cool under the shade of a coastal pine. Immediately a flock of pigeons clustered around him. The males strutted, inflated their iridescent throats, and pecked at each other. The females cooed softly. Their life was so simple. They searched for food, mated, stayed with their flock, and had no greater expectations. They watched him for a while but when he didn't feed them they wandered off. Then, as if on cue, they flew off in close formation.

Bruno opened the paper but was unable to concentrate. His mind was scattered and his body needed to do something. He had already had his swim. It was late afternoon, the time when the young people in town crowded around jukeboxes and pinball machines and *boccette* tables, the older ones played cards, and people his age with children took them to the park. None of this had any appeal. He decided to walk back to the *pensione*. It would take close to an hour and maybe would relax him enough so that he could rest.

The rhythm of his steps was soothing, and his thoughts began to gather. It was really going to happen. The decision had been made. All he had to do now was take things one at a time and survive until it would all be over and he would be with Nadia. The time would come when he would be living with her in a wood frame house in America, looking back on all this. He would wake up every morning with her by his side. Spend the long nights with her—thousands of nights like the one they had together in Lerici. Days, too, but the nights were special. Zia Carolina, one of his great aunts who had grown blind in her old age, once said that she liked the night because then she was wasn't old blind Zia Carolina any more, she was Carolina again, the real Carolina, just like everybody else because nobody could see at night. Bruno had laughed, but even then he had felt like she was touching on something that he, too, knew. There was some way in which you were less your outside self at night, less entangled in social obligations, and at the same time, because of this, more yourself.

"*Buona sera, signore,*" the proprietor of the pensione was sitting out front, when Bruno arrived. "How is the little girl?"

"Much better. They are going to send her home on Wednesday."

"We were worried."

Bruno nodded and entered the *pensione*. He was able to pass the lounge without being seen by his mother or grandmother. Once in his room, he removed his trousers and hung them up, and then lay down with his paper. The riots in America were increasing. They were burning new cities each day. Nadia was worried, he knew. It must be hard to be so far away when your country was in trouble.

He put the paper down, closed his eyes and drifted off. He woke, not really refreshed, and wanting the afternoon coffee he had missed earlier. He looked at his watch. It was six-twenty. Dinner was at eight. If he hurried, he could get a coffee at the café and walk back to the hospital in time for Ivana to have a good dinner at the *pensione*. He dressed and set off.

Annamaria was at the hospital when he arrived. Graziella was asleep and Ivana had already left for dinner. "Let's go sit where we can talk," Annamaria said.

"What if Graziella wakes up?"

"I'll tell the nurse to call us. There's a little lounge down the hall."

It turned out to be just a little alcove with two easy chairs, but it was close enough to Graziella's room for them to be able to hear her, and they could talk without worrying about waking her.

"What's going on?" Annamaria asked, once they were seated.

"Nothing."

"Come on, I know you better than that."

"Nothing. I'm just a little distracted."

"About what?"

"I've just been thinking about how much things have changed since we were children."

She smiled. "I should hope so. Remember that silly poem I had to say in school—*la vita gli dono, cosi' come un fiore*—that I would give Mussolini my life just like a flower? I always hated that."

"You were six."

"I didn't have to be any older to know my life was worth more than a flower."

He smiled. Even at that age Annamaria had seen through the fascist propaganda. He had been pulled into it a lot longer.

"But that's not what's bothering you," she said now.

"No. I don't want to go back to those years, or to the war or to the years after the war. And I'm glad that the young people today are so passionate about taking care of the poor and making a better society. I agree with them. But . . ." He paused.

"But . . . ?"

He took a deep breath. "It's this new stuff about women's equality."

"Ah," she said, smiling. "You're not so comfortable being displaced from your position of superiority."

He laughed. "You've never let me be comfortable in that position. But what I don't understand is how you can say women can do all the things men can when women can get pregnant and men can't?"

"Why should that have to stop you?"

"How can it not stop you?"

"It's all in how you look at it. If you think getting pregnant means you have to get married and stay home and take care of the baby, instead of going places and doing things, well then that's what will happen. But the only reason it has to be that way is convention. And convention can be changed."

Now Bruno saw Ivana walking down the hall to Graziella's room. He and Annamaria got up to meet her, and they all went back to the room. Graziella was still sleeping.

"Let's go find something to eat," Annamaria said to Bruno. He kissed Graziella softly, they said good night to Ivana and left. The night was warm, and Annamaria suggested a pizzeria she knew in to Forte dei Marmi where they could eat on an outdoor terrace.

The terrace was too well lit to see the stars, but fireflies were dancing in the hedge surrounding the terrace and the moon was rising beyond. Bruno was glad to be here in the warm evening talking to Annamaria. He considered what she had said about convention changing. Maybe she would understand his reasons for leaving. Maybe she would be an ally. He said, "But men and women are different. Women have to be careful about what they do when they're pregnant."

"An old wives' tale. Women are tougher than you think."

Their pizza and beer arrived. The smell of oregano, olive oil and anchovies wafted up from the platter, and Bruno's appetite awakened for the first time in days. He cut a piece of the pizza and set it on the side of his plate to cool.

Annamaria went on. "Women are tired of having men trying to oppress them, telling them what they can and can't do, how they should dress, where they can go."

Bruno put the piece of pizza in his mouth, pausing to fully enjoy the taste. Finally, he said, "Men don't want to oppress women. We want to protect them."

"From what?"

"From ruining their reputations."

"Another convention."

"But men are men, and women are women. If you turn them loose alone, it will end up in affairs and then the women will get pregnant." He lifted his mug to his mouth and took a long drink of cold Pilsner.

"Not if we have good birth control. And besides, so what if they did?"

"You don't see any problem?"

"Only if you make it a problem."

"What if the father is married?" he said, keeping his voice casual.

"Who needs the father?"

Bruno was surprised that even Annamaria would go that far. "Everyone would reject the baby if he had no father, and the family would be dishonored. The child would have a miserable life."

"Who needs a family? Italian families have been stifling their children for generations. It's time to change."

Now she was just being ridiculous. "You can say that because you've always had men to protect you. You have your career, but people make allowances because you're a woman. It's much harder for a man out in the world. Your family is who you can lean on, who you can trust."

She reached out and put her hand on his. "Dear brother, it's you who've had it too easy too long."

He stared at her. Too easy?

"It's going to change whether you like it or not."

"I know. That's what scares me." He took another swallow of beer. It hit the back of his throat in a satisfying way. "What would you do if, hypothetically speaking, of course . . . ?" He tried to think how to ask this without giving himself away. "If you got pregnant and he was married?"

"I wouldn't care what people thought. *Mamma* would help me. And even if she didn't, I promise you, I would find a way to manage alone. I'm a good journalist. If they fired me, I could wait until the baby was born and then get another job."

They ate a while in silence. Then he asked, "That's easy to say. But what if it were real? How would you feel if Ivana had to raise Graziella alone?"

"That's a different question."

"How so?"

She looked at him. "Because it's Graziella."

"So all your talk of rebellion is just talk?"

"No. Things are changing, and I'm glad, though I know people are going to get hurt in the process. That doesn't mean I wouldn't do everything possible to protect Graziella." She looked at him, her eyes fierce. "Just like you would."

"That seems inconsistent with what you said before." He tried to keep his voice light.

"It's not about being consistent. It's about being honest and being who you are, and I'm just a person who would kill to protect the people I love."

Bruno didn't think she would actually kill him, but it was clear she wasn't going to support him when she found out what he was planning. He finished his beer, but the pizza on the plate looked less appetizing now.

# 15

The next morning Bruno took *Nonna* and his mother to the hospital to say good-by to Ivana and Graziella, and then they returned to the *pensione* to pack the car. Finally at around ten-thirty, they set off, Bruno and his grandmother in the front seat, his mother in the back with the largest of the suitcases, which Bruno had not been able to cram into the small trunk of the Fiat. Bruno's thoughts were fuzzy and disjointed. He was only aware of wanting to get to Nadia.

"*Ma che ci hai?*" his grandmother asked. "Are you listening?"

"I'm sorry," Bruno said.

"He's still worried about the child," his mother said from the back seat. "*Poverino.*"

"Don't be silly. Graziella is fine," his grandmother said, but she stopped trying to engage him in conversation.

As they drove into Florence, they were assailed by the swelter and noise and soot of the city, and yet Bruno was glad to be back. He would soon be with Nadia, and his problems always seemed smaller when she was present. They passed through the city and then stopped on the outskirts at a *rosticceria* where they bought a roast chicken and some potatoes. Finally they arrived at *Nonna's* home in San Domenico. The women took the parcels of food, wrapped in brown paper, into the house, while Bruno began carrying their luggage in. On the second trip, as he brought bags through the kitchen to the living area, he saw the clogs he had bought Nadia sitting in the corner of the room. His heart skipped a beat and his breathing froze. He looked around quickly, but the women were both in the kitchen. He walked over to the corner, and, when he leaned over to set the luggage down, he picked the clogs up. Holding them down by the side of his body, he went through the kitchen to the back door, shifting them in front of him as he passed the women. He tried to look natural, but the movement felt clumsy.

"Where are you going, crab walking like that?" *Nonna* asked.

"Back to the car to see if there's anything else." The back of his neck could feel her eyes looking at him.

"We only had these four," she said.

"I just want to check."

"There's nothing to check."

He continued walking, the clogs held in front of him. "I'll feel better if I look," he said over his shoulder.

"If that's what you want." He could hear the shrug in her voice. "While you're out, get some tomatoes and basil from the garden."

He put the clogs under the front seat of the car and went to the garden to get salad. When he came back *Mamma Do'* had set out the food they had picked up. The women quickly made a salad with the tomatoes and invited him to sit down.

"I know how much you love roast potatoes," his mother said, heaping them on his plate.

"When they're fresh out of the oven," *Nonna* complained. "But these are cold and tough."

Bruno wasn't hungry, and he was anxious to get to Nadia, but there was comfort in sitting here as *Nonna* and *Mamma Do'* acted out their predictable roles. This, too, would soon be a thing of the past. When the meal was over, he stood up, saying that his lesson would be starting soon and he had to leave. He kissed them both good-by and then he was finally out the door, in the car and on his way to see Nadia.

He drove to her apartment, where the *portiere* let him in. He climbed the stairs, rang the bell and, when she opened the door, he took her in his arms. The touch of her body to his was a comfort even as it aroused him. He tried to move her towards the sofa, but she took his hand and led him into her room. It was the first time he had made love to her in her bed. She seemed to want to hold him and to be touched, but she did not climax.

"It's all right," she said afterwards. "It was good anyway."

Lying beside her, Bruno looked around, wanting to learn about this place she lived in. It was a large room with high ceilings and tall windows. It had been an elegant room at one time, but the gilt on the panel doors was chipped and the coverlet on the bed was frayed. It was sparsely furnished—a cot with a piece of cloth nailed to the wall instead of a head board; a bedside table with a bent brass lamp; a large oak wardrobe with two white modern looking suitcases on top; a nice nineteenth century painted desk with a marble lamp. He was surprised at how neat it was. A hair brush and a pile of books on the desk and a blouse hung over the door knob were the only things out of place, except for his and Nadia's clothes draped across the straight chair, his folded neatly over the back, hers thrown more casually on the seat. It gave him pleasure to see their clothes mingled that way.

"Have you told your wife?"

"I'll wait until she gets back to Florence, in a few days." His scalp tingled as he heard himself speak the words.

"Will she be mad?"

"She will be hurt, of course."

Nadia sighed. "I hate hurting other people. Sometimes I almost wish I had never met you. It would be better for everyone."

Bruno was silent.

"But at least we can be together," she said.

"It won't happen right away." He raised himself on one elbow and looked at her. It was important that she understand how complicated it would be. "I'll have to figure out some way to support two families."

"I can get a job and help."

He was silent.

"I can stay here until the end of the year. I'll cancel my ticket on Monday. We can plan to go back to America in time for Christmas."

Christmas in a strange land without his family. *Natale con i tuoi, pasqua con chi vuoi.* He had heard it all his life, *Christmas with your family, Easter with whomever you want.* "You wouldn't be willing to stay here?"

"I want to have the baby in America."

"Why?"

"I don't want to have a baby in a foreign land. And besides, the hospitals are better."

Bruno started to say that Italy was not a foreign land, but, of course, it was for her and after all she was the mother.

"I was born in Greece. I'm an American citizen, but I've lived in four different countries. It's hard. I cringe when people ask where I'm from because I really don't know. I don't want that for our child."

"What will your father say?"

"He'll be mad, but he'll get over it. I'm sure there's a way for you to get divorced once we get to America, and then we'll be married. It won't be like you're dead. You can still call and write your daughter."

"You make it seem so easy," Bruno said. And, although he knew it would not be easy, when he was with her, it seemed so inevitable that he was sure there would be some way. He checked his watch. It was after six. "I have to leave now. I need to get back to Viareggio."

"So soon?" Nadia asked, as he got out of bed and began dressing.

He came back to the bed, ran his fingers down the soft skin of Nadia's arm and kissed her on the chin. "I have to pick up some things at my apartment and then be at the sea before eight."

"Go." She held her arms out for a last kiss.

Once he arrived at his building, he parked the car and climbed the steps to his apartment. Outside the door he heard the phone begin to ring. It wouldn't be Nadia. She didn't have his number. It was probably Ivana calling to add something to the list of things she wanted him to bring. But what if Graziella had taken a turn for the worse? He fumbled with the key, clumsy as he tried to hurry, finally got the door open and rushed to the living room. He snatched the receiver off the hook and, his voice winded, said, "*Pronto.*"

"*Pronto.* Is that Professor Cassini?"

"Yes."

"It's Signorina Cohen. I've been trying to reach you all day. You have to leave."

"What?"

"You have to leave. The Germans are coming."

"What are you talking about?" Her behavior had been strange ever since the Five Day War, but now he wondered if she had gone completely over the edge.

"The Germans are coming. You have to leave. Ari, please."

"Ari? Who is Ari?"

Silence.

"Signorina Cohen?"

"Professor Cassini?"

"Yes."

"I'm sorry. I was thinking about Ari—my little brother. He stayed behind, and they took him." Her voice trailed off and he heard a sound that might have been a sob. "You have to leave. Get out of the country."

"I think you are confused, Signorina."

"No. I heard it on the radio." She was talking fast. "The Germans are coming, and the Americans are staying away because of the war in Israel. There will be no one to help us."

Now he understood what she was saying. "Signorina, they are talking about the tourists."

"No, I heard it on the radio."

"I did, too. It's the American tourists who aren't coming because of the war. The German tourists are coming anyway."

"But if the Germans come . . ."

"That war is over, Signorina. This is a different war, and we're not involved. Neither are the Germans, and they aren't our enemy anymore."

"Are you sure?" Her voice was small now.

"Yes."

"That's what Ari said. That he was sure it would be all right." The pitch of her voice rose, like the whine of a motor wound too tight. "I shouldn't have left without him."

"It's different now, Signorina. I assure you."

"I shouldn't have left. He said he was going to come later. I knew he wouldn't, but I was so afraid." This time Bruno was certain he heard a sob.

"That was a long time ago, Signorina."

"You're sure the Germans aren't coming."

"Yes, Signorina."

"I'm sorry I disturbed you," she said, her tone formal now.

"It's nothing. Good-by."

"Good-by, *professore*."

After he hung up, he stood for a moment holding the phone. Should he call someone? He knew that she didn't have any family, and he didn't know of any friends. If he called the police, they would go to her home and frighten her even more. He decided that when he got back from the sea he would go by and visit her.

Signorina Cohen was still on his mind when he reached the *autostrada*, on the way back to Viareggio. The only thing he could think of to do was call his colleague, Manucci, and have him look in on her. He resolved to do that first thing tomorrow. Then after his visit to the hospital, he would go for a swim. Maybe he could stay longer with Graziella, so Ivana could go to the beach, too. She hadn't been in days. The next morning, Wednesday, they would check out of the *pensione* and come back to Florence.

And then . . . The hair on his spine stirred. He would have to tell Ivana. And then would he have to leave? Where would he live while he was trying to arrange it all? Would *Nonna* let him stay with her? Or should he figure out some way to support two families first? Maybe he could keep his new job and take on extra tutoring while he studied English. Nadia could leave for America, and he could follow in the summer. That would give him time to try to find a job in America. When would the baby come? He thought back. Nadia would have gotten pregnant in August. The baby would be born in May. Around Easter. He might be able to get away for a week then. But how much would it cost to go? He would have to save for that, too. The more he thought about it the more it seemed it would be best not to tell Ivana until he was actually able to go. But it wouldn't be easy to live with Ivana that long without her knowing. And she would be so hurt when she found out. He shook his head. It was too much to think about. The next few days he could manage and the rest could wait. Having decided these things, he drove fast and aggressively, clearing his mind of all but the road. When he arrived at the hospital, he parked the car, walked to the nearest café and phoned Nadia.

"I told my father everything," she said, once they had greeted each other.

"You did?"

"He called the way he always does on Sunday, and I started crying, and then I had to tell him."

"Was he angry?"

"He was more interested in how to fix things. He said he was glad you were doing the right thing, and he'll help us when you come to America."

The right thing? Bruno felt a sense of outrage. Leaving his wife and child and family and running off to America might be what Bruno was going to do, but he didn't see how anyone could say it was the right thing. Was Nadia's father only thinking about what his daughter needed or did Americans think it was all right to leave one family and get another, just like they moved from one house to another whenever they felt like it? He knew that it was easy to get a divorce in America and nobody seemed to mind if you did. How would he ever fit into a world like that?

"We can live with him at first. He will help you find a job."

"What kind of job can I get if I don't speak English?"

"You'll have to learn English. I'll help you."

He sighed.

"You don't sound happy."

"There's just so much to take care of."

"Don't worry," she said. "It will be wonderful."

After he hung up, he walked back to the hospital and went to Graziella's room. She was propped up in bed with a book, and, instead of a hospital gown, she now wore her own pink pajamas with little puppies on them. He kissed her, asked how she was feeling and then told Ivana that tomorrow he would come back after his swim and stay with Graziella while she went to the beach.

"That would be nice." She smiled, but her voice sounded tired.

"I want to go swimming, too," Graziella said.

"But you're sick, little love," Bruno said.

"No, I'm all better. The doctor let me get up and walk around today. Didn't he, *Mamma*?"

"Yes, indeed, but I'm afraid you won't be well enough to swim for a while."

"I'll be well enough before we go back to Florence, won't I?" She looked from one to the other, her face anxious.

"I'm afraid not, little one," Ivana said.

"But I was just learning how to swim."

"Maybe *Babbo* can take you to the new pool in Florence." Ivana looked at Bruno. "The one in Piazza Beccheria. They say it's nice."

"Can you, *Babbo*? Can you?" Graziella sat up and leaned forward.

"We'll see," Bruno said. Surely Ivana could take her if he wasn't there.

"You will. You always do nice things for me." Graziella leaned back and smiled.

And he would, he thought. He would find some way to take her swimming.

The next morning, as he sat alone at the breakfast table at the *pensione*, he decided he would ask Ivana how long it would be before Graziella could swim. He would wait until he had taken her to the pool to tell Ivana about Nadia. He buttered a piece of bread and was just about to take a bite when the proprietor of the *pensione* called him to the phone. It was Annamaria.

"Signorina Cohen is dead," she said without preamble.

"Dead?" He could not connect the word to Signorina Cohen, at first. "Dead? Are you sure? How do you know?"

"I saw it on the news. She fell from window last night, or jumped. That's all I know. It was just a brief report on the *telegiornale*."

"I can't believe it."

"I'm glad you have another job. Who knows what will happen with the school now?"

"It's so terrible. I talked to her just yesterday."

Annamaria made a sympathetic sound.

"She was upset, but I didn't think she would do anything like that."

"Poor thing."

"I'll have to find out when the funeral is."

"Yes. Well, let me know. I can help Ivana with Graziella while you're gone."

They hung up, and Bruno returned to the dining room, a bitter taste in his mouth. What had happened? Had she lost her mind so completely that she hallucinated Nazis chasing her? Or was the guilt over her brother too much to bear? He felt a rush of anger. People said the war was over, but it wasn't for her, or for so many others. He closed his eyes, not wanting to imagine the depth of her desperation.

After breakfast, which he hardly tasted, he called Professor Manucci, who had taught at Signorina Cohen's school longer than anyone, and found out that the funeral would be the next day. Then he drove to the hospital.

Graziella was sitting up in bed, eating her breakfast. Beside her, Ivana was balancing a plate on her knee and spreading jam on a roll. A cup of coffee sat on the table next to Graziella's bed.

Ivana looked up as Bruno came in. "What's the matter?"

"Can we talk in the hall?"

She nodded, put the plate down and rose. Bruno kissed Graziella, promised to come right back and followed Ivana into the hall. He told her what had happened. "Should I have called the police? Maybe I should have gone to her house, talked more to her."

"It's a tragedy," Ivana said, her voice rich with compassion. "But there's no point in making it worse by thinking it was your fault."

"I may have been a little impatient with her."

"You've always been kind to her. That's all you could do. You won't help her by letting it depress you. You'll only make it hard for the people around you." She hesitated, then she looked down and said softly, "And we need you."

Something rose up in him, some childlike emotion straining against every fiber of his will, and suddenly he was too tired to resist. He put his arms around Ivana, laying his head on hers. She smelled of hospital soap with a hint of her own rosemary shampoo. He felt a great sigh run through her body. They stood that way a long moment in the hall.

"It's just so awful," he said, as they drew apart.

"It will be all right. Remember how it was during the war? You just endured because you had no choice. And then it got better. Things pass."

"But it could happen again. It's just a push of the button away and there's nothing we can do about it."

"That's why it makes no sense to worry about it. Do you know when the funeral is?"

"Tomorrow."

"You'll have to go, of course."

They decided he would leave the next morning. He would pack their things, check out, and stay the night in Florence. It would save them the cost of a night at the *pensione*. On Wednesday morning he'd drive back with a change of clothes for Ivana and Graziella, and they'd go from the hospital straight to Florence. On the drive back to the *pensione*, Bruno stopped at a neighborhood café to call Nadia. He told her about Signorina Cohen.

"How terrible," she said. "I never understood her."

"I don't know that anyone did."

"She didn't seem to like me. I could never figure out why. Then suddenly, right before I left, she went out of her way to be kind to me."

"She was a little crazy. The war was hard for all of us, but especially for the Jews."

"Oh," Nadia said. "I didn't think about that. I thought she was just mean."

"She could be that, too," Bruno said. "The funeral is tomorrow at eleven. Do you want to go with me? I'll pick you up."

"Yes."

He was glad she wanted to go. He didn't think there would be many people there, and this seemed very sad to him.

He ate, swam, took a walk, lay down for siesta, feeling like a zombie throughout. It was almost three when he remembered that he was going to give Ivana time to swim. He rushed over to the hospital and into Graziella's room. He kissed his daughter and then turned to Ivana. "I'm sorry I'm so late. I know you like to go to the beach in the morning, but I got distracted."

She nodded but didn't say anything. After she left, he tried to pay attention to Graziella. She had her paper dolls out. "Here, you dress these." She handed him several dolls and a pile of clothes.

Bruno sat with the dolls on his lap.

"You haven't dressed any of them," Graziella said. "You have your head in the clouds."

Bruno laughed. "Where did you hear that expression?"

"*Nonna* said it to *Mamma Do*."

Bruno put a skirt and a blouse and a hat on one of the dolls and handed it to Graziella.

"No." She shook her head. "That's terrible. They don't go together."

"Show me how you want it," Bruno said.

She explained in detail what each doll was supposed to wear.

"How am I supposed to remember all that?"

"You can't remember because you have your head in the clouds," she said laughing. "Your head in the clouds, your head in the clouds," she chanted.

Her voice was shrill and had a piercing quality that made Bruno want to put his hands over his ears. "That's enough," he said.

Graziella's looked at him, her face pale, her eyes round, and now her lower lip began to tremble. "I'm sorry," Bruno said, reaching out to hug her. She turned her head away from him.

"I love you," he said. "I never want to hurt you. I'm just very tired, and I have a headache."

She didn't say anything.

"Please forgive me." Bruno went down on one knee, hoping to amuse her.

She turned towards him and held out her arms to him. He folded his around her, and she began to cry. He buried his face in her curls. "It's all right, *piccola mia.*"

Eventually she pulled away and looked at him, tears streaking her cheeks. "Today was a bad day." Her face was solemn. "A very bad day. First they didn't have any raspberry ice cream or even any strawberry, and then I couldn't go to the beach with *Mamma*, and now you don't want to play paper dolls."

"That's sounds like a very bad day," Bruno said. How small and innocent and seriously important her problems were. "But I'll play paper dolls if you'll show me slowly just how you want them. Pretend I'm not very smart."

She laughed and agreed. She now gave exaggeratedly explicit directions for each outfit. When Ivana returned several hours later, Bruno was tired and ready to leave.

That night he dreamed again about the Duomo. He was wandering around in the dust and debris, stumbling over chunks of marble and stone, searching for something. He didn't know what it was that he was looking for, but he knew it was desperately important to find it. Then a form stepped out of the shadows in front of him. Slowly its shape began to reveal itself—the face was without features, but it was topped by the black tasseled hat of a fascist *squadrista.* Bruno began to run and the thing ran after him, brandishing its club. Bruno thought he could escape if he merged with the crowds of tourists who mill around the Duomo, but there were no tourists today and suddenly he remembered why. He looked up through the bombed out cupola and knew before he saw it that the sky was melting, like paint dripping down the side of a bucket. The whole world had changed, and he was alone and lost. He woke dry mouthed and afraid. He lay a while. The fear slowly turned to anger. He was tired of worrying. Deeply tired. There was no sense in it anyway. Being worried and afraid didn't keep you, or anyone else, safe. Nothing did.

He looked at his watch. It was a little before five. He knew he would not get back to sleep. He dressed, walked softly down the hall, opened the front door as quietly as he could and headed for the sea. The beach was deserted, barely recognizable with the deck chairs and umbrellas put up for the night. Overhead the stars were myriad, even the smallest ones bright except where the fuzziness of the Milky Way lay splattered across the sky. Bruno made out Cassiopeia high above and then found Vega, looming large, close to the horizon and nearly as bright as the lights of the fishing boats that bobbed in the distance. He stood on the sand, a little away from the sea, letting the vastness of the sky lull his mind. The distances were too great to imagine, and he felt himself as small as the grains of sand at his feet, but somehow not unimportant. Then suddenly he understood, or rather it was as though he saw, that each grain of sand was an individual and marvelous thing, of complete and terrible importance and somehow kin to him. He stood a long time, afraid to move, almost afraid to breathe because he might break the spell of this revelation.

The early morning air was chilly and eventually he began to shiver. Folding his arms close to his body, he started walking to warm up. He headed north, but the sand was deep and difficult to walk in and was beginning to get into his shoes. He stopped, took his shoes and socks off, carefully rolled his trousers up and walked towards that stretch of beach closer to the sea where it was damp enough to be firm but not so wet he would sink in. The sand felt cold and grainy on his feet and surprisingly pleasant.

Bruno had always thought of life as something that happened to you. You took the good times when they came and you did the best you could to avoid the bad ones. But now he became acutely aware of his participation in the world around him. Just placing his feet on the sand was a unique act that would never be repeated anywhere in the universe. And there was nothing disrespectful in his stepping on it; rather the sand was happily participating in this contact. In fact, everything around him appeared happy and in its place. In front of him, the Big Bear, low in the sky, dipped her tail towards the sea like a child approaching as close to the edge of the water as she dared. The sea itself rose and fell with a contented, gentle movement like the breathing of a living thing. And somehow Signorina Cohen had her part in all this. He did not know what or how, but he thought that it was enough, at this moment, to feel sad for her. That was his part.

Now there was a shift in the night—the slightest hint of light, hardly more than a lessening of the darkness, as soft and fresh as a baby's breath. Soon the light began to spread across the sky, and the stars slowly dimmed until all but the brightest had retreated. The awakening birds began to talk. Bruno stood, drinking it in, until the world around him was repainted with the hues of daylight. He turned around and headed back. By the time he arrived at his starting point, the beach was in full color. Seagulls keened as they circled and swooped; delivery trucks rattled down the road, and the voices of the *bagnini* filled the air, joking with each other as they swept seaweed from the beach and set up chairs and umbrellas.

Bruno walked slowly back to the *pensione*. His whole body was relaxed, like after a long game of *calcio* when he was a boy, or after a passionate session of lovemaking. Signorina Cohen's death was tragic, but he was too pleasantly lethargic to feel anything more than recognition of the sadness of it. *Lacrimae rerum*, he thought. The sadness of things. The phrase from the Aeneid, where Aeneas, entering a temple when he first arrived in Carthage, saw paintings of the Trojan War and thought that this city must be civilized because it understood *"lacrimae rerum."* And Bruno, after all, was Italian and so a descendent of Aeneas. It was in his blood to feel these things—this sadness of things.

But there was something else, something he had almost understood when he had placed his bare feet on the sand, something important, and it seemed to him that if he could stay quiet and not think too hard it might come to him. In this mood, he packed the car and set off for Florence.

Bruno's window was open, and the sound of the air rushing in made a pleasant backdrop for the gentle rumble of the engine. On either side of the *autostrada*, farmlands and hills rolled away softly, and their rich earthy colors, muted by a late summer haze, mirrored his state of mind. But whatever it was he was trying to remember seemed to fade farther and farther away.

Eventually the fast, open lanes of the *autostrada* gave way to the outskirts of Florence with its heat and congested streets, and, although he was leaving his family at the sea and going towards Nadia, the worries of his life returned. He was going to hurt everyone in his family. He shook his head, wanting to push the thought away, and then sighed. He was just going to have to do it without thinking about it. He had no choice. He drove though the din of the crowded San Frediano quarter to San Niccolo', where Nadia lived. It was a quieter area, inhabited by old families and artisans and foreign intellectuals, and there was usually parking available. He found a place down the street from Nadia's building, walked to her door and rang the bell. She appeared at the window and called out for him to wait and then within minutes was out the door and at his side. The short-sleeved, pale green suit she wore was fitted and showed the shape of her body. Her hair was up, she had makeup on and she wore high heels. A small gold locket nestled against her throat.

He took her arm in his and they headed towards the American

Church in via Ruccellai where Signorina Cohen's funeral was scheduled. They walked slowly as Nadia navigated the uneven stones of the sidewalk. He could feel the heat of her body close to him.

"Have you had any news?" she asked. "Do you have any idea why she did it?"

"I talked to her the day before. She seemed a little disoriented. Like she was reliving the days of the war."

"How terrible it must have been." Then after a pause, "I don't remember that much about her. Just how mad she was at me."

"That's the second time you've mentioned that. Did it bother you so much?"

"At the time it did. She liked me so much at first, and then suddenly it was like I had done something awful. I couldn't figure out what, and then just as suddenly she liked me again."

"She had a lot of crazy ideas about a lot of people. I don't think she ever got entirely right in the head after the war."

They had left the narrow streets of the old section of via de' Bardi, crossed the open square of Santa Maria sopr'Arno and were now entering the stretch of via de' Bardi that had been rebuilt after the war. A few stray tourists wandered here looking tired and lost. There would be hordes in the next block as they neared the Ponte Vecchio. There was really no way to get around them, but Bruno and Nadia were on the far side of the river, and once they got past the shops in Borgo San Jacopo they would have left the tourists behind.

"Do you think we'll have a boy or a girl," Nadia asked, looking up at him as she placed her hand on her abdomen.

"I think it will be a boy." He smiled at her. "I have a feeling."

She smiled back, her eyes happy. "What should we name him?"

"My father's name was Luciano."

Nadia was silent for a moment. "Luciano might not work too well in America," she said slowly, her voice hesitant. "Luciano is a gangster name."

Bruno could not imagine how gangster names were different from other names. "A gangster name?"

"You know, Lucky Luciano. It's the only Luciano most people have heard of. And anyway it would probably be easier for a boy living in America to have a name that didn't sound so foreign."

"What about Humphrey?"

She laughed.

"What's so funny? Don't you like Humphrey Bogart?"

"Yes, but Humphrey is one of those names that's a joke in America."

"Why?"

"I don't know. It just is."

"Do people laugh at Humphrey Bogart?"

"No. He's an exception."

So Humphrey Bogart could be named Humphrey but no one else could? What other exceptions were there? The distance between her world and his loomed like the shadow of an unknown stalking them.

They crossed Piazza Frescobaldi and Nadia caught her heel on one of the gaps between the stones of the sidewalk. Bruno felt her weight on his arm as she struggled to keep her balance. He tightened his grip and stopped until she recovered. "I hate heels," she said.

"We should have taken the car."

"No, I'm all right."

"You look very elegant, but we don't want a sprained ankle."

"Don't worry." She snuggled into him. "I'll hang onto you."

But when they emerged from the cool of the narrow back street of via Santo Spirito and crossed Piazza Nazario Sauro into the glaring sun on the Ponte alla Carraia, he thought again that it might have been better to take the car. It was going to be even hotter on the way back.

"Where are we going?" she asked.

"*La chiesa americana.*"

"St Paul's?"

Bruno shrugged. "I don't know. Everyone calls it the American church."

"St Paul's Episcopal church in Florence. I've been to functions there."

"Are you protestant?"

"I'm nothing. My mother was Lutheran and my father is Episcopalian."

Bruno had studied European history in the *liceo*, and so the concept of different denominations wasn't new to him, but he had never heard anyone actually make the distinctions. He wasn't sure he had even met a protestant before. He was musing on this fact, as they approached the church. Right before they turned the last corner, Nadia drew away from him, walking beside him now. Bruno was not sorry to avoid another occasion for gossip.

Now they could see the church. Bruno had passed it many times but was still unable to decide how he felt about it. An early twentieth century gothic revival building, it was aesthetically well balanced and had an appealing air of quiet confidence, but it seemed out of place in Florence. The iron railing around the property added to the sense of separation from its surroundings. Today the gate was open, and a small group of people stood inside. Bruno recognized several students and most of his colleagues. He and Nadia entered the gate and approached Professor Manucci.

As Manucci was remarking on how grown up Nadia was, Professor Berlazzi approached. "Do you remember Nadia Taylor?" Manucci said. Berlazzi nodded, as he leered at Nadia. Bruno had never liked him and liked him even less now.

"Why are they having the funeral here?" Bruno asked Manucci. "This is a protestant church."

"They called me to see if I knew anything about her family,"

Berlazzi said. "They wanted to bury her as soon as possible with this heat. I suggested the American Church. I couldn't think of any other foreign church."

"But she was Jewish," Bruno said.

Berlazzi shrugged.

"I wish you had called me," Manucci said. "I would have told you."

"Well, I didn't. But anyway, what difference does it make?" Berlazzi said. "She's dead. And she doesn't have any family. Who's to know?"

Now the *Misericordia* arrived with the coffin, and they all entered the church. The interior was light and simple, but there was no sanctuary light. Bruno had never been in a church without a sanctuary light. He sat, uncomfortable in this pagan and forbidden place, while the priest spoke mostly in English, and he thought about what Berlazzi had said. *What difference does it make?* And it seemed to Bruno that it made an enormous difference. It was bad enough that Signorina Cohen was being buried in a foreign land without any family to mourn her. "*Zacinto mia,*" he thought, remembering Foscolo's poem about his exile, where he begged to at least be buried in his own land. He couldn't remember the whole poem, but he did recall the phrase, "*illacrimata sepoltura,*" unwept grave. And Signorina Cohen would not only have an unwept grave in a foreign land but would not even be buried with her own people. She would be forever in the wrong place. Thanks to Berlazzi's stupidity and lack of feeling, Bruno thought.

Bruno wanted to get up and say something, but it would be an appallingly improper thing to do, and, besides, he told himself, it was not his habit to interfere in this way. Then he remembered the moment on the beach when he had placed his foot on the sand. The feeling that what he did in that moment would be something that could never be undone. It was that feeling he realized that he had been trying to recall earlier on in the car. And now, he had the chance to change something of much greater importance. He sat throughout the service, torn between knowing that it wouldn't be proper to interrupt and feeling it was important for him to do something. After the service, the priest led the congregation out and stood at the entrance of the church greeting people as they passed him. Bruno and Nadia approached. Bruno stopped and explained the situation to him.

The priest spoke very poor Italian, but the distressed expression on his face as Bruno talked made it clear that he understood. "I should have known," he said. "Her name." He and Nadia spoke a moment in English, and then he hurried off.

Nadia turned to Bruno. "He said that he will call the synagogue right away and fix it."

Relief washed over Bruno like a spring breeze, leaving him energized and happy. He smiled at Nadia. "Let's go to Fiesole for lunch. It's cooler in the hills, and we can take the bus so you don't have to walk in your heels."

It was a short walk to pick up the number 9 bus to San Marco, where they could catch the "F" for Fiesole. They arrived at San Marco a little before it was due to leave. Since they were among the first to get on, they were able to find two seats together. Bruno felt strong and ready to face anything, but Nadia sat quietly. At first Bruno thought that her silence was due to the onslaught of noise through the open windows, which made it hard to converse. It didn't help that the bus lurched and swayed its way through traffic, so that, even holding onto the poles next to them, they continually slid around on the plastic seats. But as the bus gathered people and Bruno joined the standing crowds to give his seat to an older woman, he could see Nadia's face. She was unaware that he was looking, and, as he watched, the sadness that he saw shook him. He needed to help her somehow, to find words to comfort her, but it would have to wait until they arrived. His impatience grew, as the bus jerked along slowly.

When they left town and started the run up the hill, passengers began to get off. Eventually an empty seat came up across from Nadia. Bruno sat down, and she gave him a small, distracted smile and then turned back towards the window. He wanted to touch her, but nothing in her stance invited him.

Finally the bus reached the main square in Fiesole, its last stop. Bruno and Nadia stepped out onto the main *piazza*. Although it was hot up here, too, there was a pleasant breeze, and Bruno breathed in deeply, relieved to be out of the confines of the bus. Since it was not quite twelve-thirty, too early for lunch, he suggested a walk to the old Roman amphitheater. "It's only a few blocks from the square," he told Nadia. Nadia agreed and tucked her arm in his as they set off slowly.

Five minutes later they emerged from the shade of the narrow street and entered the amphitheater, its open space ringed by the stone seats that glared white in the sun. On the top tier they found a bench somewhat shaded by a young olive tree. As soon as they sat down, Nadia removed her shoes and began to massage her feet.

"Are they too tight?" Bruno asked, taking over the massage.

"No, it's just that I don't usually wear them."

Bruno looked up from Nadia's feet. "You looked so sad on the bus."

She looked off in the distance. "It's funny," she said slowly. "In one way I miss my mother all the time, but, after she had been dead a few years, the sadness moved into a corner of my mind." She hesitated and then went on. "But sometimes it becomes an enormous thing. The day before I graduated from high school, I cried all night because I wanted her to be there so badly. And now I feel like I want to tell her about the baby." She looked at him now, her face open and earnest. "It's not a rational thing that I can talk myself out of. It's like a primitive instinct. The funeral made it worse."

Bruno took her hand. "Do you have any other women you're close to? Your grandmother raised you, didn't she? Can you talk to her?"

"I called her last night, but I didn't tell her. She's getting hard of hearing, and anyway she spent the whole time worrying about how much it costs to call from Italy. It would be good to be with her, but it isn't the same thing."

Bruno felt a great tenderness for her, so young and so alone. And anger at her father. Why had he let her wander around the world, far from her family? "You are so brave," he said, stroking her hand.

She laughed. "I don't feel at all brave. But I do feel strong when I'm with you." She looked at him. "It's amazing, isn't it, this feeling we have for each other?"

He put his arm around her. "It is." And it was. It was like a great letting go and falling but knowing you were safe, except he was only safe when he was with her, and not even then when he let himself think about the future. And there was nothing at all safe about the rest of his life. He leaned down and kissed the back of her neck, burying his face in her familiar scent.

Eventually they made their way to a little *trattoria* several blocks away that was known for its *bistecca alla fiorentina*. Although the meal was delicious, there was a quiet between them, which held as they took the bus back to the city. They went to an air-conditioned movie downtown and saw one of the silly science fiction films that were popular at the time. The earth was invaded by a race of giant cats from Mars, who thought that humans were a variety of mice. A young girl eventually saved the day by suggesting they use a long string to lure the cats into a cage. On the way home, Bruno and Nadia laughed at the absurdity of the movie but did not speak of anything else. Once they arrived at Nadia's apartment, they made love. Afterwards, together in the kitchen, they cooked *spaghetti alla carbonara*. Throughout the meal they touched hands, smiled and made frequent eye contact, but again spoke little. Bruno left early. He didn't want to take the chance that Ivana might call with a last minute request for something she wanted him to bring and not find him at home.

Once he arrived at his building he unloaded the family's things that he had brought from Viareggio. As he climbed the stairs, his arms full of Graziella's clothes and toys, Ivana's clothes, the toiletries that hadn't ended up at the hospital, he stopped suddenly, as though hit by a blast of hot air. This wasn't just about what he wanted, or what others needed, or what he might lose, or what he couldn't help. This was like his foot stepping on the sand that morning on the beach. His actions now would have consequences that would be forever. They would not only determine what the rest of his life would be like, but also who he would be. And he was the one who would make that choice. It was not something that was happening to him. He was a grown man, with a job, living in a free country. He could make choices. But he must figure it out carefully, get it right. "The right thing to do." That's what Nadia's father said when he heard that Bruno was going to leave his family. Bruno shook his head. He would never understand Americans. He was going to be hurt no matter what he did, and other people were going to be hurt, too. There was only one thing to be taken from the situation, the knowledge that he was doing what he thought was right. He resumed carrying his load up the stairs.

He moved quickly as he finished unpacking the car, keeping his mind as quiet as if some Martian cat were crouched nearby, waiting to pounce if it saw any movement. He knew what he was going to choose, but he didn't want to know it yet. He went to bed, telling himself that he would figure it out in the morning. He expected to toss and turn through the night, but his sleep was deep, and if he had any dreams he didn't remember them.

The next morning, feeling both calm and at the same time aware of a deep sadness, he packed the few things Ivana wanted, had a cappuccino at the café in Piazza Nazario Sauro and called Nadia. "We need to talk. I'm due in Viareggio this morning, but I'll be back this afternoon."

"You aren't going to leave your family. I knew it. I've always known it. I didn't even cancel my ticket. And you're probably right. It's never going to work."

He took a deep breath. "I don't know what I'm going to do. We'll talk when I get back. Can I come to your apartment? Will you be alone?"

"I'll find out. Call as soon as you get back. But hurry." She hung up. Bruno stood a moment holding the phone and then started out for Viareggio.

Traffic was light, and Bruno drove on automatic pilot. He let his mind wander, holding as long as possible onto this time before he acknowledged the reality that lay before him. The windows were half open, and they vibrated as the wind rushed by, making a sound like the flapping wings of a bird. Not a flutter, something bigger, a giant bird. A roc. That's what a roc's wings must sound like. Someone had read him a story when he was five or six years old about a boy who flew everywhere he wanted to go on the back of an enormous roc. For several years—until Bruno had discovered planes and decided he wanted to be a fighter pilot—most of his fantasies had been about flying to distant lands on a roc. Everything had been so simple then. But now there was no roc to escape on.

He went over the facts one last time just to be sure. He could continue to be an Italian husband and father and son and grandson and brother and cousin and nephew and professor in the state schools and, not least of all, a Florentine, but he would give up that deeper more alive self he felt himself to be when he was with Nadia. And he would lose his unborn son. Or he could be with Nadia and their son would be born, but who would Bruno be then? The exiled Italian husband of an American girl, the father of an American boy, the son-in-law of an American man who seemed to be entirely too comfortable deciding what Bruno should and shouldn't do. And God only knew what job he would have. He wouldn't be himself at all. He would be someone completely different and alien. His stomach felt hollow. It would be this other person who was living with Nadia and loving her. Maybe this new person wouldn't even love her. *Non dire scemenze,* he told himself—foolish thoughts. But he knew that they had some basis in reality. Going off to America with Nadia and trying to be a father to an American boy would have little to do with the time they had spent here together. His hands tightened on the steering wheel against the almost physical pain he felt, as he let himself acknowledge what he had known since last night. This was not something he was going to do.

But what would Nadia do alone? The world tightened around him at the thought. But he would hurt them both if he left with her. He had promised not to lie to her, and he hadn't, but now he knew it was about more than not lying. It was about letting her see who he was, what he felt, making her understand how deeply she was a part of him and how impossible it was for them to be together. He spent the rest of the trip rehearsing how to best explain it to her.

When he arrived in Viareggio, he went immediately to the hospital and up to Graziella's room. She was sitting cross-legged on the bed. Her things were piled neatly on the chair and Ivana was standing at the window. "*Babbo,* you came back," Graziella said, holding her arms out for a hug. "You always come back."

Bruno set the package he had brought with her clothes on the bed beside her, picked her up, kissed her and asked, "Are you ready to go home?"

"She's already been checked out," Ivana said, coming over to the bed. She helped Graziella get dressed, but when Bruno wanted to tie her shoes, Graziella pushed him away.

"No, I can do it. Look." And slowly, her tongue sticking out, she maneuvered the shoe strings into a wobbly bow that didn't look like it would last long.

"Remember how to pull the loops so you can tighten it," Ivana said. With intense concentration Graziella finally achieved a tight bow. She looked up at her parents and smiled. Then she looked down at the other shoe and sighed.

Ivana caught Bruno's eyes, a smile in hers. "I think *Babbo* would like to do the other one if you would let him."

Graziella lifted her foot for Bruno and said, "You can do it if you really want to." Bruno took her foot in his hand, tied her shoe lace, kissed it and laid it gently back down.

Once they arrived back in Florence and the car was unpacked, Bruno left to find a pay phone where no one knew him. He called Nadia. She answered right away. "I called my father. I told him you were going to leave me."

Bruno was amazed. How had she been so sure? "I'll explain when I see you."

"I can't see you. My father is going to help me, but he made me promise not to see you again."

"I'll come over and say good-by."

"No." Her voice was calm. "I promised. At least I won't be alone. He will help me."

He struggled to put meaning to her words. Finally, without really believing this was happening, he asked, "When do you leave?"

"I fly out on Friday. I'll take a train to Rome tomorrow."

"I could drive you to Rome."

"No."

"Can I at least come to the station to say good-by?"

"No." There was a silence. Then she said in a small voice, "I love you."

"I love you, too," he said, as he searched frantically for something to say. "I'll pay for the abortion."

"My father doesn't want me to have an abortion. He will help me so I can have the baby."

"Nadi, *amore* . . ."

"Good-by. Don't call back. Please."

He stood holding the silent receiver for a long time.

# 16

*May, 1970*

"Bad morning?" Ivana asked, as Bruno came into the kitchen.

"Yes." She always knew, he thought. And, in fact, it had been one of the worst. His students were rowdy and loud, listening to nothing that he said. He might as well not have been there. And then there was the letter.

After Nadia left, the days had stretched out, slow, and unreal. He had felt dried out and hollow as he struggled to manage his most basic duties. It seemed that the emptiness inside would pull him apart. The worst part was not being able to talk about this with Nadia. He told himself it would be better once school started. The beginning of the year always meant extra work, and he hoped this would provide a distraction. He didn't have to wait that long.

Several weeks after Nadia left, he received notice that Signorina Cohen had left him the school. The school was in a rented apartment. It wasn't worth much more than her business. Bruno wanted to sell it, but Ivana protested. "I agree that you shouldn't give up the job at the Galileo and lose the pension. But I think we could manage both. I'll help you." After some thought, he agreed, and it proved to be a good plan. All that year they worked long hard hours, leaving him no time during the day to think about Nadia. But there was nothing to help him through the nights.

At times he turned to Ivana, surprising her with his passion. Other times he walked the streets or stopped in some café to search the juke boxes for love songs, wallowing in melancholy. Slowly the pain lessened, and Nadia's presence faded, though some shred of her clung to him like the ghost toes that Zio Michele reported after he returned from the war. When Bruno was alone, in the movie, maybe, or driving, he would feel Nadia beside him or he'd catch himself explaining something to her. Often, when he passed the train station, he'd imagine her walking out, suitcase in hand. And he knew that for the rest of his life on the Feast of John the Baptist, when they went to see the fireworks, he would look for her on the bridge.

Now, almost three years later, a letter had arrived. It caught him off guard, and he had no doubt that the distraction it caused him had something to do with the students' behavior today.

"A little bad or very bad?" Ivana asked, as he came up beside her to wash his hands in the sink.

"Pretty bad."

She poured the pasta in a bowl and handed it to him. He carried it to the kitchen table, where Graziella sat waiting. "Hello, *amor mio*," Bruno said, leaning to kiss her before taking his place.

"Hello, *Babbo*. We waited for you, but I'm hungry."

"Well, I'm here now, and I'm hungry, too." He served her, served himself, and set the bowl where Ivana could reach it.

"Tell me." Ivana said, as she came to the table.

"Some of the students thought it would be funny to stop up all the toilets. So whenever anyone needed to go to the bathroom I had to let them go to the café across the street. Of course they all had to go and they all took their time coming back."

"Let's talk about it later," Ivana said with a sideways glance towards Graziella, who sat with her fork posed in midair, her attention riveted on the conversation.

"But I want to hear about them stopping up the toilets," Graziella said, giggling.

"And I want to hear about your day at school," Ivana said.

"I had a good day. The teacher said my handwriting was very neat." Graziella smiled and put a forkful of pasta in her mouth.

Bruno tried to think of something else to talk about, but there was nothing he wanted to discuss in front of a seven-year-old. The Americans were bombing in Cambodia. Students were rioting in Europe and the United States. Manners, morals, and decency were under assault everywhere. He couldn't think only of how the world was unraveling around him. He ate in silence as Ivana tried to distract Graziella from the subject of the toilets. Eventually, Ivana gave up and tried to explain why stopping up toilets wasn't a good idea.

After lunch, Ivana settled Graziella in her room for a siesta while Bruno remained at the table and lit a cigarette.

"The students must have thought the toilet escapade was pretty funny," Ivana said, returning to the kitchen. She came up behind Bruno and put her hands on his shoulders.

"I didn't."

"I know, but that's how you lose them. At that age, they think they're witty, and they often are really funny. If you show some level of appreciation, they usually behave better." Ivana had taken over the Cohen school last year and was making a great success of it. Bruno was impressed. He admired the way she kept her calm, even a sense of humor, in the midst of the chaos that ensued after the student uprising of 1968. He tried to follow her example, but it didn't come easy.

"I'm sympathetic when they actually have a cause like the university students do. Though I wish they would fight for it in a civilized way. Some of these younger ones don't respect anyone or anything. They just don't want to work."

"Be patient." Ivana sat beside him and reached for one of his cigarettes. "They have had so little control over their lives, so little say about the world they live in. They get a little freedom and don't know how to handle it. They'll learn."

"It doesn't look to me like they are learning."

"It's a process," she said, emphasizing the word *process*.

Their eyes met and he smiled. The word had become a joke between them since a few weeks before, when Graziella had said, "I know how you make babies."

Bruno had felt a pang of fear at this pronouncement. Graziella was seven. Had the world changed so much she would know these things at her age? Annamaria was married now, and pregnant. Bruno had seen her with Graziella a few days before, Graziella's hand on Annamaria's swollen belly, the two deep in conversation. What had Annamaria been saying to her? Ivana looked at Bruno and calmly asked Graziella what she knew.

"*Beh*," Graziella said, she paused, looking from one parent to the other. She lowered her voice dramatically, "It's a process."

Ivana caught Bruno's eye and smiled. "And how does this process work?"

"You have to be married. The mamma and daddy go in their room and close the door."

Now even Ivana looked a little startled.

"They make a flower and the flower makes a seed, and then the stork comes," Graziella went on. She was obviously enjoying the attention, and Bruno guessed she was improvising now. "If the stork doesn't eat the seed, it grows inside the mamma, and she gets a big stomach like Annamaria, and then the baby comes, and it looks half like the mamma and half like the daddy."

Bruno and Ivana managed not to laugh until Graziella left the room, but the word *process* still amused them. Now, as they shared the memory, some of the tension of the day slid away from Bruno. At least he had these two.

Ivana washed up and went to the bedroom to rest, and Bruno pulled the envelope out and read the letter once again.

*Dear Bruno,*

*We have a daughter. Her name is Lauren and she is healthy and beautiful. She has your Italian complexion, and I see something of you in her cheekbones and her eyebrows. I got married last month, and my husband wants to adopt Lauren. I think this would be best for her.*

*Because I put your name on the birth certificate, we need for you to relinquish your parental rights. I am sending you the papers to sign.*

*Also, my husband is a doctor, and he wants Lauren to have a full medical history of your family for her records. I am sending the questions we need you to answer for this. I will tell Lauren about you when she is older.*

*What can I say? I hope you are well. I cherish what we had, but I am happy with what I have now.*

*A big hug,*
*Nadia*
*PS Please fill out the papers, but don't write me.*

Bruno had known there would be a child, but now she was real. Lauren. A little girl. He imagined Nadia looking down at a baby in a crib. His need to be with them, to take care of them was like a physical urge. He wanted to get in the car and head east as fast as he could, letting nothing, not even an ocean, stop him along the way. But that was absurd and, even if it had been possible, it was not the way it had to be. He put the letter back in his pocket and sat there, letting the pain storm over him, knowing there was nothing he could do. Once again he had failed as a father. This doctor would raise his daughter, this stranger who had married Nadia. He tried to tell himself that at least Lauren would have someone to provide for her, even if it was this American man who probably talked too loud and wore plaid shorts like the ones Bruno had seen tourists walking around in. Bruno could not wish that the American wasn't there, but he hated him. And this man he hated was with Nadia. The letter had awakened his old yearning for her, but the image it brought had also created a distance between them. She was a mother and wife now and he did not know who it was that he really longed for. Was it the Nadia who had written the letter, or was it a memory of her frozen in time? He didn't like the idea that he might be making her into something static and still, almost as though he were taking her life away.

He told himself that he had his own life here—a wonderful child who needed him and a wife he loved and who had been with him through things Nadia could never know or understand. Losing Nadia had left something empty in him, but that was part of the past, like the war.

*Lauren.* The name rang in his ears, as he took out his pen, filled out the forms, signed them and put them in an envelope. After siesta, when the post office reopened, he went out, found out how many stamps were needed to send it to America, stuck them on and slipped the envelope in the mail slot. It made a small thump as it hit the pile of letters below. He came home, reread the letter one more time and then put it away in the hidden place where he kept the photograph of Adelina.

# 17

Bruno sat on the bed in his room, while Graziella sat across the room, cutting the threads that bound the black strip to the lapel of his jacket. She was hunched over, intent on her task, and Bruno could not actually see what she was doing, but he could hear the click of the scissors. Snip, snip, snip. Cutting Ivana out of his life.

It had happened suddenly. It was the second day of 1998. Bruno was sixty-eight years old and Ivana two years younger. They were retired now, and their life followed a gentle and predictable schedule, which included joining the throngs of Italians who took a walk before dinner. That day Bruno, checking his watch, had seen that it was almost seven. He put his book down and wandered into the kitchen. "Ready?" he asked Ivana. She turned away from the sink, wiped her hands on a dish towel and, a puzzled look on her face, said, "I'm feeling really tired. I think I'll rest while you go."

"Do you think you're getting sick?"

"No. I'm fine. Just tired. You go, and I'll lie down for a while."

He nodded. They had stayed up late New Year's Eve watching the celebrations on television. Ivana was probably still behind on her rest.

It had rained all day and was still overcast and cold. He walked fast, missing the warmth of Ivana on his arm. He crossed the river and went from Piazza Goldoni, down via Vigna Nuova. Then instead of heading towards the Duomo as he often did with Ivana, he looped back down via Tornabuoni and back across the river, cutting his walk short.

He was back at the apartment in about half an hour. Ivana didn't greet him when he entered. He knew she could hear the door from the bedroom, so he thought she must be asleep. He sat down in the living room and read the front pages of the evening news. When she still hadn't come out, he went to the kitchen to see what she had planned for supper. He found a plate of cold, sliced pork left over from yesterday's lunch. He cut up some tomatoes, seasoned them with oil and basil and put them and the pork on the table. Then he sliced this morning's bread, dipped it in olive oil, salted it and ran it under the broiler.

When he was done, he went to their room to call her. He knew the minute he opened the door that something was wrong. He called her name softly, then with more urgency. He crossed the room to the bed and said her name again. She didn't respond, didn't even seem to be breathing. Her face was blue. He put his hand on her chest. It was warm but there was no movement. He rushed across the hall to the apartment next door. Beppe Carlini was a dental surgeon, and his wife was a nurse. Bruno banged on the door. Beppe opened it.

"Something's wrong with Ivana. Come, please. Quick."

Beppe followed him back to the bedroom. He leaned over Ivana, feeling for her pulse. Then he removed his glasses and held them next to her nostrils. He showed them to Bruno, shook his head and said, "No mist." He laid his hand on Ivana's brow a moment. "She's dead."

The words made no sense to Bruno. "I'll call an ambulance," he said.

"It's too late," Beppe said. "I think it happened some time ago. How long has it been since you saw her?"

"Maybe an hour." Bruno was shaking.

"Who's your doctor?" Beppe asked. Bruno told him, and Beppe

called him on his cell phone.

"Do something," Bruno plucked at Beppe's sleeve. "Can't you do something?"

"It's too late. I'm sorry," Beppe said. He took Bruno by the arm, led him into the living room and sat him down in an easy chair. He crossed the room to the dining area, found a bottle of cognac and poured Bruno a glass. Bruno drank it, but it did nothing to ease his trembling.

Beppe's wife, who had come in with him, called Graziella. Doctor Bartolucci arrived soon afterwards and went to the bedroom, closing the door behind him. Bruno sat, all sense of time lost, the figures around him out of focus, unable to respond even when the doctor came out and said, "It was a massive heart attack. Probably soon after you left. She didn't suffer."

Graziella arrived then. She rushed from the front door over to where he sat, tears running down her cheeks, as she held her arms out to him. "*Babbo.*" He rose and reached out for her. He held onto her for long minutes, reluctant to let her go, as though her arms around him were all that was keeping the pieces of him together. Soon afterwards the doctor gave Bruno a strong sedative, and Bruno remembered little after that. When he woke the next day, he lay with his eyes closed, telling himself it had just been a dream. But he could feel he was on the sofa, not in his and Ivana's bed, and he couldn't stop the words in his head from saying, "*E' morta. La Ivana e' morta.*" Ivana is dead. When he finally opened his eyes to get up to go to the bathroom, he saw that Graziella was sitting in the chair next to the sofa.

"*Babbo,*" she said, standing up. "Can I do anything?" He shook his head. "I'll make some coffee."

Bruno didn't want coffee, but he didn't say anything. He went to his room to dress. Ivana was laid out, on top of the covers, her hands crossed on her breast. She looked peaceful, a gentle curve to her lips, almost as though she were smiling. He sat down next to her and put his hand on hers. It was cold. "It can't be," he said softly to her. "You can't be dead."

She didn't answer.

He lay down beside her. He remembered the first time they had met. He was a third year student, full of himself as he sat having lunch with friends at the university *mensa*. He noticed her immediately when she entered. She hesitated at the door, seeming overcome by the rowdy upperclassmen crowded on the benches at the long tables. Then she lifted her chin and marched in, her face determined and serious. *You looked so brave*, he thought. He had caught her eye, moved over and beckoned for her to sit by him. She smiled shyly and slipped in beside him. She told him she was a first year student in the *facolta'* of architecture. By the end of the meal, he had offered her one of the pins on his *goliarda*, the long pointed hats dating from mediaeval days that university students wore. First year students had no pins and were often hazed mercilessly. Sometimes the boys would make an "artichoke" of the girls, bunching their skirts above their heads. His pin would protect her.

She had been so young and pretty. Now they were both old, and she was gone, and without her everything they had together would be gone, too. It was too much to think about.

Eventually, much later, he got up and dressed. He came back to the bed, touched her cheek and left the room.

By now people were beginning to arrive. Mindlessly, Bruno greeted them, returned their embraces and thanked them for their concern. The women talked and wept and bustled around in the kitchen, while the men stood in groups of three or four, smoking and looking solemn. Finally Bruno escaped to the small balcony where his three-year-old grandson, Lorenzo, stood, looking down through the iron grill work.

Bruno came beside him and leaned on the rail. Lorenzo reached up and found Bruno's hand. "*Mamma* cried this morning," he said. Bruno squeezed his hand. "It's because *Nonna* is dead," Lorenzo went on. "Is that why all these people are here? Because *Nonna* is dead?"

"Yes," Bruno said.

"I think she's happy they all came to see her." And then, looking up at Bruno, he asked, "What's dead?"

Lorenzo's big, brown eyes, usually so full of fun, were serious. Bruno sighed. How to tell him when he didn't understand it himself? "It's when you go away," he said, stroking Lorenzo's auburn curls back from his face.

"That's what *Mamma* said. She said *Nonna* had gone to heaven. But I saw her. She isn't gone. She's in her room."

Bruno's throat was tight. He fought to get words through. "That's just her outside," he said finally. "The part that laughs and sings and loves us is gone."

"When will she come back?"

Never, Bruno thought. "Not for a long, long time."

Lorenzo was silent a while and then, "I don't like that, *Nonno*."

Bruno put his arm around the boy and pulled him close. "Let's go in. It's cold out here."

Graziella held the black strip of cloth up. It was no longer attached to Bruno's jacket. A year had passed now, he was officially out of mourning and it was time to remove his *lutto*. He knew this. But watching the process left him raw, as though a scab had been ripped from a wound before it was ready.

Graziella tossed the *lutto* on the bed, and Bruno picked it up, smoothed it with his hand and put it in his pocket. Graziella reached for his overcoat and began working on it.

The first months after Ivana's death Bruno had slept little and eaten less. He spent hours sitting, sometimes dozing, on the benches in the park. It was cold outside, even in the sun, but it didn't matter, he was cold wherever he was, and anything was better than the empty house. Cold and stiff and frail and useless, he thought. *Un vecchio babbeo.* Growing old, with all its problems, had been something he and Ivana shared, something they could even joke about, but now it seemed that the gap between this slowing of life and the end of it all had become a dark abyss, empty and hopeless, and he did not know how he could cross it.

Graziella wanted Bruno to move in with her. As a modern woman, she had moved away from home when she married, and she and her husband, Luigi, had an extra room in their apartment. Bruno didn't want to leave the home he had always lived in, the place that still had traces of Ivana. But Graziella was persistent, and eventually he found himself sorting through the accumulations, not only of his life with Ivana, but of the lives of several generations before, reducing them to what could fit in one room. The loss of his home made him feel even more like a tattered remnant of himself, something to be closeted away.

He worried, too, that living with Lorenzo would increase his sadness, reminding him of the joy he and Ivana had shared about this grandchild. But, from the first day he had arrived, when Lorenzo followed him around as he unpacked, curious about every little object his grandfather owned, Bruno found the boy's youthful energy soothing. The two spent hours together. Bruno took him for walks, answered his endless questions, and told him stories—stories about the city, about the war, about their family history. He went out of his way to mention Ivana as often as possible, finding comfort in the feel of her name on his tongue, in the knowledge of her name sounding in Lorenzo's ears, in this small way of keeping her in the world of the living.

The arrangement was good in other ways, too. Luigi was a quiet man, comfortable to be with, and Bruno found that the experience of living in a mostly male household for the first time in his life was relaxing. Eventually he even accepted the modern décor. The walls in the living room, a deep saturated grey with rich cream trim, proved to be restful. And the chrome and leather furniture was surprisingly comfortable, especially the reclining chair he soon appropriated.

Sometimes, looking at Lorenzo, he wondered if he had other grandchildren. Lauren was certainly old enough to have children. Over the years, his thoughts of Nadia had found a comfortable niche in the recesses of his mind, not exactly hidden, not forgotten, but, like the war, not dwelled on as he passed through his daily life. Lauren was different. He kept count of her age, trying to imagine what she would look like at each stage of development. As she grew up, passed her eighteenth birthday, then her twenty-first, then her thirtieth, he finally understood that she was not going to contact him. It hurt to know that she didn't want to know him, and he grieved that Graziella would never know her sister. Now that grief was compounded by the thought that Lorenzo might have cousins in America he would never know about.

Graziella picked the last threads off the overcoat. She stood up, came over to Bruno and handed him the coat. "It doesn't seem like a year, does it?" she asked.

"I dreamed about her the other night," he said.

"Tell me," she said, sitting beside him on the bed.

He had been in a dark forest, bare limbs woven into a cage over his head, roots tripping him as he stumbled through the dense undergrowth. He was calling Ivana's name, his voice tight and aching. Then she appeared in front of him, and at the same moment the sun burst through the trees, lighting up the whole forest. She looked at him, lifted one eyebrow and said in a gentle voice, "Silly man. Can't you see it's all right?"

"She looked so real," he said to Graziella.

"I know. I've had dreams, too."

Later that morning he put on his coat and left to go for a walk. It had been painful watching Graziella remove the black band from his lapel, but now, out on the street, he felt liberated. A barrier between him and the rest of the world had been removed. Much as he wanted to deny it, he was beginning to return to the living. "It's all right," Ivana had said in his dream. "It is not all right," he growled to himself, unwilling to let go of his grief. But he knew that it was better, that somehow a year made a difference.

And if it is better, he thought, as he walked, then it will continue to get better. The thought chilled him. He pushed it away, snuggled his scarf tighter around his neck and turned west down the broad avenue of viale dei Mille.

The day was clear but cold. He walked on the south side, where the sun's pale rays provided hope if not much warmth. As he passed the pizzeria that his friend Dario and his father ran, he saw lights on inside. It was too early for them to be open, but they might be preparing for the day. He stopped to look in. Dario saw him, waved and came to the door.

"How are you?" Dario asked, grinning widely. "We haven't seen you in ages."

They shook hands.

"Come in. We aren't yet open but come in and visit." Dario led him to a little table in the back. His father joined them.

"*Eh vai*, Dario, get the professor some coffee," the father said. Dario ran off to the espresso machine, while Bruno and his father talked about the weather and the *Viola*, the Florentine soccer team. When Dario returned with the coffee, he and his father went back to work, leaving Bruno with his drink and the paper. Bruno had already read most of the paper, so he sat with his coffee and looked around. He had come here once with Nadia. They had come after seeing a movie, he didn't remember which one, but he remembered being there with her, knew there was some part of him that was still connected to that time. He wondered who she was now, what she was like, was she still married. This thought opened the door to another thought he had been deliberately ignoring as it nibbled around the edges of his mind all day.

What if Nadia were free? His phone was listed, so she wasn't trying to contact him. But she wouldn't. It would be up to him. He had her old address, maybe she still lived there, or he could find her on the internet, find her number, but how would he call to America? He didn't speak English. He shook his head. He was not ready for these thoughts, not now, but maybe in a few years. In the meantime perhaps he would take English lessons. Just in case.

# 18

*April, 2003*

"This came for you," Graziella said, handing him a letter. "It's from America."

Bruno took the letter and, as casually as he could manage, put it in his breast pocket, his heart pounding.

"Lunch is ready," Graziella said.

"I'll just wash up."

"Well, hurry. Your pasta will get cold."

Once in the bathroom, Bruno slid the letter out. The return address was the same as on the one she had sent thirty years ago, but the handwriting was different. Could someone's handwriting change so much? Or was the letter from Lauren? He felt a shadow of fear, and knew he was not ready to find out what this was all about. He put the letter back in his pocket, washed his hands and went into lunch.

Graziella, Luigi, Lorenzo and Bruno made four at the table. Fortunately, Lorenzo was telling them a long story about something that had happened in school, and Bruno didn't have to say much. He had little appetite, but Graziella, for once, made no comment. After lunch Bruno told them he was going to take a walk before siesta.

Graziella's apartment was on the outskirts of Florence. Bruno took a bus to the downtown station and then found himself walking towards the café in Piazza Santa Maria Novella where he had last met Nadia. When he arrived he was glad to see that the table he was looking for was unoccupied. He sat down. The waiter arrived almost immediately, and Bruno ordered an espresso.

It had been 1999, almost two years after Ivana's death. Nadia had sat in the chair opposite the one he was sitting in now. He could almost see her, her face older, weathered, her body broader, but the eyes the same, the voice the same, the long legs the same. A shadow of the old longing rose up.

She had called without warning. Lorenzo, barely five, was not yet in school, and Bruno took care of him while Graziella and Luigi were at work. When the phone rang, he and Lorenzo were playing a noisy card game, Lorenzo dictating the rules as they went along. Bruno knew it wasn't family—they would have used the cell phone—and he considered not answering. But Lorenzo, who had just learned to say, "*Pronto, chi parla?*" ran to get it. He came back, holding the phone. "It's a strange lady. She wants to talk to you. She didn't tell me her name."

Bruno took the phone and spoke into it.

"Bruno, it's Nadia."

The room went out of focus. "Nadia?"

"I'm here in town. Just passing through, but I would love to see you."

Her voice was as familiar as if he had spoken to her yesterday. "When?" he asked. Then, still disoriented, he added, "Of course, I'd like to see you."

"What will work for you?"

"I take care of my grandson until one o'clock." He seemed to have too little breath to make his voice normal. "Any time after that."

"How about coffee at four?"

"Where?"

"I'm staying in a *pensione* near the station. Maybe that café in Piazza Santa Maria Novella? The small one."

"I will be there."

He had lain in his room after lunch, waiting for siesta to be over. He remembered how his pulse fluttered as he dressed to go meet her, wondering if it was possible that she, too, was widowed, or that she was divorced? Divorce, of course, was not the problem in today's world that it had been before. He didn't know what it would mean if she was free. Would she still want to be with him? Or he with her, for that matter? Would she find him old and repulsive? Would he find her strange and foreign?

He checked the mirror. His hair was no longer dark, more silver than gray, he thought. He was proud of how thick it still was, but the gray in his stubble left a dull shadow on his skin, and the flesh around his eyes sagged. He decided to shave again. He slapped his face with extra aftershave, hoping to put a little color in it. Satisfied that he looked as good as he could, he left the house and took a bus downtown. As he neared the café, he saw her, sitting alone at an outside table. His courage faltered. But he couldn't just stand here on the sidewalk. He took a deep breath, entered the café and approached her.

Now, as he sat here with the unopened letter in his pocket, he remembered the smile in her eyes when she saw him. She had risen and held out her arms for an embrace. His whole body had cried out not to let her go. When she sat back down, her voice was breathless. "It's so good to see you. You look wonderful." In that moment the years slipped away, but he knew, without her saying a word, that she had not come back to get together again. He felt no great sadness about it, just pleasure to be with her. She told him about her life, about how she had become a teacher in the small town she lived in. Bruno told her about Lorenzo and the Cohen school. She asked him if he was worried about Y2K, and he assured her that nothing would happen. She asked about the recent trial in Florence of the man who had killed a policeman and had been acquitted.

"In America killing a police officer is the worst thing you can do," she said.

"Someone had been murdering young couples," Bruno answered. "He thought he had evidence that a policeman was doing it and wasn't being investigated because he was a policeman. In his mind, he was saving all the young people who would be killed in the future."

"But he took the law in his own hands."

"And killed an innocent man, but why compound the tragedy by punishing him and his family with him?"

She shook her head, and Bruno laughed out loud with the joy of returning to these old conversations with her. "The thing that I want to know," he said, "is why a man as intelligent as Clinton, with the whole CIA at his command, wouldn't have his women vetted well enough to avoid a scandal?"

This time it was Nadia who laughed. "You Italians," she said and leaned back in her chair and smiled at him. They sat a while in comfortable silence, and now, finally, he was able to ask about Lauren.

"She's amazing. She's a lawyer and works for an international firm in Paris. She is happy and well, but never married and so no grandchildren." There was a brief sadness in her voice.

"Graziella didn't have Lorenzo until she was thirty-four years old. There's still time."

"I've just been to see her," Nadia went on.

"Do you have a picture?"

"Lauren asked me not to show you one."

"She hates me?"

"It's more like she doesn't want to know anything about you."

"Is your husband good to her?'

Nadia nodded. "They are very close." She hesitated. "I understand so much more now that I have my own family. I was such a baby, so stupid and selfish, when I was with you." She met his eyes. "It must have been terrible for your wife."

"She never knew."

Nadia continued looking at him. "I find that hard to believe."

"I made sure she didn't."

Nadia was silent for a while. Then she said, "It was such a changing time. We threw out all the older generation's wisdom and didn't have anything to replace it with. Lauren has much clearer ideas about life."

He nodded. "So does Graziella. It's not that everything has been easy for her, but she is so confident. She is an architect—very successful—and she does it without neglecting Lorenzo. Her husband helps her. They work together."

Nadia smiled. "Well, I guess we were pioneers in new times, and nobody ever said pioneers had an easy time. But I am not proud of our affair."

"Do you regret it?"

She laughed, her sparkling eyes so like he remembered. "I can't. There are limits to how much I've grown up."

"I don't regret it either. I can't imagine how my life would be if it hadn't happened. And yet I know that Graziella and her generation aren't as accepting of affairs as mine was, and I have to say I think that's good." He looked at her and she smiled. He reached his hand across the table to hers. She squeezed his briefly and then withdrew hers. She left soon after, and he had not heard from her since. Not until this letter that lay unopened in his breast pocket. Maybe her husband had died and she wanted to come back to him. But he knew this wasn't so. And he knew that he didn't really want it.

The waiter brought his coffee, and Bruno drank it slowly. Finally, he could no longer put it off. He took the envelope from his pocket and opened it. It was just a few lines.

*Professor Cassini,*

*My wife, Nadia, died last week from cancer of the throat. It was very quick. I promised her I would let you know.*

*Sincerely,*
*Peter Olafson*

Bruno sat stunned until the waiter came and asked him if he wanted anything else. He shook his head, paid and left. He wove his way through the back streets to Piazza Signoria and then down to the Arno. He stopped at the *lungarno* and leaned on the wall, looking down at the river towards the *Ponte alle Grazie*. This was where he had seen Nadia with her two friends so many years ago. Thirty-six years. Another image passed through his mind, frozen like a photograph, an image of the bridge in ruins after it had been mined, the trolley tracks curving up from the rubble like some sort of insect's antennae. He remembered the desperation of the boy he had been, how he had searched for Silvana. So much had changed, the war, the flood, Ivana's death. But this seemed the greatest change of all, that Nadia was no longer part of the world. He had grieved when Ivana died and missed her deeply. He couldn't really say he would miss Nadia, not in a day to day way, and he didn't expect to grieve for any length of time. But his world had made a great shift. As he stood here on the riverfront, he felt dislocated, unable to find where he fit in. It seemed that this was not the same wall he had known only yesterday, or the same river, or even the same city.

It was almost five when he finally boarded the bus home. He had walked up the back way to the Piazzale, where Mussolini and Hitler had once met, where he had gone so many years ago with Nadia, but the big square was full of touring Pullmans, stands festooned with souvenirs and throngs of loud foreigners. He climbed the steps to San Miniato, but crowds of tourists were lined up there, too, waiting to get in the church. Only in the cemetery, where he found the bench he and Nadia had once sat on, was he able to regain a sense of the past. This was where Nadia had told him about her mother's death. He remembered it had been a special moment, but he couldn't regain the feeling, only the sense of how strong the connection had been. The connection was still there, he felt it, reaching out from some place deep inside him, but it didn't go anywhere, like a phone off the hook on the other end. He sat on the bench a while and rested. Then he took the bus down into town.

His back ached when he stood to get off at his stop, and his legs seemed to cover the last half block to his building solely on will power. He unlocked the outside *portone*, took the elevator, and then climbed the three marble steps to his apartment. He opened the door, and, as he set his keys on the table in the entryway, he saw his reflection in the mirror above the table. The face that looked back at him was gaunt and creased, the eyes almost slits where the loose skin had fallen. He was an old man now, and he did not know how or when this had happened.

Graziella came out to meet him. She had on the black tights and black turtleneck she wore when she was working at home. Her hair was pulled back in a ponytail, but her face was framed by the curls that had escaped her attempt at control.

She put her arm around him. "Poor *Babbo*," she said, her voice warm.

"Poor *Babbo*?" he asked, as they walked together down the hall.

"Don't worry. I know all about it, *caro*."

"What?"

"The American woman. She's dead. That's what the letter was about, wasn't it?"

He stopped and turned towards her. "You know?"

Graziella nodded.

"How?"

"Lauren told me."

He felt his jaw loosen. "How do you know about Lauren?"

"*Mamma* told me a long time ago."

"She knew?" How could she have known? She couldn't have known.

"Of course she knew, *Babbo*." Graziella snuggled in closer to him. "Did you think that just because you put those letters behind your dresser drawer, your wife wouldn't find them?"

"I need to sit down." He entered the living room and lowered himself gingerly into his chair, not only because of the arthritis in his knees, but because he couldn't trust anything now, not even that he would find his chair where he expected it to be. Graziella perched on the arm of the chair. "Why didn't she say something?"

"Why didn't you say something?"

"I didn't want to hurt her."

Graziella shrugged. "And she didn't want to make a scene with you."

"She made a fool of me, instead."

"And what did you do to her?" Her voice had an edge to it.

What had he done to her? He lowered his head, resting it on his hand. He thought about his mother, sitting at the kitchen table after his father left on one of his escapades. Silent, her hands in her lap, her face sad. Often tears would run down her cheeks. Bruno had thought she was the most beautiful person in the world, but if she tried to talk during those times her mouth would contort, become an ugly writhing thing that took over her usually soft and gentle face. Remembering now, he could feel the old anger begin to grow in his chest, but it quickly died. What was the use? It was so long ago. His father had been dead for so many years.

Bruno had been angry at his mother, too, for not fighting back. Poor *Mamma*. It wasn't her fault. Mostly, he thought, he had been ashamed of his own impotence in front of his father's towering, god-like presence. But what chance had he had? He was a child. Even his grandmother, a formidable woman, had been powerless in front of his father. She would rant and call him names and tell him in great detail how he was going to burn in hell, but his father smiled and ignored her—unless he was in a bad mood. If he was in a bad mood he yelled back at her. He could no more be stopped than a thunderstorm.

But that was all so long ago. What had happened in the years between? He had fought so hard not to be like his father, and now. He clenched his jaw. Ivana should have told him that she knew. She shouldn't have let him hurt her that way.

"I never understood it," Graziella said now. "You wouldn't have gotten off so easily with me." The gentle teasing in her voice belied her words. "I would have kicked you out. But *Mamma* said you were a good man, that it was just a different time. She loved you." She put her hand on Bruno's knee. "And I'm glad she kept you, *Babbo mio*. What would I have done without you?"

Well, at least there was that, Bruno thought. He had not betrayed Graziella.

"I have work to do before dinner," she said, patting his knee. "I need to finish this project by next week." She climbed the steps to the loft in the corner of the room where she kept her drawing table and supplies.

Bruno was glad to be alone. He felt ugly and confused, not fit to be seen.

He remembered a time, the first year the Cohen school had made a serious profit. He and Ivana had eaten out to celebrate and afterwards made love. As they were embracing, she had suddenly pulled away, looked at him for a long time and then in a small, almost timid voice, she said, "I am so glad I have you." She had known, he thought now. But she had not shown anger. She had been soft and vulnerable. What had he done to her?

He had failed to protect her. She was the one who had protected him. He rubbed his hand down his face, over his mouth, across his chin, feeling the day's stubble. And if she had told him she knew? Was there anything she could have said that could have stopped him? And either way, how would it have been if they had spoken of it? He couldn't imagine it. That wasn't the way it was with them. But could it have been different? Could he have had with Ivana that openness he remembered with Nadia?

His legs ached. He stretched them out. He should take a *Cibalgina*. It would help the pain as well as keep his body from hurting worse tomorrow. But not now. Right now he didn't want to move. He didn't want to think. And he didn't want to admit to himself that he was trying to blame Ivana for what he had done to her. But that's exactly what he was doing, and it wasn't right, and it didn't even make him feel any better.

The worst part was that there was nothing he could do now. This was his life, for better or worse. He had done what he had done, and he was who he was and it was too late to change much. But he would give every second of the time that remained for five minutes with Ivana to tell her how sorry he was, that he had never wanted to hurt her, to tell her how much he loved her.

Then, like the crash of a powerful wave, he saw that Ivana had known him as he was, with the bad as well as the good, and had still loved him. He clasped his hands to his stomach as though in physical pain. *Don't do this to me.* He almost said the words aloud, as stitch by stitch, thread by thread he felt himself being undone down to his naked soul and saw that he had been found, not wanting, but somehow, by some miracle, acceptable.

He ached to see Ivana, to bury himself in her arms, to hear her words explaining how she could have possibly loved him. But she was gone and his love for her could no longer do her any good. He knew, without understanding why, that the only thing left to give her was to accept her love of him. He closed his eyes and leaned back in his chair.

Nadia had loved him, too, even though he had hurt her. And *Mamma* loved him and *Nonna* and Annamaria and Graziella and little Lorenzo. His father, too, and all his aunts and uncles. He did not understand why, or how, but sat in wonder, as this miracle coursed through him.

Eventually the world drifted away and now he was swimming in a vast body of water, not the sea, not a lake, just blue, clear, sweet water. There was no shore, but he was not afraid. Surrounded in all directions by this blue, blue water, he could hear nothing but the sound of his breathing and the rustle of his body moving through the water. Then he woke. He sat a while, holding onto the sensation of his muscles moving like those of a young man. The ache in his legs was gone.

The water had been so blue. So blue and so clear.

He heard Graziella moving around in the kitchen and remembered that she had mentioned Lauren. He pushed himself up from his chair and went to find her.

"Lauren told you? How . . . ?"

She threw a clump of basil in the pan on the stove. It sizzled in the hot oil. "It's not exactly hard to find people these days. We email. She's in Paris." She turned from the stove to face him. "I'm going to visit her this summer."

"You're going to visit her?" He sat down at the kitchen table. He was beyond surprise. Several chunks of his life had fallen out, and what remained had been rearranged like the chips of colored glass in a child's kaleidoscope. He was in a new world. "Is that all right with her?" he asked. "I thought she didn't want to know anything about me."

She looked at him the way Ivana used to, raising one eyebrow.

"That's different. We are sisters, you know."

His daughters were friends. His nose began to sting, and he felt tears pooling in his eyes.

"I'm working on getting her to meet you," Graziella went on. "She'll come around some day." Her voice was confident.

The water on the stove bubbled. The smell of basil and garlic and tomato filled the room. Tears flowed freely down Bruno's cheeks.

"And . . ." Graziella hesitated. "I know about Adelina, too."

"What? Did *Mamma* know that, too?"

"*Babbo*, you kept her picture. Anybody who saw it would know she was your daughter."

Lorenzo came into the room. "*Nonno*," he said, his voice concerned. "You're crying. Are you sad?" Bruno held out his arm, and Lorenzo crossed the room and leaned into him.

Bruno wrapped his arm around the boy, pulled his warm, body close and kissed him on the head, breathing in deeply the fresh smell of his hair.

"Your old *Nonno* has been a very stupid man," he said. "But it's all right. Everything's all right, *tesoro mio*."

# ACKNOWLEDGEMENTS

I would first like to thank the people of Florence, Italy who were patient with the insensitive, ignorant eleven year-old who landed in their city in 1952. I would also like to thank my parents who brought me there.

I want to thank Judy McKenzie, Connie Newman and Jeanne Bishop who were there the whole way and Erica Atkisson who was with us for a while and Carol Massahos who joined us later. Thanks to Pam Herber who suggested that what I thought was a short story was really a chapter of a novel.

Mary O'Connell, Betsy Hardinger, Rebeca Morales, Barbara Longo, Michelle Huneven, Christine Menager, Florence Mills, and Jeanne Carnini all read versions and gave helpful suggestions, as did my children, Alex, Rosalind and James, and their spouses, Andrea and Jenny.

Finally, the ideas, memories, and impressions of my sister, Marguerite Chiarenza, run through the novel, as entangled with mine as salt in the sea.

-RT

Rosalind Trotter was born in North Carolina and raised in Florence, Italy. She lives in Eugene, Oregon, where she works as a social worker, preparing parents to adopt children from foster care. She is blessed that her children and grandchildren live in Oregon, most of them in Eugene.